THE INV   ⌐ ॱ ⦧

NORCROSS SERIES

ANNA HACKETT

The Investigator

Published by Anna Hackett

Copyright 2020 by Anna Hackett

Cover by Lana Pecherczyk

Cover image by Wander Aguiar

Edits by Tanya Saari

ISBN (ebook): 978-1-922414-10-6

ISBN (paperback): 978-1-922414-11-3

WHAT READERS ARE SAYING ABOUT ANNA'S ACTION ROMANCE

Cyborg - PRISM Award finalist 2019

Edge of Eon and Mission: Her Protection - Romantic Book of the Year (Ruby) finalists 2019

Unfathomed and Unmapped - Romantic Book of the Year (Ruby) finalists 2018

Unexplored – Romantic Book of the Year (Ruby) Novella Winner 2017

Return to Dark Earth – One of Library Journal's Best E-Original Books for 2015 and two-time SFR Galaxy Awards winner

At Star's End – One of Library Journal's Best E-Original Romances for 2014

The Phoenix Adventures – SFR Galaxy Award Winner for Most Fun New Series and "Why Isn't This a Movie?" Series

Beneath a Trojan Moon – SFR Galaxy Award Winner and RWAus Ella Award Winner

Hell Squad – SFR Galaxy Award for best Post-Apocalypse for Readers who don't like Post-Apocalypse

"Like Indiana Jones meets Star Wars. A treasure hunt with a steamy romance." – SFF Dragon, review of *Among Galactic Ruins*

"Strap in, enjoy the heat of romance and the daring of this group of space travellers!" – Di, Top 500 Amazon Reviewer, review of *At Star's End*

"Action, danger, aliens, romance – yup, it's another great book from Anna Hackett!" – Book Gannet Reviews, review of *Hell Squad: Marcus*

Sign up for my VIP mailing list and get your *free box set* containing three action-packed romances.

Visit here to get started: www.annahackett.com

CHAPTER ONE

There was a glass of chardonnay with her name on it waiting for her at home.

Haven McKinney smiled. The museum was closed, and she was *done* for the day.

As she walked across the East gallery of the Hutton Museum, her heels clicked on the marble floor.

God, she loved the place. The creamy marble that made up the flooring and wrapped around the grand pillars was gorgeous. It had that hushed air of grandeur that made her heart squeeze a little every time she stepped inside. But more than that, the amazing art the Hutton housed sang to the art lover in her blood.

Snagging a job here as the curator six months ago had been a dream come true. She'd been at a low point in her life. Very low. Haven swallowed a snort and circled a stunning white-marble sculpture of a naked, reclining woman with the most perfect resting bitch face. She'd never guessed that her life would come crashing down at age twenty-nine.

1

She lifted her chin. Miami was her past. The Hutton and San Francisco were her future. No more throwing caution to the wind. She had a plan, and she was sticking to it.

She paused in front of a stunning exhibit of traditional Chinese painting and calligraphy. It was one of their newer exhibits, and had been Haven's brainchild. Nearby, an interactive display was partially assembled. Over the next few days, her staff would finish the installation. Excitement zipped through Haven. She couldn't wait to have the touchscreens operational. It was her passion to make art more accessible, especially to children. To help them be a part of it, not just look at it. To learn, to feel, to enjoy.

Art had helped her through some of the toughest times in her life, and she wanted to share that with others.

She looked at the gorgeous old paintings again. One portrayed a mountainous landscape with beautiful maple trees. It soothed her nerves.

Wine would soothe her nerves, as well. *Right*. She needed to get upstairs to her office and grab her handbag, then get an Uber home.

Her cell phone rang and she unclipped it from the lanyard she wore at the museum. "Hello?"

"Change of plans, girlfriend," a smoky female voice said. "Let's go out and celebrate being gorgeous, successful, and single. I'm done at the office, and believe me, it has been a *grueling* day."

Haven smiled at her new best friend. She'd met Gia Norcross when she joined the Hutton. Gia's wealthy brother, Easton Norcross, owned the museum, and was

Haven's boss. The museum was just a small asset in the businessman's empire. Haven suspected Easton owned at least a third of San Francisco. Maybe half.

She liked and respected her boss. Easton could be tough, but he valued her opinions. And she loved his bossy, take-charge, energetic sister. Gia ran a highly successful PR firm in the city, and did all the PR and advertising for the Hutton. They'd met not long after Haven had started work at the museum.

After their first meeting, Gia had dragged Haven out to her favorite restaurant and bar, and the rest was history.

"I guess making people's Instagram look pretty and not staged is hard work," Haven said with a grin.

"Bitch." Gia laughed. "God, I had a meeting with a businessman caught in...well, let's just say he and his assistant were *not* taking notes on the boardroom table."

Haven felt an old, unwelcome memory rise up. She mentally stomped it down. "I don't feel sorry for the cheating asshole, I feel sorry for whatever poor shmuck got more than they were paid for when they walked into the boardroom."

"Actually, it was the cheating businessman's wife."

"Uh-oh."

"And the assistant was male," Gia added.

"Double uh-oh."

"Then said cheater comes to my PR firm, telling me to clean up his mess, because he's thinking he might run for governor one day. I mean, I'm good, but I can't wrangle miracles."

Haven suspected that Gia had verbally eviscerated

the man and sent him on his way. Gia Norcross had a sharp tongue, and wasn't afraid to use it.

"So, grueling day and I need alcohol. I'll meet you at ONE65, and the first drink is on me."

"I'm pretty wiped, Gia—"

"Uh-uh, no excuses. I'll see you in an hour." And with that, Gia was gone.

Haven clipped her phone to her lanyard. Well, it looked like she was having that chardonnay at ONE65, the six-story, French dining experience Gia loved. Each level offered something different, from patisserie, to bistro and grill, to bar and lounge.

Haven walked into the museum's main gallery, and her blood pressure dropped to a more normal level. It was her favorite space in the museum. The smell of wood, the gorgeous lights gleaming overhead, and the amazing paintings combined to create a soothing room. She smoothed her hands down her fitted, black skirt. Haven was tall, at five foot eight, and curvy, just like her mom had been. Her boobs, currently covered by a cute, white blouse with a tie around her neck, weren't much to write home about, but she had to buy her skirts one size bigger. She sighed. No matter how much she walked or jogged —*blergh*, okay, she didn't jog much—she still had an ass.

Even in her last couple of months in Miami, when stress had caused her to lose a bunch of weight due to everything going on, her ass hadn't budged.

Memories of Miami—and her douchebag-of-epic-proportions-ex—threatened, churning like storm clouds on the horizon.

Nope. She locked those thoughts down. She was *not* going there.

She had a plan, and the number one thing for taking back and rebuilding her life was *no* men. She'd sworn off anyone with a Y chromosome.

She didn't need one, didn't want one, she was D-O-N-E, done.

She stopped in front of the museum's star attraction. Claude Monet's *Water Lilies.*

Haven loved the impressionist's work. She loved the colors, the delicate strokes. This one depicted water lilies and lily pads floating on a gentle pond. His paintings always made an impact, and had a haunting, yet soothing feel to them.

It was also worth just over a hundred million dollars.

The price tag still made her heart flutter. She'd put a business case to Easton, and they'd purchased the painting three weeks ago at auction. Haven had planned out the display down to the rivets used on the wood. She'd thrown herself into the project.

Gia had put together a killer marketing campaign, and Haven had reluctantly been interviewed by the local paper. But it had paid off. Ticket sales to the museum were up, and everyone wanted to see *Water Lilies.*

Footsteps echoed through the empty museum, and she turned to see a uniformed security guard appear in the doorway.

"Ms. McKinney?"

"Yes, David? I was just getting ready to leave."

"Sorry to delay you. There's a delivery truck at the

back entrance. They say they have a delivery of a Zadkine bronze."

Haven frowned, running through the next day's schedule in her head. "That's due tomorrow."

"It sounds like they had some other deliveries nearby and thought they'd squeeze it in."

She glanced at her slim, silver wristwatch, fighting back annoyance. She'd had a long day, and now she'd be late to meet Gia. "Fine. Have them bring it in."

With a nod, David disappeared. Haven pulled out her phone and quickly fired off a text to warn Gia that she'd be late. Then Haven headed up to her office, and checked her notes for tomorrow. She had several calls to make to chase down some pieces for a new exhibit she wanted to launch in the winter. There were some restoration quotes to go over, and a charity gala for her art charity to plan. She needed to get down into the storage rooms and see if there was anything they could cycle out and put on display.

God, she loved her job. Not many people would get excited about digging around in dusty storage rooms, but Haven couldn't wait.

She made sure her laptop was off and grabbed her handbag. She slipped her lanyard off and stuffed her phone in her bag.

When she reached the bottom of the stairs, she heard a strange noise from the gallery. A muffled pop, then a thump.

Frowning, she took one step toward the gallery.

Suddenly, David staggered through the doorway, a splotch of red on his shirt.

Haven's pulse spiked. *Oh God, was that blood?* "David—"

"Run." He collapsed to the floor.

Fear choking her, she kicked off her heels and spun. She had to get help.

But she'd only taken two steps when a hand sank into her hair, pulling her neat twist loose, and sending her brown hair cascading over her shoulders.

"Let me go!"

She was dragged into the main gallery, and when she lifted her head, her gut churned.

Five men dressed in black, all wearing balaclavas, stood in a small group.

No...oh, no.

Their other guard, Gus, stood with his hands in the air. He was older, former military. She was shoved closer toward him.

"Ms. McKinney, you okay?" Gus asked.

She managed a nod. "They shot David."

"I kn—"

"No talking," one man growled.

Haven lifted her chin. "What do you want?" There was a slight quaver in her voice.

The man who'd grabbed her glared. His cold, blue eyes glittered through the slits in his balaclava. Then he ignored her, and with the others, they turned to face the *Water Lilies.*

Haven's stomach dropped. *No.* This couldn't be happening.

A thin man moved forward, studying the painting's gilt frame with gloved hands. "It's wired to an alarm."

Blue Eyes, clearly the group's leader, turned and aimed the gun at Gus' barrel chest. "Disconnect it."

"No," the guard said belligerently.

"I'm not asking."

Haven held up her hands. "Please—"

The gun fired. Gus dropped to one knee, pressing a hand to his shoulder.

"No!" she cried.

The leader stepped forward and pressed the gun to the older man's head.

"No." Haven fought back her fear and panic. "Don't hurt him. I'll disconnect it."

Slowly, she inched toward the painting, carefully avoiding the thin man still standing close to it. She touched the security panel built in beside the frame, pressing her palm to the small pad.

A second later, there was a discreet beep.

Two other men came forward and grabbed the frame.

She glanced around at them. "You're making a mistake. If you know who owns this museum, then you know you won't get away with this." Who would go up against the Norcross family? Easton, rich as sin, had a lot of connections, but his brother, Vander... Haven suppressed a shiver. Gia's middle brother might be hot, but he scared the bejesus out of Haven.

Vander Norcross, former military badass, owned Norcross Security and Investigations. His team had put in the high-tech security for the museum.

No one in their right mind wanted to go up against Vander, or the third Norcross brother who also worked with Vander, or the rest of Vander's team of badasses.

"Look, if you just—"

The blow to her head made her stagger. She blinked, pain radiating through her face. Blue Eyes had backhanded her.

He moved in and hit her again, and Haven cried out, clutching her face. It wasn't the first time she'd been hit. Her douchebag ex had hit her once. That was the day she'd left him for good.

But this was worse. Way worse.

"Shut up, you stupid bitch."

The next blow sent her to the floor. She thought she heard someone chuckle. He followed with a kick to her ribs, and Haven curled into a ball, a sob in her throat.

Her vision wavered and she blinked. Blue Eyes crouched down, putting his hand to the tiles right in front of her. Dizziness hit her, and she vaguely took in the freckles on the man's hand. They formed a spiral pattern.

"No one talks back to me," the man growled. "Especially a woman." He moved away.

She saw the men were busy maneuvering the painting off the wall. It was easy for two people to move. She knew its exact dimensions—eighty by one hundred centimeters.

No one was paying any attention to her. Fighting through the nausea and dizziness, she dragged herself a few inches across the floor, closer to the nearby pillar. A pillar that had one of several hidden, high-tech panic buttons built into it.

When the men were turned away, she reached up and pressed the button.

Then blackness sucked her under.

HAVEN SAT on one of the lovely wooden benches she'd had installed around the museum. She'd wanted somewhere for guests to sit and take in the art.

She'd never expected to be sitting on one, holding a melting ice pack to her throbbing face, and staring at the empty wall where a multi-million-dollar masterpiece should be hanging. And she definitely didn't expect to be doing it with police dusting black powder all over the museum's walls.

Tears pricked her eyes. She was alive, her guards were hurt but alive, and that was what mattered. The police had questioned her and she'd told them everything she could remember. The paramedics had checked her over and given her the ice pack. Nothing was broken, but she'd been told to expect swelling and bruising.

David and Gus had been taken to the hospital. She'd been assured the men would be okay. Last she'd heard, David was in surgery. Her throat tightened. *Oh, God.*

What was she going to tell Easton?

Haven bit her lip and a tear fell down her cheek. She hadn't cried in months. She'd shed more than enough tears over Leo after he'd gone crazy and hit her. She'd left Miami the next day. She'd needed to get away from her ex and, unfortunately, despite loving her job at a classy Miami art gallery, Leo's cousin had owned it. Alyssa had been the one who had introduced them.

Haven had learned a painful lesson to not mix business and pleasure.

She'd been done with Leo's growing moodiness,

outbursts, and cheating on her and hitting her had been the last straw. *Asshole.*

She wiped the tear away. San Francisco was as far from Miami as she could get and still be in the continental US. This was supposed to be her fresh new start.

She heard footsteps—solid, quick, and purposeful. Easton strode in.

He was a tall man, with dark hair that curled at the collar of his perfectly fitted suit. Haven had sworn off men, but she was still woman enough to appreciate her boss' good looks. His mother was Italian-American, and she'd passed down her very good genes to her children.

Like his brothers, Easton had been in the military, too, although he'd joined the Army Rangers. It showed in his muscled body. Once, she'd seen his shirt sleeves rolled up when they'd had a late meeting. He had some interesting ink that was totally at odds with his sophisticated-businessman persona.

His gaze swept the room, his jaw tight. It settled on her and he strode over.

"Haven—"

"Oh God, Easton. I'm so sorry."

He sat beside her and took her free hand. He squeezed her cold fingers, then he looked at her face and cursed.

She hadn't been brave enough to look in the mirror, but she guessed it was bad.

"They took the *Water Lilies*," she said.

"Okay, don't worry about it just now."

She gave a hiccupping laugh. "Don't worry? It's worth a hundred and ten *million* dollars."

ANNA HACKETT

A muscle ticked in his jaw. "You're okay, and that's the main thing. And the guards are in serious but stable condition at the hospital."

She nodded numbly. "It's all my fault."

Easton's gaze went to the police, and then moved back to her. "That's not true."

"I let them in." Her voice broke. God, she wanted the marble floor to crack and swallow her.

"Don't worry." Easton's face turned very serious. "Vander and Rhys will find the painting."

Her boss' tone made her shiver. Something made her suspect that Easton wanted his brothers to find the men who'd stolen the painting more than recovering the priceless piece of art.

She licked her lips, and felt the skin on her cheek tug. She'd have some spectacular bruises later. *Great. Thanks, universe.*

Then Easton's head jerked up, and Haven followed his gaze.

A man stood in the doorway. She hadn't heard him coming. Nope, Vander Norcross moved silently, like a ghost.

He was a few inches over six feet, had a powerful body, and radiated authority. His suit didn't do much to tone down the sense that a predator had stalked into the room. While Easton was handsome, Vander wasn't. His face was too rugged, and while both he and Easton had blue eyes, Vander's were dark indigo, and as cold as the deepest ocean depths.

He didn't look happy. She fought back a shiver.

Then another man stepped up beside Vander.

Haven's chest locked. *Oh, no. No, no, no.*

She should have known. He was Vander's top investigator. Rhys Matteo Norcross, the youngest of the Norcross brothers.

At first glance, he looked like his brothers—similar build, muscular body, dark hair and bronze skin. But Rhys was the youngest, and he had a charming edge his brothers didn't share. He smiled more frequently, and his shaggy, thick hair always made her imagine him as a rock star, holding a guitar and making girls scream.

Haven was also totally, one hundred percent in lust with him. Any time he got near, he made her body flare to life, her heart beat faster, and made her brain freeze up. She could barely talk around the man.

She did *not* want Rhys Norcross to notice her. Or talk to her. Or turn his soulful, brown eyes her way.

Nuh-uh. No way. She'd sworn off men. This one should have a giant warning sign hanging on him. *Watch out, heartbreak waiting to happen.*

Rhys had been in the military with Vander. Some hush-hush special unit that no one talked about. Now he worked at Norcross Security—apparently finding anything and anyone.

He also raced cars and boats in his free time. The man liked to go fast. Oh, and he bedded women. His reputation was legendary. Rhys liked a variety of adventures and experiences.

It was lucky Haven had sworn off men.

Especially when they happened to be her boss' brother.

And especially, especially when they were also her best friend's brother.

Off limits.

She saw the pair turn to look her and Easton's way.

Crap. Pulse racing, she looked at her bare feet and red toenails, which made her realize she hadn't recovered her shoes yet. They were her favorites.

She felt the men looking at her, and like she was drawn by a magnet, she looked up. Vander was scowling. Rhys' dark gaze was locked on her.

Haven's traitorous heart did a little tango in her chest.

Before she knew what was happening, Rhys went down on one knee in front of her.

She saw rage twist his handsome features. Then he shocked her by cupping her jaw, and pushing the ice pack away.

They'd never talked much. At Gia's parties, Haven purposely avoided him. He'd never touched her before, and she felt the warmth of him singe through her.

His eyes flashed. "It's going to be okay, baby."

Baby?

He stroked her cheekbone, those long fingers gentle.

Fighting for some control, Haven closed her hand over his wrist. She swallowed. "I—"

"Don't worry, Haven. I'm going to find the man who did this to you and make him regret it."

Her belly tightened. *Oh, God.* When was the last time anyone had looked out for her like this? She was certain no one had ever promised to hunt anyone down for her. Her gaze dropped to his lips.

He had amazingly shaped lips, a little fuller than such a tough man should have, framed by dark stubble.

There was a shift in his eyes and his face warmed. His fingers kept stroking her skin and she felt that caress all over.

Then she heard the click of heels moving at speed. Gia burst into the room.

"What the hell is going on?"

Haven jerked back from Rhys and his hypnotic touch. Damn, she'd been proven right—she was so weak where this man was concerned.

Gia hurried toward them. She was five-foot-four, with a curvy, little body, and a mass of dark, curly hair. As usual, she wore one of her power suits—short skirt, fitted jacket, and sky-high heels.

"Out of my way." Gia shouldered Rhys aside. When her friend got a look at Haven, her mouth twisted. "I'm going to *kill* them."

"Gia," Vander said. "The place is filled with cops. Maybe keep your plans for murder and vengeance quiet."

"Fix this." She pointed at Vander's chest, then at Rhys. Then she turned and hugged Haven. "You're coming home with me."

"Gia—"

"No. No arguments." Gia held up her palm like a traffic cop. Haven had seen "the hand" before. It was pointless arguing.

Besides, she realized she didn't want to be alone. And the quicker she got away from Rhys' dark, far-too-perceptive gaze, the better.

CHAPTER TWO

R hys Norcross paused at the top of the museum steps, watching as Gia's driver pulled up in front of the Hutton. Gia helped Haven inside the car and, with a flash of taillights, the Mercedes slid into traffic.

Fuck. He shoved his hands in his pockets. In his head, he kept seeing the swelling on Haven's pretty face. He was pissed. He wanted to find the assholes who'd hurt her and pound them into the pavement.

Vander stepped up beside him. "At least you finally got her to talk to you."

"Ha, ha," Rhys growled.

His brothers and friends at Norcross found it hilarious that Rhys had failed to get Haven to interact with him. She'd caught his eye at a party at Gia's a few months back. She was pretty, with a gorgeous laugh, and secrets in her blue eyes. Something about Haven McKinney got to him.

The woman could've been a member of their old Ghost Ops team with her ability to avoid him.

Seeing her beaten, scared... Fuck, someone was going down.

"I'm not letting her avoid me anymore."

Vander raised a dark brow. "She isn't the kind of woman you play with, Rhys."

"I'm going to play with her, and a whole lot more." He dragged in a deep breath. "But first, I need to find these thieves and teach them a lesson."

"And find our brother's hundred-million-dollar painting."

"That, too."

Easton strode out of the museum's grand entrance, his cell phone pressed to his ear. "Yes. Do it." He slid the phone into his jacket pocket. "My insurance company is...not happy."

"We'll find the painting," Vander said. "I'll call Hunt and see what the police turn up."

Detective Hunter "Hunt" Morgan had been Delta Force with them. An injury had forced him out of the military early and he'd joined the San Francisco PD. He had beers with the Norcross team regularly, and they called him when they needed police involvement. He was often pissed with them.

"And Rhys is the best, and extra-motivated by a set of pretty, blue eyes and excellent legs," Vander added.

Rhys shot his brother a pointed look.

Easton glanced at Rhys. "Finally got Haven to talk to you."

Rhys shot his brother the finger.

Easton's lips quirked, but then his face turned serious again. "Be careful with her, Rhys. She's been through a lot. Not just this. She hasn't said much about Miami, but I get the feeling that it wasn't good."

Hmm, it might be time for Rhys to do a little digging on his pretty brunette. "I'm going to take care of her. First up, though, I need to find your thieves."

"You have the security footage." Easton blew out a breath. "Assholes posed as delivery drivers for a delivery that was due tomorrow."

"How did they know that the delivery was due?" Rhys mused.

Easton shrugged a shoulder. "They shot the guards, then forced Haven to disconnect the alarm on the painting before beating the shit out of her."

"She's tough," Vander said. "She hit the panic button."

Rhys' gut turned to rock. If they'd caught her while she was doing that, she might have been hurt far worse.

He'd seen a lot of fucked-up stuff in his time. Their Ghost Ops team—made up of the best of the best from all the special forces teams across different branches of the military—had been sent in to do the toughest, grittiest jobs. Like Vander, Rhys had been Delta Force before he'd joined Vander's black ops team. They'd done all the jobs that the government denied.

He breathed deeply. Ghost Ops was done. Finished. He'd loved fighting for his country, but he liked working for Norcross even better. He got shot at far less.

Vander had been an excellent commander, and now he was an excellent boss. They still had some messy cases, and some straddled the line between lawful and not. Norcross Security had no trouble venturing into the shadows to get a job done.

They all knew that life wasn't as black-and-white as people who lived in nice houses, in their safe, little worlds liked to believe.

Pressure built in Rhys' chest, white noise growing in his head. It happened whenever he started thinking of shit from old missions. Whenever it did, he usually jumped in his car or boat.

Speed made it ease.

But now, the thought of how soft Haven's skin was under his fingers made him feel better. Stroking her cheek, seeing her chest hitch, the bright flare of awareness in her blue eyes. Hell yeah, that made him feel much better.

You're not going to hide from me now, angel.

"I want to get back to the office," Rhys said. "I'll take a look at the security footage, and see if we can find the truck."

"It'll be a rental," Vander said.

"I'll find them." Rhys always did. He loved the thrill of the chase, putting all the pieces of a puzzle together.

"Anything you need from me," Easton said. "Just let me know. I want Haven safe, and I want my painting back."

"We need to tighten up on the delivery protocols," Vander said. "Make sure this doesn't happen again."

"Keep me posted, bro." Easton headed for his sleek, gunmetal-gray, Aston Martin DBS Superleggera parked on the street.

Rhys and Vander climbed into the Norcross SUV

they'd driven in. As soon as Rhys had heard what happened, he'd jumped in one of the Norcross fleet of black BMW X6s. Vander had barely had time to climb in before Rhys was speeding off to the Hutton.

Now, he drove a little slower toward the Norcross office. The Hutton Museum was right in the city, but the Norcross office was in South Beach, right at the border with the Embarcadero.

"You got your head in the right place?" Vander asked.

Rhys' hands flexed on the wheel. "Yeah. You?"

Vander had a short fuse when it came to violence against women and children. Once, on a mission, he'd abandoned their primary objective to rescue women and kids trapped in a rape house by a warlord. The warlord was no longer breathing.

"Yeah," Vander replied. "Find these fuckers, Rhys."

"Oh, I plan to." They'd hurt Haven, so he'd make them pay.

LOOKING at herself in the mirror the next morning, Haven stifled a cry.

She looked like she'd gone a few rounds in the boxing ring...and lost. Dismally.

She sighed, probing the swollen and bruised left side of her face. No amount of makeup was going to hide that. Keeping things simple, she pulled her hair up into a ponytail, and winced at the ache in her side. She touched her tender ribs. Nothing was broken, but it still hurt. She fished around in Gia's cabinet, pulled out some painkillers, and popped two pills. She'd need these today.

She'd spent the night in Gia's lovely guest room. Her friend had a gorgeous two-bedroom apartment in SoMa, with killer views of the city and the bay. Haven's place was way smaller, and while it was cute, it was nowhere as plush as Gia's light, airy space.

After Easton had retired from the military, he'd turned his attention to business. Apparently, the oldest Norcross had a knack for making money. He'd started with real estate, then invested in various businesses. He took care of investing for his siblings and parents, too.

Despite the lovely room and comfy bed, Haven had slept like crap. She'd kept rolling onto her injured side and waking herself up. Plus, she'd had a nasty nightmare. It had starred the thief who'd hit her, his glittering, blue eyes staring at her through his balaclava before it morphed into Leo shouting at her.

Blowing out a breath, Haven finished getting ready for the day. They'd detoured by her apartment in Pacific Heights on the way back to Gia's the night before, and she'd grabbed some clothes. Today's skirt was gray, and she had a ruby-red shirt on. It might take the attention off the bruises on her face.

She glanced in the mirror again and winced. Or maybe not.

She headed into Gia's bright, light-filled kitchen. It was ironic that her friend had a chef's wet-dream kitchen that she barely used. Gia could cook, she just had no time for it.

There was a scent of coffee in the air, and Gia turned

from the coffee machine. She took one look at Haven's face and her lips firmed into a flat line.

"I'm going to *kill* those assholes."

"It looks worse than it is." Haven slid onto a stool at the island.

Gia looked stunning in a fitted, white, sleeveless dress. It followed her curvy body like a determined lover. Her dark curly hair was partly pulled back, while the rest of her curls fell down her back.

"Well, it looks like you went a few rounds with a bull-dozer, and lost."

Haven wrinkled her nose, which tugged on her bruises. "Thanks for the pep talk. Now I feel beautiful."

"You aren't going to work," Gia said.

Haven stiffened. "Yes, I am. I'm bruised, not bedridden."

Her friend's brown eyes narrowed. She slammed a piece of toast down in front of Haven.

Haven's stomach churned. She really wasn't that hungry. She was worried about the security guards, and stressing about the painting being gone.

"I want to stop by the hospital and check on David and Gus."

"Of course, you do." Gia pushed a mug of coffee across the island. "As always, worrying about everyone else but yourself."

Haven grabbed her hand. "Thanks for looking after me."

Her friend was silent for a moment. "I hate that you say that with a faintly surprised tone to your voice."

Haven hunched her shoulders. Her mom had died

when Haven was eleven. Her dad was off saving sick kids in Africa. She saw him whenever he was in the States, but it wasn't often, and when he was here, he was usually busy fundraising. She'd been looking out for herself for a long time.

"I will always be here for you, Haven," Gia continued softly. "My brothers will deal with the situation."

Surely Easton was pissed the Monet was missing. He had to be angry that Haven had let the damned thieves in. Guilt felt like a thousand needles stabbing at her skin.

"I spoke with Vander this morning," Gia said. "Your guards are both conscious, and doing well."

Haven pressed a hand to her chest. *Thank God.* Gus loved reading thrillers, so she'd take him a few. And David had a weakness for chocolate-covered almonds he thought he was hiding. She'd grab them some gifts and visit them first thing.

Grabbing a knife and the jar of honey, she spread some on her toast.

"And," Gia continued, "Vander said that Rhys is hot on the case. My baby brother is pissed, and determined to find who hurt you."

Haven's heart went pitty-pat. *No. Don't go there.* She sipped her coffee, trying to keep her face blank.

Gia leaned a hip against the island, her laser-like gaze on Haven. "Nothing to say?"

"No." She took a bite of toast.

"Nothing to say about the dreamy-eyed hunk cradling your face, vowing vengeance for you?"

"You can't call your brother a hunk, there's a rule against that."

"Facts are facts, girlfriend. I, unfortunately, have had to deal with having three hot brothers all my life." Gia's gaze sharpened. "So, Rhys…"

Haven sipped the coffee too fast and burned her tongue. "I've sworn off men. Besides, need I remind you that, one—" Haven held up a finger "—he's your brother? My *best friend's* brother. That has trouble written all over it. And two—" another finger went up "—he's also my boss' brother. That's a big no-no. I already messed up getting involved with my boss' family in Miami. *Big* mistake."

Gia grabbed her hand. "I know Leo the creep hurt you."

"He taught me a lesson." Haven tossed her ponytail back. "I don't need another man messing up my life. Especially not one who won't stick around long. Men like Rhys, who can have their pick of any women, never do."

"Mmm." Gia managed to say a lot with one hum.

After a few hurried bites of her toast, Haven stood. "I'm going to work."

She was also going to do her own research on who might have taken the Monet. She might not be a former military badass, or a hotshot investigator, but the art world was her domain.

Offloading a painting like the *Water Lilies* wouldn't be easy. She had several people she wanted to call…

Gia's front door opened. Easton strode in, wearing another perfectly tailored suit, and a blue shirt that looked good on him.

"That key is for emergencies," Gia said archly. "You could knock."

"I don't knock." Easton looked at Haven. "You aren't going in to work today." He looked at his sister. "Can I have a coffee?"

Gia rolled her eyes. "Yes." She pointed. "The coffee machine is right there."

Easton tugged on Gia's hair and then started making himself a coffee.

Haven pulled in a breath. "I can go to work. I want to work."

"No," Easton said.

God, give her strength. "I don't want to just sit around."

"I'm your boss. You rest. You were attacked last night."

She swallowed. "I know that. I want to help get the painting back." Her voice broke.

Easton turned slowly, then stalked around the island. Watching him come closer, she stiffened. He rested his hands on her shoulders, and she smelled the crisp, citrusy scent of his cologne. She stared at the buttons on his shirt.

"Haven, look at me," he ordered.

She did.

"You are not to blame here."

"I let them in."

"Anyone would have made that decision. They were well-prepared. This is *not* your fault."

"Gus and David—"

"Not. Your. Fault. Now, let Vander and Rhys do the job they're very good at. I want you to go home and take it easy."

"Fine." Trying to reason with any of the Norcross

family was an exercise in futility. She'd have better luck beating her head against the wall.

Easton tugged her ponytail, just like he'd done to Gia. "Good girl."

As Gia and Easton went back to their coffees, Haven tuned out their conversation. She didn't care what Easton said, she wasn't going to relax.

Her painting had been stolen, her guards hurt, her museum invaded. She wasn't going to sit and do nothing. She was going to find the damn *Water Lilies*.

CHAPTER THREE

Rhys swiped through security footage from the museum again. All five assailants wore balaclavas. And, as they'd guessed, the delivery van had been a rental. It had been rented using a fake name and a stolen credit card.

"Who are you assholes?" Rhys tapped his fist against the desk.

He was in his office at the converted warehouse that housed the Norcross Security. He was good at running his prey to ground. He never let up, he checked every lead—large or small—and he left them no place to hide. He'd already put out feelers to his contacts to keep an eye out for anyone trying to shift the painting.

On the screen, he saw the leader hit Haven, saw her go down, and then the motherfucker kicked her.

Rhys growled. "I will find you." The man had signed up for a world of hurt. Rhys couldn't wait to deliver it.

He'd already called Hunt this morning, but the detective didn't have any solid leads. Rhys moved to the next image. Unlike Hunt, Rhys didn't have to follow so many rules. He would find these guys, one way or another.

Then he spotted something, and froze the image. The skinny guy near the painting. He had ink on his neck. Some sort of star.

Rhys had his own ink. His mother got a long-suffering look on her face whenever she saw any of her boys' tattoos. This tattoo could just be something generic, one drunk tourists got and then regretted the next day.

But it could also be something specific that could be tracked down.

His phone rang and when he glanced at the display, he grinned. He thumbed the screen. "Hi, Ma."

"You know, your father and I don't live very far away and we're getting old. You could come to visit."

He'd visited a week ago and had dinner with them. His mom made the best lasagna in all of California. "You and Dad aren't old."

Clara Norcross snorted. "It doesn't matter what my age is, you'll always be my *bambino*, Rhys Matteo."

She said that to all of them. "Where's Dad?"

"In his workshop. Tinkering."

Rhys bit his tongue. Many years ago, Clara Bianchi had disappointed many good Italian boys by falling head over heels in love with Ethan Norcross, the very non-Italian boy next door. Their dad had been a firefighter, working his way up to a Division Chief in the San Francisco Fire Department before he'd retired.

Rhys' mom had started buying him power tools as gifts and encouraged him to build a workshop. To this day, Rhys' father puttered around his workshop and didn't do much. He'd confessed he had no desire to work wood or build shit.

"Now, I heard from Gia that Haven's had some trouble," his mom said.

Rhys' smile dissolved. "Yeah, Ma."

"I want you to take care of her, Rhys."

"I'm working on it."

"That girl has shadows in her eyes. So much hurt."

"I won't let anyone hurt her."

"Good." His mother paused. "Maybe you can bring her for dinner some time."

Just what Rhys needed, his mother matchmaking. She had the subtlety of a sledgehammer and a very strong hankering for grandbabies.

"Ma, I have to go."

"Okay, dinner soon, Rhys."

"Love you, Ma."

He ended the call and stared at his laptop screen. Before he took Haven anywhere, he had to get her safe.

"You got anything?" a deep voice asked, interrupting his thoughts.

He looked up as another Norcross employee appeared in the doorway of Rhys' office.

Saxon Buchanan was Vander's best friend, and second in charge at Norcross. Saxon and Vander had met in high school, and become instant friends. After they'd graduated, they'd both enlisted—much to the horror of Saxon's wealthy family—determined to watch each other's backs.

"Not much," Rhys said.

Saxon cocked his head. His brown-blond hair was

always well cut, and his suit was custom. Despite being Ghost Ops for several years, and doing some messy, dirty jobs, Saxon came from money, and made no bones about liking the finer things in life. He liked his clothes designer, his whiskey expensive, and he had a vast collection of expensive watches. They all liked to give him hell for it.

"Haven okay?" Saxon asked.

"Her face is a mess." Rhys breathed deeply. "She'll heal. She stayed with Gia last night, and she's resting today."

"Haven's always struck me as tough. A spine of quiet steel under that gorgeous body of hers."

Rhys narrowed his eyes. "No need for you to notice her body."

Saxon grinned. "I'm male, with 20/20 vision. Hard to miss those legs and that ass."

Rhys growled.

Saxon's grin widened, making Rhys want to punch his friend in his perfect teeth.

"Side benefit is that I also get to yank your chain. You've had your eyes on her for months. It doesn't usually take you so long to track down a target."

True. And Rhys had been fucking celibate from the moment he'd looked into Haven's pretty blue eyes. He'd spent far too many nights stroking his own cock, imagining her hands on him, her husky cries in his ears.

Shit, he was getting hard. Rhys shifted in his chair. If Saxon noticed, he'd give Rhys hell.

Then his friend's smile dissolved. "I am sorry she got hurt."

"Well, the assholes who did it will pay. I'm following a few leads."

"Need any help?"

"Thought you had a security-system job today?" While Rhys was Norcross' top investigator, Saxon was their troubleshooter. He did a bit of everything, but was often the one sent into the crappy, messy jobs to find the best solution.

"Already done. Fancy house in Nob Hill, just around the corner from my parents." The corner of his mouth lifted. "Not that my parents would spend any time with the Dillons. They'd consider them far beneath them. New money. I scoped out the house and avoided the very obvious offers from the client's very young trophy wife to tour her bedroom, and then sent him the quote."

"I emailed some art dealers, and called a few of our other...contacts." Some of Norcross' contacts operated on the other side of the law. "I asked them to get in touch if they hear about anyone asking about the painting, or the Hutton Museum. Anyone trying to offload a Monet. Can you call a few more dealers for me?"

"I'm on it." Saxon flicked him a salute and strode across the warehouse.

Rhys made a few more calls, feeling edgy and frustrated. He headed for the well-stocked kitchenette, and made a coffee. The large windows offered a view of the water and a glimpse of the Bay Bridge.

Vander had purchased the old warehouse, then completely decked it out. The bottom level was parking for the company's fleet of cars, and also housed a well-equipped gym. There were also several holding rooms for when they had "guests."

The central level held the offices—it was all mostly open plan in the center, with wooden beams and metal duct work overhead. Glass-walled offices lined each side of the space. There was another level upstairs, with a roof terrace, that was Vander's living quarters.

Rhys had a place close by in Rincon Hill—it was sleek and modern, with a killer view. Easton had invested all the money Rhys had socked away while he'd been in the military, and Rhys now had a great apartment, a killer car and boat, and a nice little nest egg. He wasn't as rich as Easton, and Vander did well from Norcross Security, but Rhys was happy and more than comfortable. He didn't want the headache of running his own business, wheeling and dealing, or putting up with asshole clients.

He also had parking for his car and bike, and he rented a space near the Norcross office for his boat.

So many times, on missions, he'd been hot and tired, and had sand in places that chafed. He'd dreamed of being on the water, or just on a comfy couch watching a football game in peace.

A few times, he'd been injured, and thought he wouldn't make it back. He'd done important work, shitty work, but work that had to be done to ensure freedom for so many.

Now, he made no apologies that he worked hard, and played hard, as well.

He wanted Haven McKinney to play. He wanted to peel her out of those tight, ass-hugging skirts that gave him hot-librarian fantasies.

Some jacked up part of him wanted to erase the shadows in her eyes, as well.

Rhys snorted. He was no one's hero, but he had the skills to keep her safe, and ensure the prick who'd hurt her paid.

"Ah, Rhys?"

He glanced up at Saxon, who stood with his hands in his pockets. His friend had an unreadable look on his face.

"Yeah?" Rhys sipped his coffee.

"I don't think Haven is resting."

"Come again?" He lowered the coffee mug.

"Just got off the phone with a dealer. She'd been to see him."

Rhys stiffened.

"And another dealer said she was due to visit him at eleven."

He glanced at his watch. It was already after eleven.

He cursed. Rhys poured his coffee in the sink and set the mug down, then strode for the stairs.

"Good luck." Saxon sounded far too amused.

HAVEN STEPPED into the elegant gallery in SoMa. South of Market was home to many of San Francisco's museums and galleries.

She loved her friend Harry's gallery. It reminded her of the gallery she'd worked at in Miami. The lighting was warm, complementing pale walls, and right up front was a modern painting—garish, with bold, neon colors.

But with all art, beauty was in the eye of the beholder. It wasn't her particular style, but she could still appreciate it and know that someone else might love it.

"Haven!"

She turned.

Harry Temple, her dealer friend and the gallery owner, strode toward her. He was a handsome, trim, well-dressed man with a dash of silver at his temples. Haven had shared several great dinners with Harry and his husband, Trent. They were both fun and entertaining.

When Harry saw her face, he jerked to a halt. His horrified gaze moved over her cheek and eye. "Darling girl, what happened?"

"You haven't heard?"

He touched her arms. "No. Tell me who he is and I'll send Trent to teach him a lesson."

Trent was a personal trainer and owner of a local gym.

"Harry, we had a theft at the Hutton. They did this —" Haven waved at her face "—and stole the *Water Lilies*."

Harry gasped. "Okay, totally cannot process the multi-million-dollar painting theft, but they hit you?"

"I'm fine," she assured him.

Harry hugged her and she let herself lean on him for a second.

"Tell me Easton is tearing through San Francisco looking for this scum?"

"Well, he has his brother's security firm looking into it."

Harry shivered. "I'd let Vander Norcross look into me

34

any day, if he didn't scare the spit out of me." He patted her shoulder. "Darling girl, Easton may own most of San Francisco, but Vander runs it. He'll find them."

"The painting's gone, Harry. I can't help but feel like it's my fault. I *need* to find it."

Her friend frowned. "I haven't heard a peep. Something that big would make a lot of noise."

She sighed. "Will you keep your ear to the ground?"

"You know I will."

"Any whisper, any rumor, you call me."

"Absolutely. Now—" Harry slipped an arm through hers. "Come and sit. I'll have Tory make us some frothy lattes, and I'll show you the latest piece I got in from a local artist I think is going to be *huge*."

Haven let Harry fuss over her for a while.

When she stepped out of his gallery, she felt a little better, but the missing painting felt like a weight pressing down on her.

God, it was so damn unfair that she'd just gotten her life back on an even keel, was loving her work, had a good boss in Easton and a great friend in Gia, and then *this* happened.

Haven headed down the street. Feeling sorry for herself wouldn't help. She knew that from experience. The weather was lovely and good for a walk. It was a beautiful fall day, not hot, not cold. Whatever it took, she was getting that painting back, and getting her damn life calm and stable again.

She almost ran into a bulky man in a suit in the middle of the sidewalk. "Sorry."

She darted around him, her heels clicking on the

pavement. She wasn't sure what she could do next to find the painting. But she set her shoulders back. She wasn't giving up. The Hutton was only a few blocks away. She'd sneak into her office and make a few more calls.

Leo had screwed up her life, and for a while, she'd let him. Not anymore. Haven was in charge, and she wasn't letting anyone, especially some thieves, get her down.

But, millions of dollars, the voice in her head pointed out. Her stomach turned.

She paused, and practiced some breathing exercises from the yoga classes Gia sometimes dragged her to. No, she still felt stressed, and her face throbbed. Her painkillers were wearing off.

Then she felt a tickle of something on the back of her neck. That feeling any woman walking alone sometimes felt. Was someone watching her?

She heard heavy footsteps behind her and glanced back. There weren't many people around, just a stocky man in the suit heading in her direction. She frowned.

Wait, wasn't he the guy she'd bumped into before? He'd been going in the *other* direction.

He lifted his head—he had a buzzcut, no neck, and a really ill-fitting suit.

His gaze locked with hers.

Sucking in a breath, Haven turned and took off down the street as fast as she could without running. She fumbled for her phone. There was probably nothing wrong—

Strong arms wrapped around her from behind, yanking her backward.

"Hey!" she cried.

The man didn't say a word, and panic shot through Haven. He dragged her down the sidewalk.

Dammit, she wasn't getting snatched off the street in broad daylight. Could she have any shittier luck? Surely, she'd had her fair share already?

"Let me go!"

She was *not* going to let this no-neck jerk abduct her. She kicked him in the shin.

She felt her heel hit bone and he grunted, then he followed it up with a curse. He shook her.

Haven's shoe fell off, and her phone slipped from her fingers to the sidewalk. She heard locks bleep on a car nearby and fear shot through her. He was dragging her to a car. If he got her inside...

No. *No.*

Haven twisted and struggled. She screamed, but he stuck a beefy hand over her mouth. Why was no one around?

She let her body weight drop, but Mr. No-Neck just dragged her.

Oh, God. She could be taken anywhere. She'd seen those Liam Neeson movies. She'd be sex-trafficked, fed drugs, raped—

Then suddenly, the goon let her go.

Haven staggered, and fell to her hands and knees. Her ribs ached and her palms stung. Crap, she'd lost some skin.

She heard a thud and spun, her pulse racing.

Then she sucked in a breath and watched Rhys slam a brutal punch into her abductor's face.

Mr. No-Neck flew back, and Rhys—wearing a charcoal suit and white shirt that fit him in a mouthwatering way that only a woman would notice—advanced.

Two more punches and her abductor went down. Rhys straightened. He didn't look like he'd even worked up a sweat.

Boiling, pissed-off, brown eyes locked on her.

CHAPTER FOUR

R hys fought back his rage and scanned Haven.
She looked shaken, but had no new injuries
that he could see.

The man on the ground groaned, and Rhys took out
some zip ties and tied the man's wrists and feet.

"You okay?" he asked Haven.

"God, no. He... He..." She looked on the verge of
tears, but pulled it back. There was that spine of steel.

Rhys straightened, reached out, and stroked her jaw.

She leaned into his touch for a second, then she
swiveled. "Asshole." She glared at the mostly uncon-
scious man on the ground. Then she kicked him. The
man grunted. "He tried to *kidnap* me."

Rhys was happy to hear that she was pissed. He
yanked out his phone.

"Are you calling the police?" She wrapped her arms
around herself, running her hands up and down her arms
like she was cold.

"No."

She cocked her head. "No?"

The call connected. "Saxon, need you to come and do a pickup. A guy just tried to snatch Haven off the street."

"What the fuck?" Saxon paused. "Haven okay?"

"Yeah, just shaken." And starting to look furious.

"Is the guy still breathing?" Saxon asked.

"Yes, through a broken nose." Rhys rattled off their location.

"Okay, on my way."

The man on the ground shook his head, watching them blearily.

Haven snatched up her dropped shoe and phone, slipping her shoe back on. She still looked shaken and Rhys wrapped an arm around her, pulling her close to his chest. She was stiff at first, then she leaned into him, her forehead resting against his shirt. Damn, she felt good tucked up against him.

Then she made a small sound that sounded like a sob.

"Hey, it's all right now," he murmured.

Her hands clenched on his shirt. "Sorry," she sniffed.

"You've had a rough twenty-four hours. You're entitled to freak out."

"Yes, well, I've learned the best way to deal with freak-outs is to do it alone, with wine."

Frowning, he looked down at the top of her head. He hated hearing the resignation in her voice. He wanted her to turn to him, lean on him.

Hell, he'd never felt that way before. He tipped her chin up. "I'm right here."

Her blue gaze skittered away.

The man on the ground moved and Rhys flicked him a glance. "Don't even think about it."

At the cutting tone of Rhys' voice, the guy's shoulders slumped.

"What are you going to do with him?" Haven asked.

"Ask him a few questions."

Rhys saw the gears turning in that clever head of hers.

"Wait, you think he has something to do the theft? I don't think so. This was random."

Rhys rubbed his fingers up her arm. "Don't worry about it."

She threw a hand up. "He tried to drag me off the street and shove me in a car." She shuddered. "I'm going to worry about it, Rhys."

He tightened his hold on her.

She stilled, her gaze running over his face. "What?"

"That's the first time you've said my name."

"What? No, that can't be right."

"You avoid me like the plague, Haven. Believe me, it's the first time you've said my name." He paused. "Been waiting a long time to hear you say it."

He heard her sharp breath, then she glanced away, like the brick wall of the nearby building was suddenly fascinating. Her hands clenched tighter on his shirt.

"You going to ignore me while standing in my arms?"

"I thought I'd give it a try."

His lips twitched.

"You are pretty hard to ignore." Her gaze met his. "I do owe you a thank you. For rescuing me." A frown creased her brow. "Why were you here?"

ANNA HACKETT

"I heard that a certain stubborn museum curator was not at home resting the morning after being attacked. Instead, she's been taking gifts to injured guards in the hospital, and traipsing around the city, trying to do my job."

She licked her lips, which made him look at them. They were pink and perfectly shaped, and gave him dirty ideas.

"I'm fine. And... And I need to help, Rhys. I feel like this is all my fault. My job is to take care of the museum and all the artwork. To look out for our employees. I let those thieves in, and they hurt the guards—"

"Not your fault. The guys who took the painting are not amateurs."

A sleek, black BMW X6 SUV screeched to a stop beside them, and Saxon and Vander got out. Vander's turbulent gaze shifted to the man on the ground, then came back to them.

"Haven, you okay?" Vander asked.

She nodded.

Vander and Saxon heaved the man up. He went in sullen silence, and Saxon shoved him in the back of the X6.

"We'll put him in a holding room," Vander said. "Ask him a few questions."

Rhys lifted his chin. He wanted to go in and question the man himself, but he needed to take care of Haven.

She cleared her throat. "Ah, is *ask a few questions* a euphemism for rough him up a bit?"

The corner of Vander's mouth twitched. "No."

The breath rushed out of her. "Oh, good."

42

"It's a euphemism for, if he doesn't answer my questions, I'll beat the shit out of him," Vander said. "Catch you guys later." He slid into the SUV's driver seat.

A second later, the vehicle pulled away.

"Your brother is scary as hell."

Rhys didn't disagree. He'd grown up with Vander—who'd been an intense teenager with a strong sense of right and wrong. He'd worked alongside Vander in some bad places, under fire, with a lot on the line. Vander still had a code he followed, but it wasn't so black-and-white anymore.

"Come on." Rhys led her down the street and paused beside his silver Mercedes GTS.

She eyed the sportscar. "This looks fast...and expensive."

He helped her into the passenger seat.

"Where are we going?" she asked.

He pulled into traffic. "My place."

"What?" she squeaked.

"Your palms are scraped, and you're shaking. You're in shock."

She clasped her hands together. "Just take me home."

"Nope."

"So, I *have* been kidnapped."

Rhys took a turn, heading toward his apartment. "I'm going to clean your hands, make you a drink. Probably a shot of whiskey."

"I hate whiskey."

"This is a whiskey moment, angel."

She was quiet for the rest of the drive. Stewing. Rhys could sense it. Having Gia for a sister—a woman who rarely held back exactly what she was feeling—had given him plenty of experience.

They arrived at his building and he parked in the underground parking. He pulled in beside his Kawasaki Ninja, which he saw Haven eye with interest.

"You ever been on a bike?" he asked.

She shook her head.

He smiled. "You'll like it."

It was a quick elevator ride up to his apartment, and he let them through the front door.

She walked across his open-plan living room to the bank of floor-to-ceiling windows. He had a great view of the Bay Bridge.

"Holy cow," she murmured.

He paused for a second. He liked seeing her silhouetted against the glass. Liked seeing her in his place. It was weird, since he rarely brought women back here.

She turned, taking in his place. Her gaze snagged on the far wall and her eyebrows rose. "You collect...toy cars?"

He frowned at his custom-made shelves. "Those are models."

"You sure?"

His gaze narrowed. His siblings liked to rib him about his collection too. "They're all die-cast collectibles. Very valuable."

She made an unconvinced sound. "Do you play with them?"

"No." He saw her lips twitch and decided if teasing him made her feel better, he was okay with it. "I'll get my first aid kit."

She spun, blue eyes on fire. "I cannot believe this!"

Here came the explosion.

Haven tossed her arms wide, pacing across the living area. "I just can't think of what I did to deserve this shitty karma. Some no-neck hulk tries to abduct me. Thieves shot my guards, nice guys with families, and stole a really, really expensive painting. A *masterpiece*. And a total asshole beat me up." Her voice rose.

"Haven, baby, calm down."

She spun again. "All of this on top of a real asshole ex who was mixed up in God knows what, and who also hit me. Do I have a sign saying 'punch me here' hanging around my neck?"

All of Rhys' humor fled. He pushed away from his kitchen island. "Your ex hit you?"

His lethal tone of voice got through to her. She lowered her arms. "That's in the past."

He strode straight to her. "What's his name? Who is he?"

"Rhys—"

He wrapped his arms around her. "No man should ever lay a hand on a woman. Ever."

She swallowed. "I know." She spread her palms over his chest. "I left him the first time he did it. Things hadn't been good for a while." She patted Rhys. "It's over."

He realized with her calm tone of voice that she was trying to pacify him. "He back in Miami?"

She nodded.

Watching her, most of Rhys' fury drained. Damn, she was beautiful.

Then he realized she was shaking. Probably delayed

reaction to the asshole who tried to grab her. Rhys pulled her closer. She pressed her face against him, and he rested his cheek on her hair.

"Why am I shaking? I'm mad."

"You're upset. Have your freak-out."

She didn't cry, but she held on, and damned if he didn't like it. When her shaking stopped, he led her to a stool and grabbed his first aid kit out of the cupboard.

"Your kit is way more used than mine," she said. "In mine, everything is still in the original packaging."

Yeah, well, he got banged up on occasion, and he did anything he could to avoid hospitals. He took her scraped hand and gently cleaned her wounds. When he used the antiseptic wipe, she hissed, but didn't jerk away. Next, he put some antiseptic cream on, then did the same to her other hand.

"Thank you," she murmured.

"Not going to let anyone hurt you again." He tucked a strand of her brown hair back. He loved the light brown shade of it, with almost silver undertones.

"I think I'm ready for part two of my freak-out," she said.

He raised a brow.

"The getting angry part." She slid off the stool and strode across his living area.

Rhys' gaze dropped to her ass. That curvy, sexy ass.

"I left Miami for a fresh start." She made an angry sound. "Shit clearly follows me around."

Yes, her anger was back. She grabbed one of her shoes and threw it at his couch. It hit and bounced off one of the cushions. Then she tossed her other one.

"I'm done being a punching bag." She spun. "Hear that, universe?"

Rhys advanced. He had to touch her.

She spun and bumped into him. "Oh."

"Rant over?"

"Maybe." She sniffed. "I could probably dredge up a bit more."

"You're done for now." He yanked her up on her toes and did what he'd wanted to do from the first day he'd met her. He kissed Haven McKinney.

OH. *God.*

Rhys Norcross was kissing her.

This was a disaster, but it was also toe-curlingly incredible.

Even as her brain screamed at her to pull away, to run to Europe and join a convent, her hands dug into his hard chest and she parted her lips.

He took immediate advantage, his tongue sliding against hers. Desire filled every cell in her body in a wild, invigorating rush.

He deepened the kiss, and any remaining thoughts of escaping him flew out of her head. Haven moaned, and sank her hands into his thick, shaggy hair. She kissed him back.

"Fuck," he murmured against her lips.

The next kiss was wild. They were both groping each other, pressing their bodies together. He picked her up like she weighed nothing, and set her on the lovely wooden table in the dining area. Then he worked her skirt up enough to stand between her legs.

Alarm bells were ringing. Rhys was a danger with a very big D, underlined twice.

"Rhys," she panted.

Then his mouth was on hers again. Damn, he tasted so good, felt so good. Somehow, she got the two top buttons of his shirt undone, sliding her hands inside.

Oh, warm skin. She saw the ink on the left side of his chest. So sexy. A hard, muscled man with ink in a suit. Totally sex on a stick. She felt a flood of dampness between her legs.

His hands slid into her hair, tilting her head back. His mouth skated down her jaw to her neck.

Oh, God. She had a sensitive neck. She shuddered under the sensations.

A big, strong hand slid up her thigh, heading to where her body begged for him to touch her. Then her brain reengaged.

"No."

Rhys paused and lifted his head. The look on his face made her swallow a moan. Desire was carved hard on those handsome features.

Rhys Norcross wanted her.

Since she'd said no, he hadn't moved. His fingers were still on her leg, but they weren't moving higher. Damn, she knew that he was a good guy and he wouldn't take advantage.

She licked her lips. "We can't do this."

"I'm pretty sure we can," he growled. "And it'll be fucking amazing."

Haven pressed a hand to her flushed cheek. Yes, he wanted her. She knew he'd wanted plenty of other women, as well—who were more beautiful and experienced than her.

She also knew that he didn't keep them very long.

Haven wasn't a one-night woman. More power to women who were, but it wasn't her, and there was more to her refusal than just that.

It was the fact that Gia was her best friend, and Easton was her boss. This could get messy quickly.

"You're my best friend's brother."

Rhys raised a brow. "Gia's been telling me to make a move on you for weeks."

Haven's eyes popped open wide. "That traitor! I am so not getting her those gallery opening tickets she wanted." Haven drew herself up. "You're my boss' brother. That's messy. I've already made the colossal mistake of getting involved with a family member of my last boss."

"The dickhead ex?"

She nodded. "He was my boss' cousin."

His voice dropped. "I'm not your ex, Haven, and I don't care how many stupid excuses you throw between us."

The biggest one was the one she wouldn't tell him. That deep down, something in her knew that Rhys Norcross had the power to hurt her far worse than Leo Becker ever had. Oh, Rhys would never hit her, but her heart... *Nope.* She couldn't withstand whatever pain he would inflict.

She pushed him back and hopped off the table, shoving her skirt down.

Adult, be an adult, Haven. She made herself look at him.

God, those lips. And his scent—he always smelled like sandalwood and pine.

"That shouldn't have happened," she persisted.

He crossed his muscular arms over his chest. "It should. And it should happen again."

Damn, if he touched her again, her willpower would crumble like tissue paper. She was so weak when it came to him.

"No." She held up her hand, channeling some of Gia's attitude.

"You're going to have to do better with the excuses than Easton and Gia." Rhys cocked his head, a lock of dark-brown hair flopping over his forehead.

Oh, her hand itched to brush it away, or sink her hands into it and climb him like a...

Focus, Haven. "I've sworn off men."

He blinked. "What?"

"Men. I'm done." She made a chopping motion with her hand. "From now on, I'm flying solo, and getting my life back on track. I have no room for you."

He arched a brow. "Were you just here for that kiss?"

Haven decided it was best to stay quiet.

"You know what would've happened if we'd kept going?" His voice lowered to a deep, sexy murmur.

Haven fought back a shiver. "Don't—"

"I would have finally gotten my hands under that tight skirt that hugs your ass and makes my mouth go dry."

She sucked in a breath.

"I would have pushed you onto your back, splayed you on my table, and torn whatever scrap of silk or lace you're wearing as panties."

Her body was alive, heat washing through her. She closed her eyes.

"I would've touched your sweet pussy, then gotten my mouth on you. Had you writhing until you came on my tongue, screaming my name."

Oh. God. She was not strong enough to fight this. She wanted all that, and more.

She opened her eyes. "Rhys—"

His cell phone rang.

They stared at each other, then he yanked it out and answered.

"Sax, tell me you have good news." A pause, then Rhys cursed. "He won't talk, even with some persuasion?" A second later, Rhys grunted. "He's scared of someone. Yeah, okay, keep me posted." He ended the call, his gaze coming back to her.

Haven twisted her hands together. "Nothing?"

"No."

"He probably has nothing to do with the theft of the *Water Lilies*," she said.

She got a grunt in response, and Rhys took a step toward her. "We aren't finished."

Her pulse leaped.

Then his phone rang again. This time, he muttered a string of curses. "Norcross." Another pause. "Yeah, talk."

Well, it looked like the universe had thrown her a bone. She'd been saved from making a huge mistake with Rhys by the phone.

She wondered why she felt so disappointed.

"Okay, see you there," Rhys' face was set in serious lines.

Haven licked her lips. "What now?"

"A contact might have info on the painting."

Her lungs locked. "That's *great*. Who is he?"

"A dealer."

"What's his name? I might know him."

"You don't."

"Rhys, the art world is my area. I know loads of people."

"He's a black-market dealer."

She gasped. "A thief? You hang out with thieves?"

He snatched up his car keys. "I have a varied list of people who give me information. Now, come on, I'll drop you home."

"Oh no, hotshot investigator." She crossed her arms over her chest. "I'm coming with you."

"No."

"Yes."

His brows drew together. "*No.*"

"Yes." She *wasn't* going to be left behind to sit around and wring her hands. She sucked at hand wringing.

CHAPTER FIVE

As Rhys pulled up to the seedy bar in Potrero Hill, he wondered how the fuck he'd let her talk him into this.

He'd stopped by the office and swapped his Mercedes for an SUV. He parked the X6 on a side street, and glanced Haven's way. There was a shine of excitement on her bruised face.

Shit, she was here because he couldn't say no to her. He saw that she needed this. Needed to help in some way.

He got out and circled the car. He'd changed out of his suit into jeans, a T-shirt, and boots. This wasn't a suit kind of place.

"No talking, stay beside me," he warned her.

She tossed him a sloppy salute and with a shake of his head, he walked down the street and around the corner to the bar. They entered, and it took a second to adjust to the gloom. Even at this time of day, there were plenty of people sitting around, drinking.

Rhys headed for the booths at the back. Haven attracted way too much attention. She was still in her skirt, and looking gorgeous.

He grabbed her hand, and shot a few glares around.

Then he spotted his contact, Hammon, sipping what was probably watered-down bourbon.

Rhys pushed Haven into the booth, then followed her in.

Hammon was in his late fifties, grizzled, with short, gray hair. He'd spent way too long in the sun in his life, and it showed in his leathery face.

The man eyed Haven. "See you upgraded your side-kick, Norcross. She's prettier than that hardass Buchanan."

"Don't look at her. What have you got for me?"

Hammon shifted. "Heard murmurs of a big sale."

"Those murmurs say what was for sale?"

The older man leaned his elbows on the table. "Nope. Just that it was worth a lot of money."

Rhys drummed his fingers on the table. "Names."

"No, don't have names."

Rhys growled. "Why the fuck call me down here to this shithole to tell me nothing, Hammon?"

"Because I got a possible location where they're storing it."

Haven gasped and Hammon glanced at her, or rather, at her chest.

Rhys snapped his fingers to regain the man's attention. "Where?"

"Just down the street. Warehouse that used to be an old factory." He rattled off an address and sipped his drink. "No one there right now. I was waiting around and saw a bunch of guys leave."

"I'll check it out."

Hammon sniffed. "I don't want payment, just help when I need it."

"If this pans out, I'll owe you." Rhys rose. He was used to doing unsavory deals with unsavory people, but often it got him the information he needed.

"So, who's your girl, Norcross?"

Rhys ignored the man and kept walking, towing Haven behind him. He wanted her out of there. And he wanted to punch every scumbag in the face who was looking at her.

This possessive need was new to him. He rarely got possessive over a woman.

Outside, Haven glanced down the street. "So, are we going to check that warehouse out now?"

"No, *I'll* check it out. I need to drop you at the Norcross office first."

"Rhys, *no*." She grabbed his hand. "It's right there. Your—" she hesitated for a second "—friend said the place is empty."

"He's not my friend."

"Just a quick look." She shot him a pleading look.

"Did you just flutter your eyelashes?"

"Maybe? Did it help?"

She had thick, dark eyelashes. Shit, what the fuck was wrong with him, thinking about her eyelashes?

She fluttered them again. "Please, just a quick look."

Dammit, he didn't want to put her in danger. He shouldn't have brought her in the first place. Still, the risk was low, and she'd be with him. He muttered a curse. "Okay, a very quick look. You do exactly as I say."

She nodded.

They headed down the street, and soon Rhys saw the warehouse. It was brick that had been painted white long ago, but the paint was now faded and chipped. The roof looked like it was held up by a prayer.

There were no vehicles, or signs of activity.

"This way." He led her down the side alley between the warehouse and the neighboring building.

He paused by an overflowing dumpster. The windows in the warehouse were beyond dirty, and a few were broken. There were no cameras or other security that he could see.

He climbed up on the Dumpster and looked through. The place was mostly empty, except for some gear in the center covered by drop cloths. He waited, listened.

"Place looks empty." He leaped down. He continued on until he reached a rusty, metal side door. He pulled out his lock picks.

"You can pick locks?" Haven breathed.

"Yeah."

"Did you learn that in the military?"

"No." He and his brothers had gotten themselves into plenty of trouble as teenagers.

"Will you teach me?"

"Hell, no."

She pouted, but then the lock clicked and the door squeaked open on rusty hinges.

They slipped inside. The place was gloomy and dust

hung in the air. It had that scent of emptiness and lack of use about it.

Rhys headed for the pile of items in the center. He lifted one of the cloths and Haven lifted the corner of another.

It was furniture—a wooden table, some dressers, an uncomfortable-looking couch, some small tables with spindly legs.

Haven gasped. "Rhys, this isn't my area of expertise, but these look like antiques. French style. They're probably worth a lot of money."

He looked under the other sheets. There were no multi-million-dollar paintings by master artists. *Damn.*

Haven scanned the space. "Maybe they're keeping the painting somewhere else around here?"

Suddenly, there was a loud noise, followed by the squeal of metal and voices.

Oh, fuck. "We have company." They were coming in through the front doors.

Haven froze, and the color drained from her face.

Rhys knew they'd never get back to the door they'd used without being spotted. He lifted the cover off the couch. "Quick."

She ducked under the sheet and he followed. Rhys stretched out on his back on the red-velvet couch and yanked her down so she lay flat on top of him. The sheet resettled, hiding them.

Haven was pressed flush against him, her nose brushing his and her breasts against his chest, and her hips to his.

She licked her lips. "Oh, God, what if—?"

"Shh." He gripped her hips, digging his fingers in warning.

The voices got closer. Rhys heard grunting.

"Damn, this ugly-ass thing is heavy," a voice growled.

There was a thud of something heavy hitting the ground.

"Lucky they're paying us good," another voice rumbled.

"Let's get the next thing from the truck."

Okay, a delivery. Rhys relaxed a little. The men had no reason to look at the other furniture. They should be safe.

Haven was breathing fast, and her breaths fluttered against his lips.

"Hey," he whispered. "Relax."

She nodded, her eyes still wide.

He cupped her cheek. "Slow your breathing down and focus on me."

Blue eyes hit his.

"At least you aren't the one lying on an ugly, uncomfortable couch," he muttered.

"It's a chaise lounge," she whispered.

He grunted. Whatever it was, it was very red and hard as hell. He stroked her cheek. She was slowly relaxing.

"How long are we stuck here?" she murmured.

"Until they leave."

Her lips twitched. "This is a bit exciting."

"I shouldn't have let you talk me into this."

"How did I convince you?"

"Because you're too damn beautiful."

Her chest hitched.

"And I apparently have trouble saying no to you."

"Rhys," she breathed.

"Don't look at me like that right now." Her face was soft, desire in her eyes. He felt his cock harden.

Shit. She could hardly miss it. The thing was jabbing her in the belly.

Sure enough, her eyes widened.

Shit. *Shit.* He slid a hand into her silky hair. This wasn't the time. He had to stay alert.

Then she murmured his name again. "*Rhys.*"

He was a goner. He lifted his head and closed his mouth over hers.

OH, boy, kissing Rhys Norcross, while hidden under a sheet after breaking and entering in a warehouse, sure packed a punch.

She'd clearly lost her mind.

His tongue touched hers, and Haven lost the ability to think. She kissed him back and ground against his rock-hard body. And that rock-hard, intriguing bulge against her belly.

He murmured a curse. "Haven, baby."

Oh wow, that bulge against her felt big and extra generous. She shimmied again.

He let out another whispered curse and rolled, pinning her beneath him and the back of the chaise longue.

"Bad girl." His voice was a husky whisper.

The voices of the delivery men were muffled; they'd moved farther away.

Haven kissed Rhys again. She couldn't stop herself. He kissed so well, and made her want more. Her breasts felt full, her skin was tingling.

He kept kissing her and she felt drugged.

Then he lifted his head.

She blinked. And realized that the warehouse was silent.

The men had gone.

Rhys sucked in a deep breath, then rolled off her and got to his feet. He peeked out from under the sheet.

"It's clear." He pulled her up.

Then he was towing her across the warehouse and through the door they'd used to enter. She had to jog to keep up. He dragged her down the narrow alley.

"Rhys?"

"Quiet." His voice was deep and gritty.

Was he mad that she'd kissed him while they'd been in danger? "I—"

"Quiet, Haven." He towed her down the street and into the side street where he'd parked. They reached the SUV.

"Rhys—"

He spun her, and pinned her against the vehicle. His hand slid into her hair, and he was kissing her again.

Oh, *oh*.

Then one of his hands slid up her thigh, dragging her skirt up. He hitched her leg around his hip and his hard cock hit right where she wanted it.

Her head fell back and she moaned.

They were on a public street and she didn't care one bit.

He pushed against her. "That's all for you, babe."

"Rhys."

"Damn, I love it when you purr my name like that." He bit her neck.

Haven undulated, desire coiling low in her belly.

Then someone wolf whistled, and Rhys froze. She stilled too, heat hitting her cheeks.

Then she shoved at his chest.

Oh, God. Sense steamrolled back into her head. Kissing Rhys Norcross while trapped in a warehouse. Then mauling him against a car on the street. What was she thinking?

She shoved her skirt down, pressed her hands to her cheeks. "God."

"Haven—"

"You make me lose my mind."

He shot her a cocky grin. "I like that."

"No!" She shook her head. "I told you that we can't do this."

There was fear in her belly now. It would be far too easy to fall for him. *Way* too easy.

He cupped her cheek. "Angel, stop thinking so hard. Just enjoy the ride."

His words were ice in her veins. *Right.* Because Rhys loved a good, fast ride.

She stepped away from him, and saw him frown. "I'm not interested in being another notch on your bed post, Rhys."

He stilled. "What?"

"You have a reputation. A colorful one. You're a player."

His gaze narrowed. "I am *not* a player. I don't make promises that I can't keep. I'm upfront with women."

She hated thinking of all those women—women who'd touched him, kissed him.

And were now probably nursing their broken hearts, and drinking too much to drown the sorrow of not getting the hotness of Rhys Norcross in their bed again.

"So, you give them a ride and then you're done with them." She shook her head. "That's not for me."

"This is what you think of me?" His low tone sent a shiver up her spine.

"You're an adrenaline junkie, always looking for the next adventure," she said. "Fast cars, boats, women. Even your job is dangerous. You're always looking for the edge, and once you conquer one thing—" one woman "—you're looking for the next." That wasn't her. She couldn't just be a plaything to him.

His eyes darkened. "You know what, I'm thinking I was actually lucky that you were avoiding me."

His angry words hit her like barbs, and she swallowed the growing lump in her throat.

He swiveled on his boot and bleeped the locks to the SUV. "Get in the car, Haven."

He stalked around to the driver's seat.

Haven felt a little sick now. No, this was for the best. She bit her lip and got in.

Rhys waited until she'd buckled her seatbelt, then he revved the engine and they pulled off. He drove fast, but with an air of competence.

As they took a corner, Haven braced her hand on the door. He whipped through traffic. The silence in the vehicle was thick and uncomfortable.

Before she knew it, he jerked to a stop in front of her apartment building.

"Stay inside. No more traipsing around the city playing detective." He didn't look at her, just stared straight ahead. "Your apartment has an alarm?"

"Yes," she whispered.

"You get inside, you make sure your doors are locked and your alarm is on. Vander or somebody else from Norcross will be in touch about the guy who tried to grab you. Let you know when it's safe to go out."

Clearly that wasn't going to be him. She felt like a rock had settled in her chest. "Rhys—"

"Get inside, Haven."

She hesitated.

He banged a palm against the steering wheel. "Go!"

Haven flew out of the car and raced into her apartment building.

This was what she'd wanted, to protect herself from Rhys.

So why the hell was she crying? She dashed the tears away from her cheeks and headed up to her empty apartment.

CHAPTER SIX

He slammed into the Norcross office and stomped to his office. Rhys was pissed as hell with Haven.

For months he'd wanted her, thought she was smart, sexy, sweet.

All that time, she'd thought he was an asshole. He knew people talked about him. Hell, half of what they said was pure fabrication. And the other half... He dropped into his chair. Well, he wasn't going to apologize for being a single man with a healthy sex drive.

He logged onto his laptop. He had work to do. Whatever was between him and Haven didn't affect his investigation.

He did some searches on the warehouse, his temper calming after a while. Hmm, it was owned by a string of shell companies. He'd need Ace Oliveira, Norcross' tech guru, to take a look.

Shit, he'd also ask Ace to tie into Haven's alarm system and keep an eye on her place.

"Hey."

Rhys looked up at Vander. "Hey."

"Anything new?" his brother asked.

"Got a lead from an informant. Checked the warehouse. It's being used to store stolen goods, but no painting."

"How's Haven holding up?"

"Fine."

Shit. At his clipped tone, he saw Vander's eyes narrow. His brother was beyond perceptive. On missions, Vander could almost sense things before they happened. It was spooky.

"Problem?" Vander asked.

"No. Dropped her at her place, and told her to arm her alarm and stay put until she heard from someone."

Vander just stared at him.

Rhys sighed. "We argued. Let's just say, you guys can quit ribbing me about striking out with her. I'm done."

"Rhys—"

"She thinks I'm a player, Vander. I don't have time for shallow women who listen to shit and can't be bothered to get to know me."

Vander was silent for a moment. "You know about Miami?"

Rhys stiffened. "I know she had a bad ex who hit her."

"Mmm."

"Enough with the cryptic shit, Vander."

His brother just raised a dark brow. "Haven's would-be kidnapper is in the holding room, and is still not talking. I have a meeting with Binary Tech."

That was one of Norcross' big corporate clients—

Norcross supplied all of Binary Tech's security systems, cyber security, and, when required, bodyguards for their executives.

Once Vander was gone, Rhys tried to concentrate. He kept remembering the taste of Haven, the feel of her.

Fuck.

His phone rang and he pulled it out. "Norcross."

"Hey, Big R, it's Jerome."

A boat-racing buddy. "Hey, Jerome. Where are you? Got a race on?" Jerome was always on the move. They'd met on the boat racing scene a year back.

"I'm in San Fran. I've got some parties I'm going to. You should come. Prime women, good booze, fun times."

Rhys leaned back in his chair. Maybe a distraction was what he needed. Go get laid, and get a certain brunette out of his head.

"I've also got a climbing trip planned, if you're interested," Jerome continued. "A few of us are hitting Yosemite."

"I'm on a case right now, but I can carve out time for a party or two."

"Knew you'd be up for a good time, man."

Instead of smiling, Rhys frowned. Shit, did everyone think he was only a good-time guy?

"I'll text you the addresses and dates," Jerome said. "See you soon. Be good to catch up."

Rhys ended the call, but he had a bad taste in his mouth. He decided it was time to go and question their "guest."

When he headed into the holding room, he saw the man sitting at the desk, handcuffed to one table leg. He was rumpled, his nose swollen. He lifted his head, and when he saw Rhys, his eyes glittered.

"Just tell us who you are and who you work for," Rhys said. "Then you can go."

Silence.

"You tried to snatch an innocent woman off the street. Cops don't like that. You keep your trap shut, that's your next stop."

More silence.

"You know, my day has turned pretty shitty, and I'm looking for a distraction." Rhys let his fingers curl into a fist.

Mr. No-Neck didn't miss it. "I talk, I die."

"Was the woman random, or were you after her specifically?"

There was a brief struggle on the man's face. "Her. Haven McKinney."

Fuck. It didn't matter that she'd pissed him off, Rhys still wanted her safe. "Why?"

The man shook his head.

There was a knock on the door, and Rhys opened it. Ace was in the doorway.

Rhys slipped outside. Ace Oliveira's long, dark hair was pulled back in a stubby ponytail. He was the same height as Rhys, a shade leaner, but kept in shape. He'd spent several years working at the NSA, and hadn't met a system he couldn't hack, bug, or take down, depending on his mood.

"His name is Joseph Cowell." Ace's voice held a faint touch of Brazil. He'd grown up in the US, but both his parents were Brazilian. "I ran some searches and he popped." Ace handed over a piece of paper.

Rhys scanned it. "Thug for hire."

"Yep. Got links to Petrov."

Rhys stiffened. Damn, Russian mafia. Boris Petrov ran a steady business of money laundering in San Francisco. He usually steered well clear of Norcross, and kept out of their business. Rhys frowned. The mafia couldn't be linked to Haven.

He turned and peered through the glass, then back at Ace. "Thanks."

"Vander also asked me to give you this." Ace held out a slim file.

As Ace disappeared, Rhys frowned at the file and flipped it open. His stomach clenched. They were pictures of Haven.

They were from a while ago. She looked thinner, stressed, her face pinched. From the background, he could tell she was in Miami.

In one, she had bruises on her face.

Motherfucker. He could make out finger marks. Fury was like acid in his veins. Some of them showed her arguing with the slick, good-looking blond man. Leo Becker, the ex.

She'd run from this man. She'd left Miami because this asshole had hurt her.

Rhys closed the file. She might have had a rough time, but that didn't mean she got to take that out on him. He looked at Cowell through the glass. He'd give the guy a bit longer to stew. Turning, Rhys headed back upstairs to his office.

He saw he had some new emails, and one was from the tattoo artist he'd contacted. The guy had done some of Rhys' ink in the past. He'd sent the man an image of the tattoo that had been on the neck of the thief from the museum.

Rhys scanned the information and stiffened.

The guy had tracked the star tattoo down. It was a mafia tattoo, common in the Bratva.

The guy in the museum had a Russian mafia tattoo. The kidnapper downstairs had links to the local Russian mafia.

Rhys felt that little tingle when an investigation started coming together.

And this time, he didn't like it one bit. The Russian mafia was involved, and somehow, Haven was right in the middle of it.

HAVEN LAY ON HER BED, staring at the ceiling, trying not to think of anything.

She closed her eyes. For a few months, life had been good again. Peaceful.

Now...

Images flashed in her brain like someone taking photographs—the painting, the theft, the man hitting her, Rhys, Rhys kissing her, his face at the end when they'd argued.

Her stomach cramped.

He was done with her. She saw that. He'd shut down and turned off like she disgusted him.

Her stomach tightened even more. *Don't think about him.*

She rolled, pressing her face into her pillow. God, she'd been a bitch to him. Who was she to judge how he lived his life?

Ugh. Enough. Rhys Norcross was not for her. She needed to stop wallowing.

She pushed herself up and then tied her tangled hair up in a messy bun. When she'd gotten home, she'd changed into yoga pants and an oversized T-shirt with a large neck that slipped off one shoulder.

Now, night was falling. She wondered if they'd gotten her kidnapper to talk.

Shaking her head, she headed into her living room, glancing out the windows. Where was the *Water Lilies* right now?

The lights of San Francisco winked back at her, but didn't have the answer.

She just hoped they were treating it right. The smallest wrong move could damage the masterpiece. She released a breath. Art meant a lot to her. She still remembered her mom taking her to a museum for the first time when she was six. It had been their special day. Haven had learned that art was a way to express human skill, imagination, and emotion. You could capture a moment, a feeling, and make someone feel that again. There were some paintings that just a glance made her remember her mom—shared giggles, warm hugs, their love.

Haven couldn't afford the kind of art she truly loved, but she had a few pretty prints, and one small sculpture on her coffee table—a gift from an artist. It was two people entwined in an embrace, the man holding the woman close to his larger body.

She averted her gaze from the statue. All that did right now was make her feel worse.

In her compact kitchen, she opened her fridge. She had no desire to cook, and her fridge was looking a little bare. Haven didn't love cooking, but she had a few meals that were her go-tos, and usually came out pretty well.

There was a knock at her door and she froze. She wasn't expecting anyone, and no one had buzzed up.

Frozen with indecision, she stood there, staring at the door.

"Open up, Haven," Gia called. "I've got food and wine."

Relief punched through Haven.

She opened the door and her best friend bustled in, paper bag in one hand, and a bottle of red wine in the other. Her large, Fendi handbag was slung over her shoulder, and she was still in her work clothes—her sleek, white dress with sexy Louboutin heels.

Gia looked at Haven's face and her mouth hardened.

"I'm okay," Haven said. "The bruising is just getting worse."

Gia dumped her things on the kitchen island. Then she hugged Haven. Haven wrapped her arms around her friend and held on tight.

"Hey." Gia patted her back. "What's going on?"

"I went to see Harry today."

"You were supposed to rest."

"I have to try and find the painting, Gia. Anyway, some no-neck guy tried to drag me off the street."

"What?" Gia stiffened. "I'm calling Vander—"

Haven grabbed her arm. "Rhys arrived and stopped the guy. He's in a holding room at Norcross."

"Rhys arrived?"

"Yes, he saved my ass."

"Well, he is partial to watching your ass."

"*Gia.*"

"I'm just glad you're okay." Gia squeezed Haven's fingers.

"I went with Rhys to help track down a lead…"

Gia watched her with deep-brown eyes so like Rhys'.

"God, Gia, he kissed me. I kissed him. More than once." Haven dropped her head into her hands.

"It was a long time coming," Gia said.

"G, he's your brother—"

"Like I've told you before, I'm well aware that all my brothers are hot. It's my cross to bear." She grabbed Haven's hands and pulled them away from her face. "Rhys is gorgeous, yes. All of his life he's never had to put much effort in with women. They drop at his feet like flies."

Haven made an unhappy noise at that thought. "That's kind of a gross analogy."

"Except you. You've kept him on his toes. He's like a starving wolf that spotted a pretty doe when he looks at you."

"I'm not sure that's a very good analogy either," Haven said. "Anyway, it's just the thrill of the chase. He'll lose interest—"

Gia shook her head. "I've never seen him look at anyone the way he looks at you."

That made Haven's throat go tight. "I was a bitch to him. I said nasty things." She pulled in a shuddering breath. "He won't be looking at me like that again."

Gia opened the wine and grabbed two glasses from the cupboard. She poured generously. "So, your finely tuned survival instincts kicked in."

Haven took a sip of wine. "I...I can't risk myself again. I was falling for Leo, or at least I thought I was, and he betrayed my trust. More than once."

He'd turned from charming boyfriend to edgy, anxious, short-tempered man who yelled, and refused to tell her anything. And when she'd caught him getting a blow job from a waitress in his office at the club, they'd fought, and he'd hit her.

"Rhys is not Leo," Gia said.

"I know that, but Rhys can have anyone he wants, and I don't... I can't watch someone else catch his eye."

"Haven—"

"No. I don't want to talk about it anymore, Gia."

"Then just listen. Easton was always the bossy Norcross brother, running some scheme to make money. Vander... Well, even in high school, I suspected my brother was plotting to invade some small nation. Rhys was always the easygoing, charming brother. He was smart, sporty, everyone's friend."

Haven took another sip of wine. Maybe she'd have a bottle or two.

"Then he enlisted, and followed Easton and Vander as soon as he could." Gia smiled. "He hated being left out." Her smile faded. "It changed him, Haven. He believed in what he was doing with the military, but they never, ever talk details, even to Mom and Dad. But it changed him. Whatever he had to do, it left scars. On all three of them."

Haven swallowed and set her glass down, a horrible feeling sweeping through her. She hadn't gotten to know him well enough to see under the good looks. Hell, she'd been too busy thinking about herself, protecting herself, that she hadn't thought much about Rhys' feelings. Guilt stabbed at her.

"It's like he has this need to go fast and keep moving," Gia said.

Haven bit her bottom lip. She understood that need. The need to outrun your demons.

"I want to see him slow down," Gia said. "Breathe and appreciate the small things."

"I... We fought, Gia. It was ugly."

There was a knock at the door and Haven stiffened again. "Now who is it?"

"Let me check." Gia stood, going into mother-hen mode. She was a Norcross as well, and clearly, they were born to protect.

She heard Gia talking and demanding to see ID.

A moment later, her friend was back holding a huge bouquet of blood-red roses.

Haven sucked in a breath and her heart thumped. "Oh, wow."

"They smell delicious." Gia set them down on the island and snatched up the card from among the greenery. Then she frowned. "No name."

Haven took the card. *I'll keep you safe, Haven.*

A cold shiver ran through her. For some reason, that

message made her feel the opposite. "These aren't from Rhys."

"I doubt it. I don't think Rhys has ever sent flowers. Easton, yes, but this is not Rhys' style."

A bad taste filled Haven's mouth. "Leo used to apologize with flowers. Big, glossy, expensive flowers."

"You think these are from him?"

"I don't know. I don't want them. Can you—?"

"I'll take care of it." Gia slid her phone out and snapped a picture of the flowers, then she picked the vase up. "I bet old Mrs. Girard down the hall will like them."

The widow lived alone and often invited Haven in for a cup of tea. She was sweet and friendly. "She'll love them."

Gia hustled out the front door and Haven wrapped an arm around her middle. Her belly churned. She couldn't think about Leo right now. God, her life was a mess. Dragging in a deep breath, she tried to empty her mind. She didn't want to think about Leo, or the Monet, or the mess she'd made with Rhys.

When her stomach did another sickening roll, she dropped onto her couch.

As soon as Gia had regifted the flowers, she was back. She took one look at Haven, sat beside her, and tossed an arm around Haven's shoulders.

"Now, let's eat Chinese, have more wine, and not talk about anyone with high levels of testosterone." She gave Haven a squeeze.

Haven managed a smile. "Or stolen paintings."

"Deal." They clinked their glasses together. "Let's talk about the party I'm throwing this weekend."

"Gia, my face—"

"Will be healed enough that with my deft hand with makeup, no one will see anything other than your gorgeousness."

Thank God for her friend.

Tonight, Haven wasn't going to think about exes, or thieves, or men who kissed like sexy dreams.

She was just going to drink and hang with her friend.

CHAPTER SEVEN

God, it was so nice to be at work. It made her feel normal.

Haven carefully moved some jewelry around on the black velvet. She was working on a new display of jewelry from the Golden Age of Hollywood.

She nudged a necklace into the right position. *Perfect.* Next, she grabbed the description card and set it in place.

Then she turned, carefully lifting a set of dangly, pearl earrings once worn by actress Rita Hayworth and set them in the case.

She glanced around the exhibit room. It was a smaller, more intimate space than the main hall. Her stomach was still churning at the thought that someone might break in and steal these.

She dragged in a deep breath, then blew it out. Security had been beefed up at the Hutton since the theft. They had more guards, more cameras, and new protocols for deliveries. She tucked a strand of her hair that escaped her twist back behind her ear. The museum's treasures were safe, she was safe.

The giggling of children made her look up. She moved to the doorway and saw a harried teacher, along with some parent helpers, herding an excited group of schoolkids down the hall.

"Leila, can you finish up here?" Haven said.

The assistant waved. "Sure thing, Haven."

Haven headed down the corridor and saw the kids in the main hall—where the empty wall that should hold the *Water Lilies* mocked her.

Then she heard footsteps and the low murmur of male voices. She turned and her chest froze. Vander and Rhys had just entered the museum.

Vander saw her and lifted his chin. "Hey, Haven."

"Hi."

Heart pounding, she looked at Rhys. Damn, why did he have to be so damn good to look at? She felt a tingle right through her body. He was wearing another suit today. It was blue, and fitted him in a way that made her toes curl. His gaze went to her injured cheek and eye, and his jaw tightened.

Then his gaze went blank, like he was looking straight through her.

Ouch. It was like she'd ceased to exist for him. That hurt.

He nodded, but didn't say anything.

"Any news on the painting?" She forced herself to talk around the pressure in her chest. *Pull yourself together, Haven.*

"Nothing yet," Vander replied. "We're here to see Easton."

She forced herself not to look back at Rhys and cleared her throat. "He's up in his office."

With a nod, the men moved past her.

Once they were gone, she pressed her face to one of the stone pillars. *Damn.* At least the marble was cool on her skin.

Then she straightened. She had work to do. She was *not* thinking of Rhys Norcross.

She headed down the corridor and heard the kids peppering their teacher with questions.

Haven's cell rang, and she saw that it was Harry. "Hi, Harry."

"Darling girl, how are those bruises?"

"Even more spectacular. Now there's some purple thrown in."

He made a sympathetic noise and then lowered his voice. "Well, I got wind of something."

"Oh?" Her heart thudded against her ribs.

"The faintest rumbles about a private auction of a very expensive painting. Invite is going out to...let's just say, less-scrupulous dealers than myself."

Her pulse did a little dance. "People who don't mind buying a stolen painting."

"Ding-ding. I don't have confirmation that it's your stolen masterpiece, though."

"Okay." But the chances were pretty high.

"I have a gallery assistant whose sister's friend is seeing this guy. He's not nice, and has a club where some of San Francisco's criminal element like to frequent.

Apparently, he's great in bed, that's why she won't dump his shady ass."

"What club?" Haven asked.

"Doll face, the kind regular, law-abiding citizens like us don't know about."

"Okay, thanks Harry. If you hear anything else, let me know."

"Sure thing, Haven."

She ended the call and stared blindly across the main hall. Her gaze fell on a man in the main gallery, not far from the schoolkids. He'd already circled the room once, and he wasn't really looking at the art for very long. She frowned. He wore jeans, a jacket, and motorcycle boots.

Art lovers came from all walks of life, but she wasn't getting the right vibe from him.

She moved closer, pretending to survey a display case of ceramics. The man was close, and leaned a hand against one of the pillars.

The blood in her veins turned to ice. She saw freckles on his hand, in a spiral pattern.

He was one of the thieves! The man who'd hit her.

She took a step back. She needed to get upstairs to Rhys, Vander, and Easton.

At her movement, the man's head whipped up.

Familiar cold blue eyes she'd seen in her nightmares hit hers.

Shit.

She spun. "Security!"

The man lunged. He grabbed the back of her shirt and yanked. She spun and kicked at him. Kids started screaming.

The man spun her and wrapped an arm around her waist, with her back pressed to his front. She jerked and twisted.

Then she saw him lift a gun and press it to her head.

She went still. The kids' screaming intensified. Haven's mouth was dry as dust, and she realized that panic had a really bad taste.

"Come with me, or I'll shoot the kids," he said, voice low.

Haven gulped in air, panic bubbling up in her throat. She couldn't stop a whimper escaping.

"Let her go," a deep voice said.

She turned her head. *Thank God.* Vander stood there with a gun drawn, held easily in his hands. Easton was one step behind him, a gun also in his hands. There was no sign of Rhys.

"I'm leaving with her," the man growled. "No one needs to get hurt."

Vander's face was a blank, scary mask. "Let. Her. Go."

"Just back off," the thief snapped, pulling her back a step.

"You know who I am?" Vander asked.

Okay, Haven didn't think Vander could get scarier, but he looked like he was going to cut this man open, slowly, and surely, and enjoy every minute of it.

"Don't give a shit," the man said.

"Not from around here, then," Easton murmured.

"Name's Norcross," Vander said. "Now, let her go. You aren't leaving here."

"I *will* hurt her." The man gave her another yank and the gun dug into her temple.

Then she heard the squeak of shoes on the marble and turned her head an inch. Two kids stepped through a doorway right beside them. As soon as they saw the man with the gun, they froze, shaking in terror.

His arm shifted, the gun moving away from Haven and toward the kids.

Screw this. Haven was so sick of being beat up and pushed around. And she wasn't letting this asshole hurt innocent children.

She reached back, grabbed a handful of his junk and squeezed hard.

The man made a strangled sound, his arm loosened. Haven yanked away, and the gun went off, right by her head.

Damn, that was loud. Heart pounding, ears ringing, she turned and kneed him between the legs. He cried out.

Suddenly, Rhys came out of nowhere and tackled the man.

Haven managed to stay on her feet, but Rhys and the man hit the polished floor, sliding a few feet.

Then Vander and Easton were there. Easton pulled Haven away.

"You okay?" he asked.

Her ears were still ringing, but she nodded. Pressure built in her chest. *Oh, no,* she didn't want to have a major freak-out right now.

She needed a distraction, needed to do something. If she didn't, she was going to splinter apart.

She turned and saw the kids still standing there, terrified.

"It's okay." She went to them, holding out her arms. "Come on, we'll find your teacher. It's over now."

"We had to go to the bathroom," the boy said.

"The man had a gun," the little girl whispered.

"I know." Haven had felt that, up close and personal.

"You're talking loudly," the boy said.

Haven touched her ear and tried to speak a little quieter. "Come on." She grabbed the girl's hand.

She quickly led the kids over to a panicked teacher, who was herding the children out of the main hall with the help of several of Haven's museum staff.

"Get them out of here, Ron," Haven ordered. "Ensure they get free tickets to come again."

The man nodded.

Once they were gone, Haven started shaking. She glanced back, and saw that Vander had her attacker cuffed, and was yanking him to his feet. He glared at her.

Oh, shit. She twisted her shaking hands together.

Rhys stepped in front of her—his handsome face set like stone.

She stared at him. "I... Um... Can't stop shaking."

Then he yanked her to him. Her face pressed against his chest and she breathed him in. She felt the warmth of him through his shirt.

God, he was so warm, and she suddenly realized that she was so cold. Frigid. She wrapped her arms around him, sliding her hands under his jacket. Then she held on.

The best thing was, his strong arms wrapped around her and he held her back.

RHYS LED A STILL SHAKEN Haven into her office. He was pissed as hell that she'd been in danger— again.

She'd held it together during the attack, but now she was dealing with the aftermath.

Haven's office was like her—neat, tidy, with touches of class. She had a wooden desk with a shiny surface, and nothing out of place. A pretty painting hung on the wall, and an interesting twist of a sculpture rested on a cabinet nearby.

"I'll be fine." She swiveled on her heels, tucking some hair back behind her ear. Her face was impossibly pale which made her bruises stand out even more. "You don't have to stay. I know...you don't want to be near me."

She sank back against the desk, still shaking.

Rhys moved closer. "Just breathe, Haven."

She nodded, and dragged in a quick breath. He got closer and she stilled. Her big eyes locked on his face.

"Rhys—?"

"What the hell were you thinking?" he snapped.

She jerked. "What?"

"He had a gun to your head and you grabbed his balls? He could have killed you!"

Something sparked in her eyes. "There were *kids* right there. He threatened to shoot them."

"Vander, Easton, and I had it under control."

"I couldn't risk the kids, Rhys." Her lips trembled,

and she pressed her hands to her cheeks. "Why won't the shaking stop?"

He was still pissed, but he pulled her close again. Fuck, he liked the feel of her. She fit against him perfectly.

Her hands clutched his shirt, twisting. "Thanks for tackling him."

"Be quiet."

She was for a beat. He drew in the scent of her shampoo. Coconuts. Made him think of a tropical island, and Haven in a bikini.

He'd just watched her risk her life for two kids. He tightened his hold.

"Rhys? I...I wanted to say sorry for what I said yesterday. I have no right to judge you and twist things about you to keep myself safe."

His heart thudded. He pulled back to look at her face. She wouldn't meet his eyes, instead staring at the buttons on his shirt.

"I, um, well, you know I had a bad ex. That still colors a lot of stuff. I don't—"

"Shh." He tipped her chin up. "I know about Becker."

She grimaced.

"He sounds like an asshole."

"He is. Grade-A."

"He played you."

"He cheated on me. It's not nice to catch your boyfriend getting a blow job in his office."

"Shit." The guy was clearly an idiot to have Haven and cheat.

"Anyway, that spilled over, I took it out on you. So, I'm sorry." She fiddled with a strand of her hair.

"Okay," he said.

She managed a tremulous smile. "Great. I'm glad we cleared the air."

He circled her narrow waist with his hands and lifted her onto the desk. She gasped, and her mouth dropped open.

He pushed closer, and traced his fingers along her cheekbones, the shell of her ear.

"Rhys," she breathed.

He ran his fingers over her lips. Damn, so soft, and gave him so many ideas.

Then her tongue darted out and brushed his fingers. He felt it all the way to his cock and groaned. "I've got to kiss you."

"*Yes*," she breathed.

He took her mouth—hot and hard. The taste of her exploded in his mouth.

She wrapped her arms around him, sexy moans coming from her throat. She tried to get her legs around his hips, but her skirt was too tight. She made a frustrated sound.

Rhys reached down, gripped the hem, and jerked it up.

"You like me kissing you on your desk?" he growled.

"Yes." With more freedom, her legs clamped onto his hips and she undulated against him.

"Got a naughty side, Haven?" He leaned over her and ground his cock against her. She cried out.

She was a hot little thing. All class on the outside, with sexy hidden underneath.

"Um, just with you," she said.

That confession made his cock throb. He was damn glad to see the fear and shock bleed from her face. Now her features were flushed, her eyes bright with desire.

He cupped her breast and she bit her lip.

"We can't do this here," she panted.

"Probably shouldn't."

"Easton and Vander will probably be up here soon."

"Yeah." God, he could smell her arousal. He slid a hand between her thighs.

She bucked. "*Oh.*"

All she had on was a tiny thong, and she was soaked. "This wet for me, baby?"

She made an incoherent sound.

Screw it. Rhys needed a taste of her. He dropped to his knees.

Her eyes widened. "Rhys?"

He nudged her thighs apart, shoved the scrap of cloth aside, and then his mouth was on her. Haven moaned and her thighs clamped on his head.

He slid his hands under her skirt and cupped her ass. He licked her. She tasted like heaven. He explored her pretty pink folds, then sucked on her clit.

Soon, she was riding his face, her hands tugging in his hair. "Don't stop. *Please* don't stop."

He licked her again. "I'm not going to stop, baby. I want you to come."

Her husky cries were driving him crazy. His cock felt like steel.

"*Rhys!*"

He felt her release coming. He gave another hard suck of her clit, and she shattered for him. Her body convulsed and she cried out his name.

Oh, yeah, he planned to hear that again, soon. When he had his cock lodged deep inside her.

He held her as she came down. Her hands released from his hair and she blinked at him.

He pushed to his feet and kissed her. He knew she tasted herself on his lips, but she didn't hesitate. She kissed him back with hungry need.

Then she yanked her head away. "Rhys, we shouldn't have done that."

In her eyes, he saw the walls he'd shattered slowly rebuilding. He cursed Leo Becker to hell and back.

Straightening, he pulled her skirt back into place. He saw her trying to avoid looking at the bulge in his pants.

"We won't talk about this now." But later, for sure. "We need to discuss what happened downstairs."

He watched her pull herself together. "The man was the leader of the thieves who took the *Water Lilies*."

Rhys' pulse leaped. "You're sure?"

She nodded. "Same eyes. I'll never forget them. And he has freckles on his hand that I recognized."

Another piece of the puzzle clicked into place.

"Why did he attack me?" she asked.

"Maybe he was worried you could ID him." Rhys slid his hand into his pockets. "Haven, there's a link to the theft and the mafia."

Her eyes went huge. "Mafia? Like wise guys and gangsters?"

Rhys fought back a laugh. "Like dangerous organized criminals. These ones are of the Russian variety."

"Rhys, I don't know anything about the mafia."

"I know, baby. Another member of the robbery crew has a Russian mafia tattoo on his neck. The guy who tried to snatch you off the street also has links to a local Russian mafia contact."

She rubbed her face. "This makes no sense."

But Rhys knew it would as he kept putting the pieces together. "When you get home, you make sure your door and windows are locked, and your alarm is on. Me, or someone else from Norcross, will take you to and from work from now on."

"Rhys—"

"At work, you'll have a security guard with you at all times."

She bit her lip. "Rhys, are you sure—?"

He held up a hand. "It's the way it needs to be for now." He put his hands on either side of her hips on the desk, and leaned forward so their noses brushed. "I will keep you safe, Haven."

"Why?" she whispered.

"You know why."

There was a flash of fear in her eyes. "I can't be with you. I've sworn off men, remember?"

They'd see. He didn't bother arguing with her now, especially when he had the taste of her on his lips.

"We'll work it all out. Haven, don't worry." He pressed a quick kiss to her lips. "It'll be okay."

CHAPTER EIGHT

Vander dropped Haven off at home.

He did a sweep of her apartment, his dark-blue eyes like storm clouds. "After I leave, lock the door and set your alarm."

Haven nodded.

"Rhys or I will be here in the morning to pick you up."

She nodded again. "Thanks, Vander. I appreciate all the trouble."

He got close and used one long finger to tip her chin up. It was the first time he'd touched her. Vander Norcross wasn't a toucher. He was way too intense and solitary.

"You're one of ours, Haven. You work for Easton, you're Gia's friend, and you're Rhys'."

"I am not Rhys'."

Those dark eyes stared at her until she wanted to squirm.

"We'll keep you safe. Lock the door, alarm on."

"Okay." She closed the door after him, but knew he was still standing there in the hall. His presence practically vibrated through the door.

She flipped the locks and set the alarm. Okay, her life was officially off the rails. She'd been attacked *again*, and then Rhys Norcross went down on her on her desk and gave her the best damn orgasm of her life.

Haven pressed a hand to her forehead. She needed a glass of wine and a hot shower.

Shower first. Once she was under the hot water, she let it beat down on her head, and she relaxed a little. Until she started thinking of Rhys' hands and mouth on her.

Dammit. She flicked the water off and got out.

She changed into her pajamas. Who cared that it was only three o'clock in the afternoon? Her short-shorts and tank top were comfy. She tugged on a loose, gray knit cardigan. In her kitchen, she poured herself some wine, then forced down some cheese, crackers, and prosciutto.

Haven flopped onto her couch. She was pretty sure Rhys was not giving up. She'd have to find some strength to fight the pull of him.

Now, she needed to do something to find her lost Monet. Damn, she'd forgotten Harry's call. She needed to tell Rhys about the rumors of the auction.

Her phone rang. She snatched it up and recognized the number instantly. Her stomach clenched, a sour sensation washing through her.

Leo's number.

Her phone was brand new, and her new number was

for San Francisco. He shouldn't have it. Unease skittered through her. Leo was *not* what she needed right now.

Ignoring it, she slid the phone in the pocket of her cardigan. Leo was her past, and she wanted him to stay there. He didn't exist for her.

She slumped down onto her back. When she closed her eyes, she could feel Rhys' hands pushing her thighs apart. Felt his mouth on her, his stubble scratching the sensitive skin of her inner thighs.

Groaning, she squeezed her thighs together. She might need to get her vibrator out later.

A smell tickled her nose. Was that gas? Had she left the stove on?

Heaving herself up and off the couch, she headed for the kitchen. She checked everything and ensured all the burners were off.

Spinning, she frowned. The smell wasn't stronger in the kitchen. She wandered back to the living room and sniffed. Maybe she'd imagined it?

The next second, the world erupted in noise and flames.

Something hit Haven's head, and with a scream, she dropped to the floor. She rolled under her dining room table.

Everything was shaking. *Oh God. Oh God.* Fire. She smelled burning, saw flames and smoke. Everything in shambles around her.

And there was a freaking hole in the floor of her living room.

Panic made her throat tight and her movements jerky. She quickly crawled toward the door.

She had to get out. She had to warn others in her building.

Mrs. Girard. The old lady used a walker and wasn't very steady on her feet.

With a goal in mind, Haven's head cleared. She got her front door open and wondered if her alarm was still operational.

She crawled into the hall. There was more smoke, more destruction. She reached Mrs. Girard's door and banged her fist against it.

"Mrs. Girard!"

"Haven?" The door opened. The woman's terrified face peered back, her halo of gray hair a mess.

"There's a fire. We need to get out."

Rising, Haven slipped her arm around the frail, older woman and helped her maneuver her walker into the hall. They hobbled toward the stairs.

"We can't use the elevator," Haven told her.

"You should go," the old woman said. "You'll move faster without me."

"I'm *not* leaving you."

The smoke was growing and Haven coughed. Her eyes stung. She nudged open the doors to the stairs.

"Come on, hold on to me and the railing." They abandoned the woman's walker at the top of the stairs.

Then they started down.

It was slow going. Mrs. Girard was shaky, and started coughing too.

"One step at a time." Haven needed to try a distraction. "Maybe we'll meet some hunky firefighters waiting for us at the bottom?"

That got a rough laugh out of her elderly neighbor.

She heard shouts echo in the stairwell below. Other people evacuating.

They rounded the landing, and smoke poured through a door from a lower floor.

"Keep moving, Mrs. Girard. Think of those firefighters."

"You need a man, Haven."

"No one needs a man. I had one. He wasn't good. I don't need another one." Oh boy, at least Mrs. Girard couldn't tell she was lying.

"They're not all bad. My Mr. Girard was a good one. Even on the days that he drove me crazy. Once I had to hit him with my frypan."

"You miss him," Haven said quietly.

"Every day, my dear. But the pain is worth every minute we got to spend together." Mrs. Girard broke into a coughing fit.

They negotiated more stairs, and the old woman leaned heavily on Haven. She had to focus on keeping them both upright. Her eyes were stinging, tears streaming down her face.

Please Lord, not much farther. Haven's head was starting to feel woozy.

"There is a guy," she found herself saying.

"Ah-*huh*." Mrs. Girard coughed some more.

"He's way too good looking. Every time I see him, my body goes haywire. I've been trying to avoid him."

"Just like when I first saw Mr. Girard. That tingle. The knowing."

"Oh, no. I'm steering clear of Rhys. I'm not the only woman who likes the look of him."

Mrs. Girard clutched Haven's arm. "I know you're afraid, but Haven, to live, to love, you have to take some risks."

The old lady stumbled, and Haven lunged and caught her. The dizziness was getting really bad. She needed to get them out. Her lungs were burning.

The smoke was getting thicker, and they managed to get down two more stairs. Then she saw movement.

Two firefighters in bulky suits, helmets, and masks appeared.

Thank you, Jesus. The men helped them out of the building. Outside, a crowd had gathered around the fire trucks, police cars, and ambulances.

One firefighter took a coughing Mrs. Girard toward one of the ambulances.

"Your head's bleeding," the other firefighter said to Haven.

"It is?" She swiped at her temple and saw red on her fingers. "I'm fine."

"Get the paramedics to check you over."

Her head was still foggy and she couldn't think straight. She realized her legs were bare, and her feet were bare. She tugged her cardigan around her.

It was chaos. There were so many people. The firefighter started to turn away.

"Hey, what happened?" she asked.

"Looks like an explosion."

Explosion? A chill went down her spine, and she tugged the cardigan tighter around her body.

Then she scanned the crowd and froze.

There were two men in suits, looking at the building, then the crowd. They gave off the same vibe as the man in the museum.

Oh, God. Had they done this?

That couldn't be right. She was overreacting. Then she watched the men split up. One touched a woman's shoulder, looked at her face, then turned away. The other one approached another woman.

Haven's stomach turned to stone. The women they were talking to were about the same age as Haven, both of them with brown hair.

Quickly, Haven spun away, walking into the crowd.

She had no idea where she was going. Her head throbbed and she couldn't think clearly.

All she knew was that she had to get away.

RHYS PACED THE NORCROSS OFFICE. Vander was questioning the scumbag from the museum down in one of the holding rooms.

Vander refused to let Rhys in on the interrogation because Rhys wanted to rip the guy's head off.

The asshole had held a gun to Haven's fucking head. He'd hit her. Rhys pressed his hands to his hips and dragged in a breath. She was home, she was all right.

He needed to step up this investigation. He had to find the damn painting and get Haven safe.

He heard footsteps and turned. Vander stalked up the stairs.

"What did you get?" Rhys demanded.

"The crew works for the Zakharov family."

Sounded Russian. "Mafia?"

Vander nodded. "Sergei Zakharov is the head of the family. They're out of Miami."

Rhys stilled. "What?"

"Yeah, we need to see if this links back to Haven's ex. Maybe she's in contact with him and—"

"She's not. He cheated on her, hit her. Fuck."

"For now, we—" Vander's cell pealed. He yanked it out. "Norcross." Vander stiffened. "What? *Fuck.*" He gripped the back of his neck. "Yeah, okay."

His brother's gaze shifted to Rhys. Vander looked cautious.

A chill hit Rhys and spread. "Tell me?"

Vander's face twisted.

"Vander," Rhys prompted.

"There was an explosion," Vander said slowly.

Rhys' mind went blank. "Say again?"

"An explosion. At Haven's apartment building. There's no news on Haven."

No. *No!* Rhys spun and ran for the stairs.

"Rhys, wait!"

He took the stairs two at a time. At this time of the day, traffic to her place in Pacific Heights would suck, as everyone was headed home from work.

Once he hit the garage level, he bypassed the SUVs and went for his bike.

He climbed on, yanked his helmet on, and gunned the engine. Then he flew out of the Norcross warehouse.

An explosion. *Be okay, Haven. Be okay.*

He'd only gone a block when Vander's BMW motor-cycle roared up beside him. His brother's black visor looked his way, and he lifted his chin.

The two of them sped off down the road.

It wasn't long before he saw the smoke, and his gut turned into a tight ball.

They reached Haven's apartment building, and out front, he counted several fire trucks and ambulances. There was also a sizable crowd. He and Vander parked and climbed off their bikes.

Rhys jogged over. He looked up and the damaged building made his mouth go dry. It was only six stories high, and the explosion had done a lot of damage.

"Rhys." Vander was staying close, watching him carefully.

"The damage is centered on Haven's apartment," Rhys said woodenly.

Where the hell was *she?* He scanned around. Lots of bedraggled people, but no Haven.

"We'll ask around," Vander said.

Rhys nodded. "Vander, she's mine."

Vander's lips quirked. "I know, bro. I've known for a while, even if you haven't."

His brother strode off toward the firefighters and police. Rhys circled through the crowd, searching for a pretty brunette with gorgeous blue eyes.

His panic turned from an itch to a burn. There was no sign of her. His gaze went back to her destroyed apartment.

Then Vander came back, his face grim. Saxon was with him.

"Hey." Saxon's body was tense and alert.

"Why is Saxon here?" Rhys asked.

"I called him before we left the office," Vander said.

"Why?"

"In case you lose it."

Rhys felt like the ground moved under his feet. "Tell me."

"Rhys—"

"Tell me!" he barked.

Vander's jaw tightened. "The explosion was in an empty apartment below Haven's. It's looking like a faulty gas line. The arson investigators aren't done yet, but they think it was rigged."

Rhys dragged in a breath. "Haven?"

"No sign of her. They haven't recovered any bodies, yet. Four people went to the hospital. An old lady, a mother and toddler, and a boy who broke his leg evacuating."

Rhys' chin dropped to his chest. "They searched her apartment?"

Vander hesitated. "Not yet. The fire's too intense, and it's too dangerous."

The news was like an arrow to his heart. "So, no one would have survived."

"She might have gotten out," Saxon said.

"Then where is she?" Rhys said.

Suddenly Gia pushed through the crowd, her face twisted with panic. "Where's Haven?"

Vander turned. "Gia—"

Their sister froze, reading Vander's tone. "No." She shook her head. "Haven *isn't* dead."

Dead. The word reverberated in Rhys' head.

He sat on a nearby brick retaining wall, and dropped his head to his hands. He'd pushed her away, said ugly things.

Images of Haven—smiling, sipping a glass of wine, laughing, avoiding him, crying his name as she came—cascaded through his head.

"Gia." Saxon moved toward her.

"Don't touch me, Saxon Buchanan." She smacked him away. *"Find* her. This can't be a coincidence. Someone did this."

Rhys squeezed his eyes closed. Now was not the time for the Saxon and Gia show. Since they were teenagers, the pair fought like snarling cats. They made oil and water look compatible. Rhys had promised to keep Haven safe. Pain tore him apart and he rose. Emotions swelled inside him like a tidal wave.

Vander and Saxon eyed him. Gia looked stricken. Her gaze met Rhys' and she flinched.

Vander pulled her into his arms.

"I have to go." Rhys swiveled.

"Rhys." Vander's voice was laced with warning.

Fuck. He was going to lose it.

"Saxon, follow him," Vander ordered.

Rhys went straight to his bike. He had no idea what he was going to do, where he was going to go.

His cell rang and he yanked it out. "What?"

"Whoa, Norcross. It's Hammon."

"I'm busy."

"Saw your girl. The classy one who was with you the other day. Thought you'd want to know. She's in pajamas and no shoes, and wandering in the Tenderloin. She looks drunk or high, or something."

Rhys went still. "What?" His hand clenched on his phone so hard that the plastic creaked. "Haven?"

"Yeah, and she's not in a nice part of town." He rattled off a street corner.

"I'm coming. Hammon, don't let anyone touch her or I'll kill you."

Rhys looked at Saxon. "Informant saw Haven."

"Go. Call us when you've got her."

Rhys jumped on his bike and sped off. He ran a red light and ignored the speed limit. He roared down Van Ness Avenue, then turned again. A second later, he spotted her.

The weight that had been choking him lifted. She was sitting at the curb, staring at nothing. She had soot on her cheeks and her legs were bare.

Rhys pulled up beside her and leaped off the bike. "Haven!"

She blinked. "Rhys?"

"Yeah, baby. People are worried." *I was fucking destroyed.*

Then she leaped up and ran at him.

He caught her and she burrowed into his chest.

"God, baby, I was so worried." He held on tight.

"There was an explosion, smoke, fire." Her voice hitched. "I got Mrs. Girard out."

Of course, she hadn't worried about herself, and had made a point of helping others.

Blankly, she pulled her phone out of her pocket. She blinked like she was surprised to see it. "I should have called." Her voice lowered to a whisper. "But then I saw them."

"Who?"

"Two guys in the crowd. They were looking for me."

His arms tightened on her. "You're safe now."

She was shivering and he scooped her up into his arms. She pressed her face to his neck.

Rhys smelled coconuts and smoke. Then he spotted the blood smeared on the side of her head. "Haven, you're bleeding."

She made a sound and looked up. That's when he realized her eyes weren't fully focused.

"I think...something hit my head in the explosion." She blinked. "Where are we?"

His heart clenched. She was probably concussed, and she'd been wandering around, out of it and hurt.

"Come on, I need to get you checked out."

"Okay. I feel safe with you, Rhys."

Her words were so quiet he barely heard them.

"Come on, baby." He managed to get his phone out. "Vander, I found her. Can you meet me with an SUV?"

As Haven snuggled close into Rhys' chest, he held on tight.

CHAPTER NINE

H aven sat quietly on the hospital bed. She'd been checked over, and now the nurse was taking care of the cut on the side of her head.

It was small, but it had bled a lot.

She'd been asked lots of questions about her bruised face, and she'd finally convinced the nurse that Rhys hadn't given them to her. Then a police detective had arrived to take her statement about the explosion. She hadn't mentioned the men in the crowd, but she'd told the detective everything about how she'd gotten out of the building.

The older man had eyed her carefully before giving her his card and leaving.

Rhys sat in a chair beside the bed. He was staring at her, hadn't taken his eyes off her the entire time.

She fidgeted a little. The painkillers had kicked in, and had helped clear the fog in her head. She wasn't sure if she wanted to be pissed off or scared about what had happened. At least she'd heard that no one had been killed, and Mrs. Girard's family were with her and she was recovering.

"All done." The nurse pulled off her gloves. "I recommend no more adventures for you."

Haven choked out a laugh. "I didn't want any of the ones I've had. Believe me, robbery, beatings, attempted kidnapping—twice—and now my apartment exploding... Not fun."

The nurse's eyes widened.

Haven felt something pumping off Rhys and glanced at him. His face was hard, his brown eyes glittering.

Her chest locked. Right now, he looked as scary as Vander—all that easygoing charm gone.

"Get some rest," the nurse said. "You have a mild concussion, so you need someone to stay with you."

"Okay." Hopefully, she could stay with Gia. She glanced at the bed and saw her cell phone. That was all she had left of her stuff. *God.*

With a nod, the nurse left.

"Well, I—"

Rhys dragged his chair closer, startling her. He took her hands, holding them tight enough to hurt.

"Rhys?"

His forehead dropped to her thigh. "I thought you were dead."

His harsh voice and his words made her belly clench. She rested her hand on his head. "I'm okay," she said softly.

"There was no sign of you, your apartment was in ruins and on fire..."

His voice cracked.

Oh, God. She tangled her fingers in his hair. "Rhys, I'm right here."

He lifted his head. Then he rose, his mouth on hers. He kissed her like he couldn't breathe and she was air.

A shiny sense of relief flooded her. Just being close to him made her feel better.

His fingers moved up to press against the side of her neck. He lifted his head, his gaze intense and turbulent as it locked on hers. He pressed his fingers to her pulse.

Her heart skipped a beat and she knew he felt it. His hand slid down until his palm rested on her chest, over her heart.

"I'm okay," she repeated again.

"I'm going to keep you that way. From now on, I'll be your own personal bodyguard. Keep you alive and breathing."

She swallowed. "I—"

"No arguments. No negotiations. This is the way it's going to be."

Haven nodded, and saw his shoulders relax a little.

"I'm not letting you out of my sight." He rested his forehead against hers.

"Okay, Rhys."

"Let's get you home."

He bundled her up, and then when he looked at her bare feet, he lifted her into his arms. He carried her through the hospital and outside to the SUV. It was a short drive back to his place.

Realization flooded her. "I have nothing." Her mother's bracelet. It had likely been destroyed. A searing pain filled Haven's heart. Her clothes, her jewelry. "God, all my things—"

He reached out and touched her hand. "We'll take care of it."

She nodded, fighting back tears.

"You have insurance?"

She nodded again. "I had a bracelet of my mother's, some photos, my clothes. They're gone."

He squeezed her hand.

Once they reached his place, he carried her into the elevator. He set her down in front of his door to unlock it, and it swung open to reveal Easton.

Her boss shouldered his brother aside and pulled her against him.

Her lips trembled.

"Shit, Haven," Easton murmured.

Gia strode in from the kitchen. "My turn."

As her friend hugged her, Haven spotted Vander and Saxon in the kitchen. Vander was dressed all in black and as always, Saxon looked aristocratic and elegant in a custom suit.

"I bought you some supplies." Gia nodded her head toward what Haven guessed was Rhys' bedroom. "Clothes, underwear, toiletries, and makeup. Just a few days' worth. We'll get more."

"Can I stay with you?" Haven asked.

There was a deep growl behind her, and Rhys wrapped an arm around her. She found herself pressed against his body.

"No," he clipped out.

"Rhys—"

"You're staying with me."

No. *No.* There was no way she could fight the pull of him if they were living together. "I don't—"

"It's not safe. You could put Gia in danger."

Horror rolled through Haven. She hadn't even thought of that. "Then you'll be in danger, too."

He cupped her cheek. "I'm trained. It's my job."

"No one is going to get you, Haven." Vander's hard tone wasn't just a promise, it was a vow.

And she saw the echo of that in Rhys' eyes.

Okay. She could do this. She'd sleep on his couch. And she'd keep her eyes, hands, and lips off Rhys' body. Somehow.

"I have drinks with a client tonight," Gia said.

"What client?" Saxon demanded. "It's late for a business meeting."

Gia pinned him with a look. "I don't run my schedule through you, Buchanan."

A scowl crossed Saxon's handsome face. "I think—"

Gia held up her hand. "I don't care what you think."

Sexy, elegant Saxon growled. Haven watched the pair eagerly. What was this? How had she missed the tension between these two before? Maybe because she'd been too busy avoiding Rhys.

Gia focused on Haven. "I'll cancel—"

"No," Haven said. "Go. I'll be fine."

"She needs to rest anyway," Rhys added.

Gia gave her a tight hug. "I'm already sorting through stuff to get you a replacement license, ID, credit cards."

Haven smiled. "Thanks, G."

"No more danger for you."

Haven snorted. "I'll see what I can do."

"I don't want a world without you in it, girlfriend."

Tears pricked Haven's eyes. "Don't make me cry."

"He'll take care of you." Gia's voice was a quiet murmur.

"I know, but as soon as it's safe, I'm out of here."

Gia smiled that maddening smile of hers. "We'll see."

Why could no one understand? "He's your brother, my boss' brother—"

Gia kissed her cheek. "Sleep well." She winked. "Or not."

After blowing kisses to her brothers, and shooting a glare at Saxon, Gia left.

"I think I need a shower," Haven said to the sexy man-huddle at the kitchen island. She wanted the blood and soot gone.

Rhys broke away. "Let me show you where to find everything."

His bedroom had white walls, and the same warm, wood floor as the living area. A bed with an industrial-style, metal headboard faced floor-to-ceiling windows that highlighted the Bay Bridge. He pointed through to the spacious bathroom, with lots of gray granite and a large shower.

His hands reached into her hair, tugging her ponytail loose.

"Take your time," he said.

Soon, Haven was naked in Rhys' shower. She closed her eyes. She was in so much trouble, and she didn't just mean exploding apartments and art thieves.

Grabbing one of Rhys' fluffy, gray towels off the rack,

she dried off. She dug through the bags Gia had left on Rhys' bed, and found that her friend had bought all of Haven's favorite toiletries. She pulled on a pair of yoga pants and a cute blue T-shirt. She studied her hip. Hmm, she had a few new bruises appearing. Well, she'd just add them to the collection.

She headed back into the living area and heard the men talking, their voices low.

"We need to drill into the Russian mafia link." That was Vander.

"I'm already on it," Rhys replied. "I'm digging into everything on the Zakharov family."

"What's the link to Haven?" Easton asked, clearly not happy.

"Don't know, but I'll find out." Rhys' voice was hard, dark. "And neutralize it."

"So you're all-in for her?" Saxon asked.

"Yes."

"You sure? You've been dancing around this."

Dread filled her, her heart pounding as she listened. She was so screwed up. She wanted him to want her, but she knew she should stay away.

"Haven's mine. I'll do whatever I have to do to protect her."

She closed her eyes, trembled. No one had ever said anything like that before. When she'd met Leo, it had been fun. He'd liked collecting art. He'd wanted a pretty woman on his arm in his club, and to have a good time.

He never put himself on the line for her. The opposite, in fact.

Her father loved her as much as he could. But after

her mom had died, he hadn't been there for her in the way she'd needed. As soon as she'd gone to college, he'd left on his trips overseas to provide medical services in developing countries.

She'd had no one to protect her but herself.

Haven waited, listening, as the men kept talking.

They talked some more about the investigation, until she finally decided that she'd eavesdropped enough. She set her shoulders back and walked into the kitchen.

"Well, at least I don't smell like smoke anymore."

Rhys moved toward her. He slid an arm around her and pulled her close.

She glanced around at the serious faces. "What's going on?"

"You don't need to worry, but we're working on this mafia link," Rhys said. "The Zakharov family out of Miami is involved."

Miami? Her skin went cold. "I don't know anyone in the mafia, here or in Miami."

Vander almost smiled. "We didn't think you did, but there's a link somewhere. Rhys will find it. He's the best."

"We questioned the man who hit you. He gave up his crew." Rhys pointed to a sheet of paper on the island.

There were photos. No, mugshots. "These are the thieves?"

Rhys nodded.

Looking at the photos, she stiffened.

"Haven?"

"This one." She tapped one man with a scar on his face. "I've seen him before."

"Where? At the museum?"

She sucked in a breath. "No, at my ex's club in Miami."

Rhys and the others didn't appear surprised.

"I'm already pulling information on your ex," Rhys said. "He's got his fingers in a lot of not-exactly-legal pies."

"Oh, God." She sagged against the island.

Rhys squeezed her. "Don't worry—"

"He dragged me into this." Her voice rose.

"We don't know that yet."

"He tried to call me earlier."

Rhys' face hardened.

"I didn't answer." She pressed a balled hand to her throat. "I left. I've been gone six months! I live on the other side of the country."

Rhys yanked her to his chest. "Calm down."

She dropped her forehead to his chest. "My fucking ex did this. See, this is why I've sworn off men."

She ignored chuckles from the others.

Rhys tugged on her hair. "We'll see."

RHYS WOKE to the smell of coconuts and smiled.

He was lying flat on his back in his bed, with Haven clamped onto him like she wasn't planning to let go.

He glanced down. Her arm rested across his chest, one of her legs was thrown over his thigh. She was wearing another tiny set of pajamas. The very short shorts gave him a hint of ass cheek. Her hair was every-where, her breath puffing against his chest.

Damn. He didn't usually spend an entire night with a woman. He didn't really like someone in his space. In the military, he'd spent many an uncomfortable night sleeping with his entire team in some pretty rough places. It made him appreciate his own space.

But he'd happily wake up with Haven McKinney wrapped around him any day.

She stirred and made a cute sound. Then her fingers stroked his chest, her lips pressing against his skin.

Shit. Was she even awake?

Then she slowly peppered kisses across his pec. *Fuck.* Blood filled his cock, and need throbbed hungrily through him.

"Haven," he growled.

She froze. She looked up his chest, sleepy eyes clearing. He was happy to see that while her bruises were changing to ugly greens and yellows, they were getting better.

"We're in the same bed," she said.

"Yeah."

"We weren't," she squeaked.

No, last night, when she'd faded, he'd put her to bed. She'd babbled about him sleeping on the couch, which he'd neither confirmed nor denied. But he was six foot three, so he sure as hell hadn't been planning to sleep on the couch.

She pulled back, and her gaze snagged on the tattoo on his chest. An American flag. He'd gotten most of his ink after he'd left the military. A way to celebrate his service, and the change in his life. A new start and freedom.

Haven bit her lip, and his cock throbbed even harder.

"You can touch me," he said.

She squeezed her eyes closed. "No."

"I want you to touch me."

She made a sound that was mostly a whimper. "I'm so weak." Her eyes opened. "Damn you for being so hot, Rhys Norcross."

He grinned at her and her gaze dropped to his mouth.

"What do you want, Haven?"

"It doesn't matter what I want, life rarely gives it to me. I wanted my mom to get better, but she died from cancer."

Rhys' smile faded.

"I wanted a loving dad, and I got one dedicated to saving the world, instead. I wanted a man, a partner, a home. I ended up with Leo. I don't get what I want, Rhys." Her hand moved over his chest. "I get a taste of good things, then they're taken away."

He swallowed a growl. He hated that she'd suffered all of that. She deserved better, more.

He wanted to give it to her.

"What do you want, Haven, right now?"

"To be safe."

"You feel safe right now? Right this instant?"

She hesitated, then she nodded.

"What else?"

"I want to touch you." A whispered confession that sounded torn from her.

"So, touch. I'm not going anywhere."

"I'm afraid." Her eyes closed. "I told myself no men.

Especially not gorgeous ones who are closely related to my boss and my best friend."

"Touch me. Take what you want."

She shivered. "Okay. But you can't touch me."

Dammit. He saw in her face that she expected him to balk.

All right, sexy Haven. Rhys raised his arms above his head and grabbed the slats on his metal headboard.

She sucked in a breath, her gaze locked on his torso. In this position, it drew the muscles in his arms, chest, and abdomen tight.

"No one should be as hot as you. It's so unfair."

Her gaze wandered down, over his abs to his black boxers. It lingered. Yeah, she could hardly miss his rock-hard erection.

"Haven, less looking, more touching."

She leaned over him. "I can do both."

She smoothed her slim hands up his chest. She found his tattoo and traced it. Then she lowered her head and licked it.

Fuck. His body bucked.

Her blue eyes looked at him. "I like having control."

She'd had control of her life stripped away. He was happy to give her some back, even if it killed him.

She flicked at his nipple, then nibbled at it, her nails pricking the skin of his abs.

He pulled in a shuddering breath. She looked lost in a pleasurable daze. Then her fingers skimmed down once, running along his hipbone, then slid into his boxers.

Her hand circled his cock.

He growled and lifted a hand.

"No." She stilled. "Put it back. I'm in charge."

Shit. He grabbed the headboard again.

She freed his throbbing cock. He wanted to shove her back, thrust himself deep inside her. But he knew she wasn't ready, and seeing her bruises and scrapes, he didn't want to hurt her. He was fucking hungry for her. It wouldn't be slow or gentle.

She pumped his cock. "God, even your cock is perfect."

"Faster, Haven," he groaned.

She gripped him harder, stroked him faster.

Oh, yeah. Rhys pumped into her fist. He had enjoyed sex in lots of different ways, and this was almost innocent in comparison to some of the stuff he'd done. But she was so focused on him, his cock, and the need inside him was white hot.

"Haven," he growled.

"I want to watch you come. Do it, Rhys. For me."

With another pump, he groaned her name. Her other hand slid in, cupping his balls. He came hard, spilling all over her hand and his gut. Hot sensation coursed through him. She watched him through hooded eyes, her chest rising and falling, pretty breasts pushing against her tank. There was fire in her eyes.

With a growl, Rhys reared up. She gasped.

He yanked her into his lap, his hands sliding straight up the wide leg of her shorts.

"Rhys!"

His hands slid under her panties, two fingers pumping inside her.

She moaned, her hips moving.

"You're drenched," he said.

She made a husky sound and rocked.

"Yeah, ride my hand, baby."

She did and he gripped her hip, helping her move.

"Oh God." Her head fell back, giving him a view of her long neck.

"That's it." He thumbed her clit.

"*Rhys*." She rocked harder.

"Look at me, Haven. Now."

Her head fell forward, their gazes locked.

"Come," he ordered.

He watched her orgasm roll over her. Her thighs trapped his hand, and she shuddered and moaned his name.

Pure beauty, right there. He earned this. Every dirty fight, every dusty hellhole, every cursed mission had brought him to this.

She collapsed against him, her face pressed to his neck.

He liked holding her limp, well-pleasured body as much as he liked pleasuring her. He stroked his hand down her back.

"We need to shower and get to work." He needed to find the thieves and whoever the fuck was pulling their strings.

"Uh-huh," she mumbled.

"That includes you, beautiful."

"What?" She blinked at him.

"You're coming with me to the Norcross office. Shower first."

She lifted her head. "Am I showering alone?"

"Yes, otherwise I'll spend the next few hours fucking you, and we'll be late."

She licked her lips and he felt it in his gut. He slapped her ass. "Move it, and I'll go make some breakfast."

"You can cook?"

"I can toast bread and scramble an egg." That and grilling were about the extent of his cooking abilities, much to his mother's dismay. Clara Norcross loved to cook, preferably hearty Italian food, but it hadn't rubbed off on Rhys.

He gave Haven a slow kiss, and took his time. He waited until she had that dazed look on her face. It made him smile.

"Now, get moving, babe."

CHAPTER TEN

She'd never been to the Norcross office before.

As Rhys led Haven inside, she took it all in. Unsurprisingly, it was a gorgeous space. Huge and open, with an industrial vibe. There were touches of wood and metal, with a polished-concrete floor. It definitely said "badasses work here."

Rhys' office was all glass walls. His desk was...messy.

"How do you find anything?" she asked.

He shot her a smile. "I know where everything is."

"I don't buy that, at all."

There were sticky notes everywhere, stacks of files, half-scribbled-on notepads, and pieces of paper dotted all over.

Her gaze fell on his smile. He had a really, really nice one. It made her remember what they'd done in his bed that morning. Her body tingled. It wanted more. Meanwhile, her brain was screaming at her to run.

"Haven, if you're still trying to go with the sworn-off-men thing, stop looking at me like that."

She licked her lips.

"Stop that, too," he said.

She looked away. Across the space, she spotted a man and froze. *Wow*. He was really muscular with smooth, brown skin, and cropped, dark hair. He glanced her way, and she almost swallowed her tongue. He was gorgeous, with strong features, a hard jaw, and pale green eyes. He nodded at her and she waved.

He looked like a movie star. He looked like he should be in an action movie, scaling cliffs and leaping out of planes.

"You can stop drooling now," Rhys said, tone amused.

"Who is that?" she asked.

"Rome. He's our main guy for bodyguard duty. Guy has a sixth sense for trouble." Rhys pushed a chair over to her. "Sit."

She sat and watched as Rhys dropped in his chair. He pulled a file across his desk and opened it.

"I forgot to mention that my friend Harry called," she said. "He's an art dealer. He heard a rumor of an underground auction of a very expensive painting."

Rhys' gaze sharpened. "He have any details?"

She shook her head.

"How good of a friend is this Harry?" Rhys' tone turned growly.

"Very good. He's handsome, a good dresser, kind, funny, and an art lover."

Rhys gripped the arms of her chair and wheeled her closer, scowling.

"I get on very well with him and his husband, Trent."

Rhys relaxed. "You're a pain in my ass. That's earned you some punishment."

She just smiled at him. God, it was nice to feel safe. To know that this man was looking out for her.

"I need to make some calls to Miami," he said.

Her good feelings plummeted. "About Leo."

"Yeah. Kitchen's over there." He pointed. "Get yourself some coffee. And you need to call your insurance."

Leaving him to his calls, she puttered around in the glossy kitchen and made herself a latte. She turned, and through the glass wall, saw Rhys leaning back in his chair, deep in conversation on the phone.

She hadn't realized that watching a man work could be hot.

She wandered back, wondering idly where everybody was. Although from what she knew of Vander, Rhys, and no doubt the other men who worked at Norcross, they were out doing badass security things.

Pulling out her cell phone, she sucked in a breath and called her insurance company.

After being put on hold and shuffled around to a few different people, she had her claim in. When she got back to Rhys' office, he was scowling hard.

"What's wrong?" she asked.

"Apparently your ex is in deep to the Zakharov family."

"Oh God." She dropped into her chair.

"He was having problems at his club, and started bleeding money. Looks like it started about nine months ago."

Haven closed her eyes. That was about the time he started to change.

Rhys took her mug and set it down. He pulled her closer until her legs bumped his.

"That's when he got moody, mean," she said. "That's when he started cheating."

"He borrowed money from Sergei Zakharov."

"Took money from criminals," she spat.

"Yeah. Instead of manning up, he took the easy path. Or what he thought was the easy path. Now, they own him. My contact said he's even more in debt now."

"God." She rubbed between her eyes.

Rhys' fingers slid up her thighs. "It's not your problem."

She nodded.

He cocked his head. "You still feel something for him?"

"No."

"Good."

Her cell phone rang. She pulled it out of the cute tote Gia had gotten for her. She stiffened.

Rhys cocked his head. "Haven?"

"Leo. He tried to call right before the explosion..."

Rhys' face turned dark. "Answer."

"What?" She stared at him.

"See what he's got to say." Rhys yanked her forward, pulling her into his lap.

She thumbed the button. "What?"

"Haven, babe, thank God."

"Leo." Her skin crawled.

Rhys' hand on her thigh squeezed, and that move steadied her.

"Why you're calling me?" she demanded.

"I know you've had...some troubles. I wanted to make sure you were okay."

"How do you know about my troubles, Leo?"

There was a pregnant pause.

"Would it be because *you* happened to land these troubles on me? And when I say troubles, I mean theft, beatings, kidnappings, and someone blowing up my apartment with me in it!" Her voice rose to a yell.

Vander appeared in the doorway, a troubled look on his face.

Rhys waved his brother off.

"I'm sorry, babe," Leo continued, voice wheedling. "I love you, and I never wanted you hurt."

"You *love* me?" Her voice turned incredulous.

Beneath her, she felt Rhys stiffen.

"If this is your idea of love, you've lost your mind. If you love someone, you don't cheat on them, you don't hit them, and you don't bring shit down on them."

"Babe."

She shook her head. "Don't call me babe. Just tell me what you did, Leo. I'm in danger."

His breathing was harsh across the line.

"I'm in deep, Haven. I owe a lot of money. I've kept tabs on you. I wanted to make sure you were safe."

She snorted. "Well I'm not."

"I saw the article in the paper about the Monet."

She stilled. "What did you do?"

"I still remember you bitching about how easy it was

at Alyssa's gallery for someone to sneak in as a police officer or delivery driver. I remember you told me about that famous robbery."

Oh. *God.* The robbery at the Isabella Stewart Gardner Museum in Boston. The thieves had posed as police officers. The thieves stole over half a billion dollars' worth of paintings. She'd used Leo as a sounding board, trusted him, and he'd used it against her.

"You're an *asshole.*"

"I was in bad trouble, Haven. They were threatening to break my kneecaps."

"They *blew* up my apartment!"

"They're trying to get to you to control me—"

"Tell them I'm nothing to you."

"I love you, Haven."

"Well, I do *not* love you," she snapped.

"You don't mean—"

Suddenly, the phone was gone from her hands.

"Haven is not yours to protect anymore," Rhys growled into the phone. "You tell Zakharov and his thugs that she's out of this."

"Who the fuck are you?" Haven heard Leo's tinny, irate voice through the phone.

"I'm Haven's man," Rhys said. "She's mine now."

Rhys' words sent a tingle through her.

"I'm the guy who won't cheat on her, or hit her." Brown eyes met hers. "Who'll keep her safe."

She felt the words deep inside. Rhys would do all of that.

But eventually, he'd lose interest, and move on and leave her in tatters.

"She's mine," Leo growled across the line.

Haven scowled. Like she was a bone to fight over.

"You fucked up," Rhys said. "You're still fucking up, Becker. Call Zakharov off her."

And with that, Rhys ended the call. He tossed her phone onto his desk.

"You okay?" he asked.

"No. My ex is still ruining my life."

Rhys cupped her jaw. "We'll get you through this."

Maybe. But Haven wasn't sure what the bigger danger to her was—Leo and his criminal troubles, or Rhys Norcross.

"I'M NOT sure I'm in a party mood."

Gia leaned forward, dabbing makeup on Haven's face.

"You deserve some fun." Gia made a humming sound. "Your bruising is looking much better."

"It is not. It's green and yellow. I look like a zombie."

"It's easier to cover now. There." Gia turned Haven toward the huge, well-lit mirror in Gia's swanky bathroom. The gorgeous space looked like a spa.

Gia had almost hidden all the bruising completely. *Oh.* She'd also given Haven sexy, smokey eyes.

"My brother will want to drag you out of here and into his bed to do naughty things."

"Gia!"

Gia wrinkled her nose. "Which I never want you to tell me about in detail, because *ew*."

"I told you I'm not going there." Haven couldn't go there. "Look what the last man I let into my life has done. I'm a mess, my life's a mess."

"Let Rhys make it better."

"*I* need to make it better."

Gia cocked her hip. She looked gorgeous in a red dress that showed off some wicked cleavage. She was like a pocket-size Sophia Loren.

"You don't have to do it alone," Gia said quietly.

"I do." Haven's heart squeezed. "I'm always alone."

Gia cursed in Italian. "Your stupid father."

"Gia."

"No. You're not alone anymore. You're my best friend. And whether you want to admit it or not, you and my brother are a thing."

"We are not."

"Where did you sleep last night?"

"That's not the point."

"Where?" Gia persisted.

"There were extenuating circumstances—"

"Where?"

"Fine. At Rhys' place."

"Where exactly?"

Haven sighed. "In Rhys' bed."

"Was he in the bed?"

Haven's teeth clicked together. "You are a pain. Yes."

Gia smiled like a queen who was well-pleased with her subjects.

"I hate you," Haven muttered.

"No, you don't, you love me."

Haven sighed. "I do."

125

Gia hugged her. "Come on, let's get some champagne. Good champagne makes everything better."

Haven let herself be dragged out of Gia's bathroom and bedroom.

In the living area, Gia's brothers were in the kitchen around the huge island. They were all holding beers, and huddled around the platters of food that Gia had done up for the party.

"Why do they have to be so hot?" Haven said.

"I've bemoaned the same thing lots of times," Gia said.

Easton—in one of his expensive suits—was rocking the hot-businessman look. Vander was in a suit as well, but he'd lost the jacket, and had his shirt sleeves rolled up, showing off the tattoos on his muscular forearms. He had the "mouthwatering badass" look cornered.

And Rhys...

Haven's belly went hot and melty. He'd changed into dark jeans, with a forest-green shirt that fit him like a glove. His sleeves were rolled up as well, and his hair was shaggy like he'd just rolled out of bed. He looked like a sexy rock star.

He smiled at her, his gaze heating. It skimmed over her silver dress, which had long sleeves, and although he couldn't see it yet, dipped low at the back. Very low.

He grabbed two glasses of champagne off the island and handed one to his sister, then one to Haven.

"You look good enough to eat," he murmured.

She quickly took a sip of her drink.

The doorbell rang. "I'll get it." Easton strode that way.

A moment later, Saxon entered. He was in suit pants as well, with a crisp, white shirt. He looked like a sexy, wealthy Norse God. *Move over, Thor.*

Haven watched Gia's eyes flash, then her face smoothed into blank lines.

"Mr. Buchanan has graced us with his presence," Gia drawled.

His green gaze skimmed over Gia, something predatory on his face. "I wouldn't miss out on free food and drink."

"No surprise there. You're richer than God, but like mooching off me."

He nabbed an olive off a platter. "You do know how to make good food."

Gia arched a brow. "And a woman's place is in the kitchen?"

Saxon smiled at her. "Ah, there are those sharp claws of yours, Contessa."

Contessa? Fascinated, Haven watched the pair. They'd completely forgotten anyone else existed.

"And no, my woman's place is in my bed." With that comeback, Saxon turned and headed towards the fridge.

Hmm. Haven watched Gia struggle with her temper and shoot daggers at Saxon's broad back. Holy smokes, the sexual tension was turning Haven on a little bit.

The doorbell rang again, and more people arrived. Most were connected to Gia's work. Someone put some music on.

For a little while, Haven forgot about Leo, the painting, everything.

Anytime she looked up, Rhys was watching her, and it

made her feel warm and jittery inside. She heard Gia and Saxon sniping at each other again. She was totally grilling her friend as soon as she could. How two people could devour each other with their eyes, while flinging shit at each other, she didn't know, but Saxon and Gia had it down to a fine art.

Needing some air, Haven headed out onto Gia's balcony. She leaned on the railing, the breeze cool on her face.

She sensed Rhys before she felt him behind her. She clearly had a finely tuned Rhys radar.

He dropped a kiss to her shoulder, and she shivered.

"If I'd seen the back of this dress when you'd first come out, I wouldn't have let you wear it."

She tipped her head back. "It's not the Dark Ages, Rhys. Men don't get to dictate what women wear."

He trailed a finger slowly down her spine, sensation igniting in its wake. "I hate any man looking at all this honey-gold skin."

She leaned into him, and felt herself losing herself in him.

He spun her around, and his lips were close to hers, just a tiny fraction away.

"Rhys—"

"I love it when you say my name like that. Like you want so much, but you're fighting so hard."

He lowered his mouth to hers, nibbling her lips. His hand slid around her ass as he kissed her. She rubbed against him, her tongue stroking his. She was so weak.

Then she pulled back. "I can't risk this, risk you."

"Haven, trust me."

"You'll break my heart."

He froze, staring at her.

"You want a good time, but for me—" She shook her head. "I'll be left fumbling with pieces that will never go back together. And it'll be a mess, with Easton and Gia—"

Rhys kissed her again. She clung to him.

"It's worth the risk," he murmured. "We can't predict the future, but I want you, Haven. In my bed, in my arms."

She was totally going to cave. "I...I need another drink."

She ducked under his arm and made it back inside before he stopped her.

Gia's apartment was filled with laughter, music, and conversation. Haven pushed through the crowd and set her glass down on the island. She needed a break from Rhys' orbit. He continued to pull her in, and she couldn't seem to stop it.

What if she just let go? What if she let him claim her?

Temptation trembled through her.

The doorbell rang. Some late arrival.

No one was headed for the door, so she reached it and opened it.

A smiling, young woman, wearing a little slip of a blue dress, beamed at her. "Hi. I have some stuff for the party. Can you give me a hand bringing it in?"

"Sure." Haven stepped out.

The woman's friendly smile shifted to something that

made Haven frown. Then the woman gave Haven a shove down the hall.

"Hey!" Haven squeaked.

"Good work."

The male voice made her turn, and she saw Leo. Her eyes widened.

He pressed a cloth to her mouth, his arm snaking around her.

"What the hell!" Her words were muffled and thick. She struggled against him.

Then dizziness hit her, her legs turning wobbly.

Leo's face turned wavy. This couldn't be happening.

Then there was nothing.

CHAPTER ELEVEN

Taking a swig of his beer, Rhys scanned the party for Haven. Gia always put on a good spread. It had been at a party just like this one that he'd first seen Haven.

She'd been standing in Gia's living room, smiling, wearing a sexy, green dress that hugged that sweet ass of hers. She hadn't laughed much, had been a little tense, but Rhys had still felt like he'd been hit by a flash-bang grenade.

Now, he'd finally had a taste of her, and experienced the smart, sexy woman beneath.

He wanted her. All of her.

His hands tightened on the beer bottle. He needed to get her safe first.

He still couldn't see her in the crowd and frowned. He'd known that she'd needed a moment after the balcony. She felt their connection, but she was fighting it.

That damn ex of hers had her spooked.

He spotted Gia talking with her friends. Center of the party, as always.

"Hey, Gia, have you seen Haven?"

His sister frowned. "No, check the bathroom, maybe?"

Rhys strode that way. Saxon caught his gaze.

"You look like you want to smash someone's teeth in," Saxon said.

"You seen Haven?"

Saxon straightened. "No."

Together they quickly checked Gia's condo. Panic—hot and burning—hit Rhys' chest. There was no sign of her.

They met Vander in the kitchen.

"Haven's missing," Rhys said.

His brother grabbed his phone and put it on speaker.

"This better be life or death," Ace's voice growled from the phone. Ace hadn't come to the party as he'd had prior plans.

Rhys' gut churned. "Haven's missing from Gia's party."

"Shit." The rustle of sheets, then a muffled female voice in the background. "This is work. You should head out, babe. Right. Vander, I'm getting my laptop now."

A few moments passed.

"Pulling security footage." There was a pause. "Shit. Damn. *Fuck.*"

Vander's phone pinged, as did Rhys and Saxon's.

Rhys yanked out his phone and stared at the image of Haven outside Gia's door, struggling with a man. A woman in a blue dress watched with a faint smile.

"A man carried her out of the building," Ace said.

"Ace, I need his face," Rhys growled.

"Here."

Another ding, and a new image appeared on Rhys' phone. It was a perfect shot of the man's face, with Haven's head lolling over his arm.

Leo Becker.

"He drugged her." A roar started inside Rhys' head.

"Keep a lock on it," Vander said.

"Hey, the woman in the blue dress is still here." Saxon jerked his head toward the living room.

Rhys swiveled. He spotted the woman amongst the partygoers, then he exploded across the living room.

"Rhys!" Vander barked out.

The woman lifted her head, her eyes widening as Rhys barreled down on her. She backed up and Rhys pressed a hand against her shoulder and shoved her against the wall. Gasps and murmurs broke out.

"Rhys!" Gia snapped. "You can't—"

"What did he pay you?" Rhys' tone was low and deadly.

"Rhys?" Gia said again, confusion in her voice.

"He paid you to lure her out of the party. He drugged and abducted her."

Gia hissed out a sharp breath. "Haven? Oh, God. Leah, what the fuck?"

Leah licked her lips. "It was all in fun. He's her boyfriend, and he wanted to surprise her." The woman was talking fast, babbling. "He asked me to find some way to get her into the hall, but I got lucky and she answered the door. Apparently, she's into kinky stuff, likes being kidnapped."

"Fuck!" Rhys exploded.

Vander and Saxon gripped his arms and pulled him away from the woman.

Leah rubbed her shoulder.

Easton pushed forward. "What's going on? Where's Haven?"

"Becker kidnapped her," Rhys said through clenched teeth.

"Shit." Easton muttered.

Leah's face drained of color. "He's...he isn't her boyfriend?"

"He's her abusive ex-boyfriend." Gia's voice was as sharp as a blade.

The woman slapped a hand against her mouth. "Oh God, I didn't—"

Rhys turned away. "We need to get searching."

Vander put his phone to his ear. "Ace, find what Becker is driving, and where the hell he took her."

Rhys strode onto the corridor. He *had* to find Haven.

If that prick hurt her...

Vander gripped his shoulder. "Becker won't hurt her."

"Becker's a wildcard," Rhys snapped. "He hit her before, dragged her into this fucking mess, and now he's drugged her."

Standing waiting for the elevator, Rhys turned and punched the wall. His fist went through the drywall.

"We'll find her," Vander repeated.

Rhys nodded, but his throat tightened. He wouldn't relax until Haven was back in his arms.

HAVEN BLINKED HER EYES, fighting through the grogginess wrapped around her like a thick blanket. How much wine had she drunk?

She opened her eyes and found herself sprawled on a couch in a small, not-so-nice apartment. The couch had an awful floral pattern with dubious stains on it.

What the hell? She jerked upright.

Then she spotted Leo sitting in an armchair across from her.

She jolted. "Leo? What the hell?" Memories came back to her in a rush. "Oh, my God, you kidnapped me!"

"Haven—"

"Shut up." She dropped her head into her hands. Her friends would be out of their minds with worry.

Rhys.

Shit, Rhys would be tearing the city apart.

Leo, looking bad-boy disheveled, leaned forward in the armchair. She noted the lines of stress and tiredness on his face. She jerked back, not wanting to get too close to him.

"I left," she said. "I want *nothing* to do with you. Why won't you leave me alone?"

His handsome face twisted. "I never wanted to hurt you. I love you, Haven."

She laughed harshly. "You're kidding me." She saw from his face that he was serious. "God, you aren't." Her eyes narrowed. "Did you love the cocktail waitress who gave you a blow job in your office, too?"

Leo closed his eyes. "That was a mistake."

Haven made an angry sound. Why wouldn't her past leave her alone?

"I was under a lot of stress. You kept pushing—"

"I was your *girlfriend*. I was worried. I wanted to help you." She sat back, and worried for a second what she might catch from this damn couch. "I guess being in debt to the Russian mafia is stressful."

Her ex dragged in a breath. "You know."

"I'm in danger, Leo. I've been hurt, a hundred-million-dollar painting I'm responsible for was stolen from my workplace, my apartment exploded. Yes, I know."

"That's why I'm here. I want to keep you safe. You need to come with me and—"

"You can't be serious." She rose and her head swam. *Dammit.* She locked her legs to keep from swaying. "I want *nothing* from you. I don't want to be anywhere near you. You're the one who put me in danger." She took two steps away. "I need to contact my friends." Rhys would be going crazy. "They'll be worried. Where the hell are we?"

"Airbnb I rented. And your friends can't worry for you, or care for you, like I do."

Was he serious? Had he always been this self-centered? "You are absolutely right. They care for me *way* more than you ever did. I'm leaving."

Leo leaped up. "No. It's too dangerous. Zakharov's men—"

She cocked her head. "Your Russian friends."

"They're after you," he said.

"Why?" Anger was a burn in her throat. "How do they even know who I am?"

"I told you, I'm desperate. I needed to pay them back, and when I told Sergei about the painting..." Leo swallowed. "They've got it, but they're finding it hard to sell a painting like that."

"It's a stolen masterpiece. No shit."

"They need someone reputable to guarantee that it is what it is, and not a fake. They know how knowledgeable you are..."

Her eyes widened. "They blew up my apartment and tried to kill me!"

"You weren't supposed to be there." He shoved his hands through his hair. "It was the afternoon and you should have been at work. They just wanted to rattle you, limit your options..."

She shook her head. "I can't believe this."

"They think you can help them shift the painting." He rubbed the back of his neck. "They're also not happy with me. They have some San Francisco security firm on their ass."

"My boss is a wealthy, influential businessman, Leo."

"He the one you're fucking?"

Haven ground her teeth together. "No, not that it's any of your business. One of his brothers runs that security firm, and the other one works there. They want the painting back. They're also my friends, and they want me safe."

"Zakharov wants to use you to try and control me."

"Why?" she screeched.

"Because he knows I love you."

"Stop telling people you love me. I don't love you!"

Hurt filled his features. "We were good, Haven."

"For about thirty seconds, Leo. We had fun. Then it wasn't fun, and now it's *really* not fun. I've moved on. Please. Leave. Me. *Alone.*"

He stared at her with those clear-blue eyes she'd once thought were beautiful. "Moved on with that asshole on the phone?"

Haven wanted to scream. "That's what you got from what I said? Not me telling you how I feel and what I want?"

He paused. "Are you with him?"

"I'm leaving, Leo."

"No!" He lunged at her.

They wrestled for a second and she jabbed her fingers into his eyes. He yelped and fell, and they both went down in a tangle, rolling on the dirty carpet. They hit a coffee table, and pain flared in her hip.

"Let me go!" she yelled.

"I have to keep you safe!"

Haven managed to get on top of him, and rammed her knee into his gut. Leo stayed in decent shape, but he was nowhere near as hard and muscled as Rhys.

The air whooshed out of him and he grunted.

Haven scrambled up, then yanked the front door open. She'd lost her heels in the fight, but she didn't pause. She raced barefoot down the dingy stairwell.

She hit the street, looked left and right, then went left. The cool air hit her and she shivered.

She wanted Rhys. She wanted those muscular, tattooed arms around her. For once, she wanted to lean on someone and trust them to help hold her up.

Stifling a sob, she turned a corner. She had no idea where she was, but she saw lights and shops ahead.

She broke into a jog and spotted a Walgreens. She needed to call Gia and Rhys.

The doors swished open.

"I need help."

A middle-aged woman and a teenaged girl stood behind the counter, their eyes widening. The woman raced around to Haven. "Oh, honey. Are you okay?"

Haven nodded. "Can I use your phone?"

The woman patted her back. "Of course."

Haven was so glad she knew Gia's number by heart. She held the phone in her trembling hands. It rang.

"Hello?"

"Gia!"

"Haven! Are you all right? The guys are out searching everywhere for you."

"I'm okay. Leo—"

"We know, we saw the security footage. Where are you?"

"At a Walgreens. Hang on." She put her hand over the phone. "Where are we?" The teenager rattled off the address, and Haven gave it to her friend.

"Sit tight, girlfriend. Are you sure you're all right?"

"Yes."

"Okay, let me call the cavalry."

"Thanks, G." Haven handed the phone back to the woman. "Thank you. Someone's coming."

"Do you want to call the police?"

All Haven wanted was to not be here. "No, that's okay."

A few minutes passed and she saw movement at the door. She looked up.

A wild-eyed Leo stared at her through the glass.

Oh, hell. The doors opened and she pushed away from the counter.

Leo strode in. "Haven, we need to go now."

"Leo, leave me alone. I don't know how else to say it."

He grabbed her arm. "You need to—"

"Hey," the Walgreen's lady interrupted. "Leave her alone."

Leo ignored the woman and jerked Haven forward. She shoved at him, but he moved closer.

Suddenly, a candy bar sailed through the air and smacked Leo in the forehead. He blinked, shocked, and Haven glanced to see the teenage girl grabbing another candy bar off a display near the counter.

"Haven," Leo growled.

"Just *leave*," she yelled.

He yanked her again and she pulled back. They spun in an unwieldy circle and crashed into a display. Hair brushes and accessories flew everywhere.

She fell to the floor and Leo landed on top of her. The air rushed out of her.

"My God, what did I ever see in you?" she cried.

She shoved at him, then suddenly, he was yanked off her and he went flying, smacking into a set of shelves.

She scrambled up to see Vander and Saxon standing in the doorway, their faces like stone.

Vander crossed his arms over his chest. "Haven, you all right?"

She nodded.

Then she turned. Rhys had Leo on the ground, one tattooed hand fisted at the front of Leo's shirt, while he punched Leo in the face with his other hand.

Oh, God.

She raced over. "Rhys, let him go. He's not worth it."

That got her no response. Leo moaned.

"Rhys!" She clung to his side. "Please."

He hesitated.

"I need you. I feel a huge freak-out coming on." Not really, she was more pissed than upset, but she did a pretty good job of making her voice shake.

Rhys dropped Leo. He turned to her, face like thunder and his eyes boiling.

"Rhys," she whispered.

He yanked her up and kissed her. She sank into him, feeling a punch of emotions—relief, desire, anger. His tongue touched hers and she slid her hands into his thick hair.

When he finally pulled back, he pressed his forehead to hers and she clung to him. Then she let out a happy, little sigh.

He tilted his head. "What happened to the freak-out?"

Oops. "Oh, well, your kiss chased it away."

His dark eyes narrowed, but then his lips twitched. "You wouldn't be trying to distract me from beating the shit out of your ex, would you?"

"Who, me?"

He shook his head, his lips twitching.

"You said you weren't dating your boss." Leo's voice was nasally and his nose was bleeding.

"He's not my boss," she huffed. "He's my boss' brother."

Leo scowled. "He's an asshole—"

Rhys shifted, and quickly, Haven stepped in front of him to block his view of Leo.

"Be quiet," she snapped at Leo. "You don't exist for me."

"But this asshole does?" Leo scowled at Rhys.

Behind her, Rhys tensed. She pressed a hand to his hard gut, and was momentarily distracted by feeling his six pack through his shirt.

"He does. Tell your friends I have nothing to do with you." She turned. "Can we go home now?"

"Yeah, angel."

Rhys picked her up and she snuggled into him.

"I can walk," she said.

"I know." He didn't set her down.

She leaned into him as he headed out the door.

CHAPTER TWELVE

As Rhys unlocked his front door, his chest held a knot of residual anger and a whole lot of relief.

He held Haven tucked under his arm. She was alive. Safe. Breathing.

She looked fine despite her ordeal. He wanted to take care of her.

And he definitely didn't want to feel the fear that had hit him knowing she'd been taken again.

They walked in and he flicked the lights on.

"Why don't you take a bath?" he said. "Relax—"

"I don't want a bath." She walked into his place and his gaze took in the back of that damn dress. Or rather lack of a back.

She spun, her blue gaze on him.

Then she ran at him and jumped.

He caught her with a grunt, sliding his hands under her ass. "Haven."

"I know what I want." Her mouth hovered over his, not kissing him. Yet.

Anticipation was hot and hungry. Her breath mingled with his.

His cock went hard in an instant. Then he dug deep and dredged up some control. It was minuscule. "You've had a rough night—"

She licked her lips and her tongue brushed his. They both groaned. His fingers bit into her ass.

"I'm not thinking of anything but you," she murmured.

Rhys gritted his teeth. He was known for his control. Iron hands on the wheel of a fast car, on the controls of a speeding boat, on a rifle in battle.

Right now, those hands were shaking.

Because of her.

His Haven.

When he didn't move or say anything, he saw uncertainty cross her face.

"Um, if you don't want—?"

He slid a hand up and tangled it in her hair. He tilted her head back, just rough enough to get her attention. Her pretty lips parted.

"What do you want, baby?" he drawled.

Something twisted inside him, a beastly part of him that wanted to throw her on the ground, and tear that damn dress off of her.

"I want to be safe," she murmured. "I want your hands on me." Her mouth brushed his lightly. "I want you inside me."

Rhys' growl was loud. His cock was hard and throbbing, trapped in his damn jeans. Sharp need twisted in his gut.

He'd never wanted to claim and possess a woman like this before.

"You going to let me sink my cock deep? You wet for me, angel?"

She squirmed against him. "Yes."

"It won't be polite or gentle." He ground his cock against her. "You've got me hot and hard."

"I want hard. I want it *all*." She was breathing fast.

Rhys strode across the room to the dining table, filled with barely leashed hunger. He set her down on her feet, then pushed the dress off her shoulders.

The fabric fell to her waist and she gasped, but Rhys could only see those gorgeous breasts. They weren't big, but they were perfectly formed, and topped with pink nipples.

"Rhys—"

He slid an arm around her and pushed her back, arching her spine so her breasts pushed up at him.

"Look at you." He ran his knuckles across her nipples, watching them turn to hard, little beads.

She made a hungry, desperate sound.

He lowered his head and sucked one nipple into his mouth.

"Oh... *Yes, God.*"

He rolled his tongue over her nipple, loving how she squirmed. Then he moved across to the other one. Her skin was so smooth, so damn sweet.

She slid one hand into his hair, and gave a small yank. He sucked harder, and she moaned and bucked against him.

"Need you inside me," she pleaded.

Desire made everything in him hot, tight. If he didn't have her soon, he'd implode. He felt like he'd wanted her forever. He couldn't remember not wanting her.

He pushed her dress down and it slithered into a pool at her feet.

She wore a tiny wisp of bronze lace beneath.

He gripped her hips and lifted her onto the table.

"Oh." She gripped his biceps. Then she grabbed his shirt and yanked.

Buttons flew everywhere, and her gaze locked on his chest. She pushed the torn shirt off.

"My God, you're Grade-A fantasy material." She pressed a hand to his abs, her nails scratching his skin.

Rhys made a sound that made her gaze meet his. He saw the answering need in her eyes, the same desire that was strumming through him.

Then she touched the tattoo on his chest—the American flag. A reminder of why he'd fought, why he'd given up little pieces of his soul.

Then before he realized what she had planned, she palmed the large bulge in his trousers. *Fuck.* He felt his balls draw up, and for a second, he worried that he'd come in his jeans.

He moved fast, pressing close between her legs and shoving her back on his table. Damn, he'd never seen a better sight than a naked Haven McKinney laid out for him.

"Baby, my cock is on a hair trigger when it comes to you. I plan to come deep inside you, not in my jeans."

She arched up, and he stroked his hands down her

belly. Then under the edge of her thong. She was drenched and his gut clenched.

"Baby, so wet. I can slam inside you and I'll slide right in."

"*Rhys.*"

He hated even the tiniest barrier between them. He yanked and tore her thong off.

She gasped. "No one's ever torn my clothes off me."

He smiled darkly. "You started it. You ripped my shirt off."

She bit her lip. "I'm not sorry."

He leaned over and kissed her. A kiss that demanded everything. Their tongues stroked, both of them grabbing at each other, pressing hard. Her long legs clamped on his hips, and she writhed against his cock.

Rhys slid a hand between them. Then he slid two fingers along her sweet, wet folds. She cried out. Then he thrust his fingers inside her welcoming warmth.

Her hands clenched in his hair, pulling hard. She made a desperate sound, then chanted his name.

He could tell that she was close. He stilled and pulled his hand away.

"*No,*" she complained.

"I think you should come on my cock, not my fingers."

"Rhys, please." Her body arched.

"Or maybe, I'll make you come on my hand, then again on my cock." He slid his fingers back inside her. His thumb found her clit.

"Rhys!"

She rocked against his hand, and her scream felt like

a prize. Her body squeezed down on his fingers as she came, and he kept working her, watching every emotion that crossed her face.

So damn expressive.

Finally, she slumped back, panting, her lips swollen.

Rhys yanked his belt free. He had to have her. *Now.*

He pulled a foil packet out of his pocket, then shoved his jeans down and kicked them off. Then his boxers followed, and his cock sprang free.

Haven rose up on one elbow, her hungry gaze on him. She took in his naked body, then stared at his cock. He fisted his erection and pumped.

Her chest hitched. "You're big."

"It's all yours, baby." He grabbed her and slid her toward the edge of the table.

She gasped.

He pushed up against her, his hands spreading her thighs. "What are you going to do with it?"

"Mine," she whispered.

"Yours."

He quickly tore the condom package open, and rolled it on. Then he pushed forward, sliding his swollen cock against her wet warmth.

She moaned. He pushed until the head of his cock was inside her. They both moaned.

Her arms and legs wrapped around him.

"Do it," she ordered.

Rhys plunged into Haven—hard and deep.

Her cry was loud, her nails digging into his shoulders.

Tight, hot. He gritted his teeth. "Haven."

"So big. So good."

Rhys reared back and thrust hard. The table rocked beneath them. He picked up his pace.

"Hold on, Haven." His hips slammed into her, in and out of her wet heat. He felt sensation building in his gut, balls, the base of his spine.

"*Yes*, Rhys, harder."

"*Baby*."

Their eyes met.

"Connected," she whispered.

Hell yeah, connected. He was deep inside her. So fucking good.

"Come again," he growled.

"I'm not sure—"

He changed the angle of his thrusts, tilting her hips. Her husky cries filled the air.

"Damn, need you, Haven."

"Rhys!"

She came again hard. She whimpered, her body shuddering, pussy clenching on him.

Rhys' release hit him like a knockout punch. A roar echoed through his head and every muscle in his body locked.

With one last thrust, he ran his teeth along her neck. Then he sank his teeth into the tendon there, and heard her cry out as his body shuddered through his white-hot release.

HAVEN DID NOT CARE one bit that the table was hard against her back.

Her body tingled everywhere. Her breathing was still fast. Rhys' body was slumped on hers, his face against her hair.

Wow.

She stroked a hand down his back. He shifted and pressed a kiss to the side of her neck where he'd bitten her.

Their gazes met, then his head lowered and he kissed her.

Oh.

Her hands drifted to his hair, lazily massaging as he kissed her. This time it was slow and deep, with a surprising edge of sweet.

She hummed into his mouth and shivered.

"Got to take care of this condom," he said. "Be right back."

He pulled out of her and she let out a little sound.

He grinned at her then stalked away, and she had just enough energy to stare at the hardest, most amazing ass she'd ever seen.

Haven guessed she should feel embarrassed, lying naked on Rhys' table. She waited a second. *Nope.* Post-the-best-sex-that-she'd-ever-had bliss was in full effect.

Rhys came back, still gloriously naked, and pressed his hands to the table either side of her body.

"You going to sleep on the table?"

"Maybe," she answered.

He grinned and a curl of heat ignited in her belly. *Oh, boy.*

He lifted her and she found herself tossed over a hard shoulder. A big hand pressed to her ass.

"Rhys!"

That earned her a grunt. He walked down the hall and into his bedroom. He laid her on the bed and she stared up at him. Out the window, she saw the lights of the Bay Bridge.

He reached over and flicked on the lamp on the bedside table, washing them in a warm glow.

It just made him look better. The light caressed his hard body, making it a fascinating pattern of gold skin and shadowed dips. She wanted to explore all those intriguing tattoos. She'd never had a thing for tattoos before, but on Rhys...yum.

"Can check the table off the list of places where I want to fuck you." He pressed a knee to the bed.

She saw his long, thick cock getting hard again.

"Bed next," he said.

Haven fought a rush of dampness between her legs. "How many places are on this list?"

His eyes flashed. "Everywhere."

She thought he'd reach for her, but instead he leaned back against the pillows lined up against the metal headboard.

Then one strong hand circled his cock, and he started stroking himself.

Her belly went tight.

"What do you want now, Haven?"

Her chest filled with air and desire hummed through her. *You. Everything.*

He lifted his other hand and crooked his finger.

She crawled across the bed toward him. God, he had a beautiful cock. She knelt between his legs, and looked up his powerful, sexy body. His bronze skin was a beautiful contrast to the white sheets. On his face, she saw desire and, more than that, a need to possess.

This man wanted to possess her.

She wrapped her hand around his cock and made a fist. He grunted. She dragged her hand up from root to tip.

His grunt turned to a groan. "Baby."

"I like this big cock." It swelled in her hand.

"It likes you, too. Now, you going to suck it?"

She lowered her head. "Is that what you want?" Her lips brushed the tip.

Rhys hissed out a breath. He shifted, and the swollen head brushed across her lips. Haven opened her mouth and sucked him deep.

He muttered a curse, his hips pumping up. She slid up, then sucked him back in. One big hand slid into her hair. Not to direct her, but like he needed to ground himself.

She hummed on his cock. She loved the salty, musky taste of him. She licked and sucked, laved her tongue along his hard length.

"That's so good, angel." His voice was deep and raspy. "I love your sweet mouth."

As she kept working him, his big body tensed. She saw the muscles in his abs straining.

Then suddenly, he yanked her off him.

"No." She wasn't done. She wanted to watch him come.

He pulled her up his body. God, she loved how

strong he was, that he could so easily move her around. He pulled her thighs either side of his head.

Haven's eyes popped open. Oh, *oh*.

"Prettiest pussy I've seen." His mouth closed over her.

"Rhys!" Haven grabbed the headboard, her knuckles turning white.

His tongue plunged inside her and she couldn't even cry out his name, all she could do was make hungry, desperate sounds.

He licked and sucked, lavishing her clit with attention. His stubble scraped her skin. Soon, her hips were bucking.

"Yeah, ride my face, baby."

With a deep groan, she came. So damn hard. Her back arched, her head fell back, and she screamed.

Her body was still shaking, pleasure coursing through her like the sweetest drug, when Rhys lifted her again.

She found herself on her hands and knees in the center of his bed.

"Look, Haven."

She lifted her head. The mirror on the wall gave her the perfect view of the two of them.

Rhys was on his knees behind her, and she heard the crinkle of foil before he rolled the condom on. Her belly contracted.

His hands slid between her cheeks, stroked, and she moaned.

Then his hands slid up her spine to her shoulder blades. He pushed and she lowered her head to the bed, pressing her cheek to the covers so she could watch them in the mirror.

Haven shivered, and watched one of his hands wrap around her waist, while the other one circled his cock.

He looked like a conquering king, about to claim his spoils of war.

He thrust into her.

Haven moaned.

"You like my cock, angel?"

She moaned again.

He moved inside her, not fast, but deep and firm. "You are so damn beautiful. I have the perfect view of your body taking my cock. You were made for my cock, Haven."

Rhys leaned over her, covering her body with his. One of his hands slid down her arm, their fingers tangling together.

How could she feel this connected to him? Like they were one. She was surrounded by him—his strength, his power, his possessiveness.

Right now, there was only Rhys. The rest of the world did not exist.

He picked up speed, powering inside her. Haven felt her release building again. She shoved back against him, needing more.

"Can't get enough, can you?" he growled.

"Can't get close enough to you," she panted.

She felt his fingers convulse on hers.

Then she came in a blinding rush. She shoved back against his strong body, his name torn from her lips. "*Rhys.*"

"*Haven*." Another hard, violent thrust and he came. His roar echoed in her ears as she rode through the shockwaves of her orgasm.

Rhys' arms wrapped around her as they collapsed on the bed. She looked into the mirror and saw one muscled, tattooed arm banded across her naked body.

Warmth unfolded inside her chest. She felt a prick of panic in the back of her head, but she pushed it away.

There was nowhere else she wanted to be right now except in Rhys' arms.

He kissed her shoulder. "Sleep, baby."

Warm, well-pleasured, and feeling safe, she did.

CHAPTER THIRTEEN

R hys woke and stretched one arm over his head.
Damn. They hadn't gotten much sleep, but he
didn't regret a thing.

He reached out and found no warm, soft body beside
him, but he heard water running in his bathroom.

He stuffed a pillow under his head and eyed the bed.
The sheets were nearly torn off. He pulled the corner of
one sheet over his naked body and smiled. Haven
McKinney hid a hot, wild, sex kitten under her tight
skirts.

He heard her humming as she brushed her teeth, and
his smile widened. He liked this—feeling good, lazy, his
woman in his bathroom.

Now he just had to convince her not to be scared
of it.

He heard the water shut off. As he lay there, Rhys
realized that for the first time in a really long time, he
didn't feel that gnawing need in his gut to leap out of
bed and get moving. The urge to get out, find some-

thing to distract himself, to stay in motion. He knew that it was when you stopped that old demons caught you.

But right now, his demons were quiet.

Haven sauntered out of the bathroom. She was in one of his T-shirts. It was too big for her—it hit her at mid-thigh, and the neckline slid down one shoulder.

A silky-smooth shoulder. His cock woke up. Shit, when was the last time a shoulder had turned him on?

Her hair was a sleep-mussed mess. All that brown hair gave him ideas.

Her steps slowed. "Hi."

"Hey."

Her gaze ran over him. He just had the twist of the sheet covering his hips, one leg uncovered.

She swallowed. "You look like a debauched rock star."

"Well, the debauched part is right."

Color flared in her cheeks. She twisted her hair up in a messy pile on her head and fastened it with a band. "I'll cook us some breakfast. Then I want to go over everything we have on the *Water Lilies*."

Rhys was momentarily distracted. As she lifted her arms up to do her hair, the hem of the T-shirt lifted. He saw several more inches of those slender thighs. Was she wearing panties?

"Rhys?"

Her words registered. "We?"

"Yes." Her chin lifted. "I'm going to help you find the painting."

He was tempted to lock her up somewhere safe, far,

far away from San Francisco, and anything to do with the painting.

But he knew she'd fight him.

The only other alternative was to stick to her every second.

"Come here," he said.

She hesitated, but then she moved and pressed a knee to the bed. "Rhys—"

Using his lightning-fast reflexes, he yanked her on top of him.

"You got panties on under that?" She was half sprawled on him, and he reached out and gripped her leg, just above her knee.

"I'm not answering that." She sniffed. "I told you, you have nothing to do with any decisions on what I'm wearing."

He slid his hand up, saw her chest hitch. "But I have some say in the clothes you take off." His hand danced under the hem of the T-shirt, moving toward the juncture of her thighs. "Your skin is so soft, Haven."

Then he found out that she definitely wasn't wearing panties.

"My angel's got a naughty streak." He slid a finger inside her warmth.

She moaned, her head dropping forward. She pressed her hands to his chest and he loved the bite of her nails on his skin.

Rhys thrust two fingers inside her, his thumb strumming across her clit. Her hips moved restlessly, and she cried out.

"Get there, baby," he murmured.

She panted, her hips rocking on his hand. "Rhys."

"Come."

"*Oh, God.*" She ground down.

He pinched her clit and she came. He felt a rush of wet on his fingers and her tight pussy squeezing. Her husky cries were the sweetest music. She collapsed onto his chest.

Rhys reached out to the bedside table and grabbed a condom. He tugged Haven back up to straddle him. With a noise, she shifted her thighs on either side of him, her heavy gaze finding his swollen cock standing up between them.

He was so damn hard for her.

"Put it on." He handed her the foil packet.

She fumbled and opened it. Then she took her sweet time rolling the latex over him.

Rhys felt like a wild beast. He *needed* her. He needed her skin against his. Needed her scent in his senses. Needed her warmth.

He reached up and yanked the shirt off her. Then he fisted his cock and Haven's eyes glazed with need. She lifted her hips.

His gut was in knots, blood hammering through his veins.

"Take what you need, baby. What we both need."

She rocked against him, rubbing against his cock. He hissed out a breath.

"Haven, do it." He clamped his hands on her hips.

She lowered down, and the head of his cock slipped inside her. They both groaned, their gazes meeting.

"That's it," he said. "Work me inside you, angel."

She lifted up, then drove down. She cried out.

Rhys gritted his teeth. He was lodged deep inside her —every hard inch. Desire hammered inside him, then she made an incoherent sound and pressed her hands to his chest.

She started to ride him, her hips rolling.

Fuck. Her tight pussy gripped him hard. With every thrust, she let out a harsh breath.

"Faster, Haven," he growled.

She picked up the pace. Her pretty breasts bounced with her moves. He reached up and tugged her hair free.

It tumbled around her shoulders. She was the most beautiful thing he'd seen. Haven riding his cock, taking her pleasure.

"Rhys?"

"Baby?"

"Please...rub my clit."

His gut clenched. His sexy girl asking for what she wanted. "You want me rubbing your clit while you ride my cock?"

"Yes."

He found the sweet nub, and with one roll, her pussy clenched. She made a strangled cry and her back arched.

Fucking beautiful.

Her orgasm triggered his. Rhys yanked her down, his cock buried deep in her. His vision grayed—narrowing to only her and the climax tearing through him.

With a roar, his release shook his entire body.

She collapsed on him, and he wrapped his arms around her, tucking her close against his chest.

He turned his face into her hair and breathed her in.

He listened as her breathing slowed, and let his hand trail up her back.

He wanted more. Turning his head, he found her neck. He kissed her, tasting her skin and the faint trace of salt. He saw the tiny bruise he'd left the first time they'd fucked and he smiled.

His mark. He gently kissed it and she made a happy, contented sound.

Then he smacked her ass. "You mentioned breakfast."

This time, she made an annoyed sound.

"Come on, McKinney. I need sustenance."

"Because you fucked me most of the night. I'm surprised we didn't both lose ten pounds."

He reached over and found the shirt he pulled off her. He urged her up, he pulled it back over her head.

She gave him a small smile, and Rhys stilled. Emotion moved through him.

In that moment, sitting on his rumpled bed with an equally rumpled Haven, he realized that he'd kill for her. Die for her.

She tilted her head. "Rhys?"

"Come on, angel. I need bacon."

HAVEN FINISHED SCRAMBLING THE EGGS. She eyed Rhys at the coffee machine, and added way more bacon to the frypan.

She'd gathered her hair back up on her head, and this time, she'd pulled some panties on under his T-shirt.

Rhys could not be trusted.

He was wearing a pair of loose sweatpants and had no shirt on. All those muscles and ink were a huge distraction.

Her belly tightened. She'd had sex—so much delicious sex—with the man. There should be no belly tightening.

He turned and handed her a mug of coffee, then dropped a kiss to her bare shoulder.

She shivered. How could one man be so devastating to her senses?

Quickly, she turned back to the frypan. She was in *so* much trouble. She was getting in deep, and a trickle of fear skated down her spine. She closed her eyes. Despite the fear, she wanted him. She'd wanted Rhys Norcross for a long time, and he was going above and beyond to keep her safe.

"You finished up with all the reasons why you can't be with me?"

She turned to look at him. "Not yet."

He smiled at her—slow and sexy.

"Go away." She made a shooing motion with her hand. "And stop looking so sexy."

Even his deep chuckle was sexy.

"Go play with your toy cars."

He shot her a glare. "They're models."

She rolled her eyes.

By the time she'd plated up their food, Rhys was sitting at the island, staring at a sleek, black laptop.

Haven froze.

He was wearing glasses.

A hot, muscled badass in glasses. Her panties went damp in a second.

"Haven?" He was looking at her.

"You wear glasses?" she said.

"Not often. Sometimes I need them for computer work." He cocked his head. "Why?"

"Nothing." Resisting the urge to fidget, she pushed his plate to him, then sat on the stool beside him. She pressed her thighs together.

Rhys' grin was cocky. "You like the glasses."

She ignored him. He hardly needed his ego stroked.

"I need to fuck you again?" he asked.

She dug her fork into the eggs. "No. We'll never find the painting if we're always—" *don't look at the glasses* "—in bed."

"I still have a long list of places where I need to fuck you."

She shivered.

"And Haven, I can wear my glasses."

She shot him a look and then set to work on her eggs. He ate as well, tapping one handed on the laptop.

"I've called all the dealers I know," he said.

"Me, too." Apart from the vague rumor of the auction, they had nothing else to go on. "At least it seems they're having trouble finding buyers to attend the auction. That's why Leo needed me. To authenticate the painting."

Rhys' jaw tightened. "We'll keep tugging on the strings. Sooner or later, someone will see or hear something."

He pulled the laptop closer and Haven spotted the

appraisal photo of the *Water Lilies* on the screen. She'd taken it herself.

She let out a gusty sigh. "It's so beautiful. If they ruin it..."

Rhys made a sound.

"It *is* beautiful," she insisted. "What I like is that you need to look deeper than just a first glance. The good stuff always requires more effort."

She saw that he was looking at her with an intense look.

"Rhys, the *Water Lilies*. A stolen Monet you have to find." She touched his jaw and turned his head back toward the computer. "Look at the brushstrokes. The shading to give depth. The colors."

His brow furrowed. "Makes you wonder what's under the water."

"Exactly." She beamed at him. "Yes. And look at the lilies. You can almost feel the breeze on your skin. It's like a hidden message."

"A puzzle," he murmured.

"Yes, but there's no right or wrong answer. It invokes different things in different people."

He made a humming sound. "What's it invoke in you?"

"Emotion. Feeling. A sense of belonging to something bigger than myself."

His gaze was on her like a laser. "You don't feel like you belong?"

She felt a pain under her heart. She'd forgotten that he was a very good investigator. She shifted on her stool. "Rhys..."

"I've always had my family, my siblings," he said. "Then I joined the Army, and I had another place to belong."

"You're lucky," she whispered.

"But I do understand that feeling of wanting more. Of wanting something that clicks and feels right. That makes all the noise in your head stop and things just go still." He reached out and took her hand, turned it over.

She swallowed. "In the Army, I know you were on some super-secret team."

"It's classified."

"Right. But I still know that the work you did must have been dangerous." She hesitated. "Hard and difficult."

He gave her a small nod and she saw nightmares echoed in his eyes.

"That's what causes the noise?" she asked quietly.

Another nod. "Keeping busy dulls it for a while."

She smiled. "Fast cars, fast boats, and fast women."

His fingers clenched on hers. "Yeah. But now I've found a woman who slows me down and quiets the noise just by looking at me. And who makes me look at brush-strokes."

The air lodged in her chest. What was he saying?

Suddenly, Rhys' cell phone rang. He glanced at her for another beat, then pulled the phone closer and put it on speaker. "Ace."

"Hi, Rhys. I know it's Saturday, but I might have something on the painting."

"What?" Haven blurted.

"Hi, Haven." There was amusement in Ace's voice.

"The warehouse you guys broke into, I dug through the shell companies that own it. It was a fucking tangle, but I found a link to a guy called Aleksandr Volkov. A big art collector."

Haven frowned and tapped her nails against the counter. "The name's vaguely familiar."

"He has a private collection," Ace continued. "Although not all of it is legitimately sourced."

Anger flared in Haven's gut. She *hated* thieves. "How do you know all this?"

"Babe," Ace said. "I'm the best hacker in the Northern Hemisphere."

And so modest too.

"Name sounds Russian," Rhys noted.

"You are a crack investigator, Norcross," Ace said.

"Fuck you," Rhys replied good-naturedly.

"Volkov was high up in the Soviet government. After the fall of the Soviet Union, he ended up with lots of land. He sold it, made millions, and eventually ended up in San Francisco."

"Any overt links to the Zakharov family, or Boris Petrov here in San Francisco?"

"Nope, but I'm guessing I won't have to dig far to find them."

"Okay, keep digging. Thanks, Ace."

Haven swiveled on her chair. "This Aleksandr Volkov might have the painting. Maybe he'll run the auction."

"Maybe," Rhys said. "But we don't jump the gun. We need to gather more intel and check him out."

Frustration gnawed at her.

Suddenly, Rhys' phone rang again.

"Hey, Rhys," A jovial male voice said.

"Jerome," Rhys replied.

"There's a party tonight on a friend's yacht. You said you wanted to come. Guy owns a slew of boats. There'll be free booze flowing, and no doubt willing models everywhere. That's usually Kellerman's style."

Haven stiffened, her eggs turning to dust in her mouth.

"Something came up, Jerome," Rhys said.

He'd planned to go to a party. Haven swallowed. "Go if you want," she whispered. "I'll go and stay with Easton."

Rhys' face darkened.

"Or Vander," she said.

"Rhys, you got someone there?" his friend asked.

"Yeah. Look, I can't make the party, Jerome. Have fun."

"Sure thing, Rhys. Another time."

"Yeah." Rhys ended the call.

"Go," she insisted. "You've made plans." To party with models.

"You aren't staying with my brothers," he ground out.

"They can keep me safe. I know Easton has excellent security at his house." She'd been to a couple of parties at Easton's gorgeous house near Billionaire's Row in Pacific Heights. "I don't know where Vander lives." She dredged up a smile, even though her breakfast was sludge in her belly. "But it's probably a bunker built into a hill that can withstand a nuclear blast."

ANNA HACKETT

Rhys shook his head. "Don't try to be funny when I'm pissed."

"Rhys."

He dragged her off her stool and between his legs. She was surrounded by him, felt the heat pumping off him.

"I agreed to the party when I was pissed with you."

She stared at him.

He fingered her hair, rubbing it between his fingers. "I don't want to go to the party."

But one day, he would.

"Did you hear me?" he asked.

"Yes," she whispered.

"I don't think you're hearing me, or getting it." He kissed her—slow and sweet. She clung to him, and soon, he was all she could think about.

He nipped her bottom lip. "Vander lives above the Norcross office."

"Really?" She hadn't known that.

"He's got an awesome rooftop terrace, but he rarely lets anyone up there. Vander's a little paranoid about his privacy and security."

"Vander, paranoid? No way."

Rhys grinned and tugged on her hair again.

The doorbell rang and he frowned. "Stay here."

She shifted back onto the stool, watching as he strode to the door.

He checked the peephole and his face hardened. He opened the door. "What the hell are you doing here, and how did you get up here?"

A woman strode in. She was tall, blonde, and fabulous. She wore a short, snug skirt, and a knit top that draped her lean torso. Her blonde hair was an artfully styled mass of curls.

"I haven't seen you in a long time, lover." She ran a long nail down the center of Rhys' bare chest.

Haven wanted to leap up and scratch her eyes out.

"You never returned my calls," the blonde continued.

"Guy doesn't return your calls, Heidi, it usually isn't a sign that he'd appreciate a visit."

Haven sat frozen. *Oh, God.*

The woman spotted Haven and stilled. All the sexiness drained from her face. "Oh, someone new. Not one of your regular friends with benefits."

"Heidi, leave," Rhys bit out.

"And here I thought I was special." A flicker of real emotion crossed Heidi's face and it made Haven feel bad. "You brought me home. People told me that you never do that."

So, she'd felt special. Haven's belly tightened to a hard ball.

"Yes, and it didn't mean anything except that you had an annoying roommate I wanted to avoid," Rhys said. "I'm seriously regretting it now."

Haven saw that he looked stiff and unhappy.

"She's here." Heidi waved a hand in Haven's direction.

"She lives here."

Heidi's eyes widened so much Haven expected them to roll out of her head and plop on to the ground.

"Right, well, take it from me," Heidi said. "It won't last. Enjoy him while you can."

Rhys growled. "Heidi, go. Forget my number ˌand address. And I'll be having words with whoever the fuck you charmed to let you in."

The woman tossed her head.

Something in Haven shriveled. She knew all of this. She knew everything Heidi was saying was the truth. She turned to look at Rhys. He was blank faced, and that made her go still. He wasn't mad, or making a joke.

He turned to look at her, his dark eyes empty. But Haven thought she could see a hint of... Panic? Pleading?

She remembered what he'd said earlier, about quieting the noise.

Dredging up her courage, she slipped off the stool. She strode over to him and when she got close, he quickly wrapped an arm around her pulling her back against his chest.

Heidi's gaze sharpened on them.

"I get it," Haven said. "You want him. You want more of him."

The woman stayed silent.

"Well, you can't have him, because he's mine."

Rhys' arm convulsed on her.

Heidi sniffed. "I'm just doing you a favor. He'll get rid of you. It won't last."

Rhys spun Haven around and pulled her up on her toes. "I don't want to let you go. I want you right here. I've wanted you right here since I first looked into your eyes."

"Rhys," Haven breathed.

"Get out," Rhys said, not even looking at the blonde.

"Oh, I'm gone." Heidi spun, and stalked out like she

was on the catwalk. She slammed the door closed behind her.

Haven blinked. "Do you think she practices how to walk like that?"

Rhys lowered his head, running his nose along Haven's. "I know we didn't finish breakfast, but I need to fuck you again."

She felt a little spasm between her legs. "Okay."

"Let's check the shower off the list next."

Another little spasm. "Okay."

CHAPTER FOURTEEN

R hys sat at his laptop, researching the art collector Aleksandr Volkov.

He couldn't find much information about the man, and Rhys didn't like it. Everyone left a trail, and if you didn't, you were hiding something on purpose. He tapped his pen against his notepad.

The guy had a big house in Sea Cliff, and a winery in Napa. If he was holding the painting for the Zakharov family, it was likely at his house.

He heard Haven muttering and glanced over. She was sitting cross-legged on his couch. She'd changed into yoga pants and a pink top. All of it hugged her body.

His cock twitched. Shit, the damn thing was trying to kill him. He liked sex a lot. It was fun and felt good. But what he and Haven had been doing was something else. It was intense, mind-blowing, well beyond just fun.

He watched her shift, her legs tucked up beneath her. She was using his tablet, and earlier had called her dealer friend, Harry. The man hadn't heard anything else. He did know about Volkov, though. Apparently, Harry preferred *not* to do business with the man. Harry had confirmed that Volkov was a serious collector.

Knots began to form in Rhys' gut. He really didn't want Haven near the man.

She huffed out a breath. Her hair was still piled up on top of her head, but several strands had escaped, framing her face.

So damned beautiful. Rhys wanted to tumble her onto the couch and—

The doorbell rang.

Her head shot up, and he sensed her anxiety from across the room.

"I've got it." He rose. Through the peephole, he saw his sister.

"Morning." Gia breezed in on a cloud of her favorite perfume.

"It's just ticked over afternoon," Haven said, and Gia shrugged nonchalantly.

The women hugged.

"You're okay?" Gia asked.

Haven nodded. "Yes."

Gia's gaze moved between Haven and Rhys, then back to Haven. "The stubble-burn and the massive hickey on your neck tells me that you're *really* okay."

Haven threw a cushion at Gia.

Grinning, Rhys sat back on the stool at the island.

"Shut up, G, or I'll give you play-by-play detail of how good your brother is with his hands, his tongue, and his—"

Gia made gagging noises, then her face turned serious. "You're really okay?"

"Yes. I don't think Leo would really hurt me—"

Rhys growled. He didn't have the same confidence in Becker. "You're *not* getting near that fucker again. You see him, you run away."

"So," Gia said. "I know you'll have to wait a bit for your insurance payout, but you need more than one party dress and some activewear. I'm here to take you shopping. We're hitting the mall and replenishing your wardrobe."

Rhys frowned. "Gia—"

"That means you're on bodyguard duty, dear brother. And coming shopping."

He groaned. He'd seen his sister shop.

But then he saw the way Haven's face lit up. She did need things, and he figured this was a good distraction from everything going on.

Damn. Looked like he was going shopping.

An hour later, Rhys was trailing Gia and Haven through a department store. He was already carting several bags for them.

His phone rang, and he juggled purchases to pull it out of the pocket of his jeans. "Hi, Vander."

"Hey. Where are you?"

"Mall, with Haven and Gia."

His brother snorted.

"Laugh it up." Rhys saw Haven hold up a shirt, then laugh at something Gia had said. "It's not too bad. Haven needs more shit."

"Still, I've seen Gia around clothes and shoes, so I'm glad it's not me. Look, I'm still running down a lead, but I spoke to a few people, and there have been more rumors about an auction. Apparently, there are out-of-town buyers coming in."

"Shit. We need to find the painting."

"My gut says this Volkov's the key."

And it paid to trust Vander's gut. "Yeah, the dealer friend of Haven's confirmed he's a big collector. Kind of guy who could pull off an auction of a stolen painting."

"We'll keep an eye on him. Well, have fun looking at shoes."

Rhys laughed. "Lingerie's up next, bro."

"Lucky bastard."

"You need a woman, Vander."

Vander made a sharp noise. "I haven't found one I wanted to keep." He paused. "Is this the one for you?"

Rhys' throat tightened and he swallowed. "She's special."

"She is. Sweet, smart, deserves some good. Treat her right, brother."

"Yeah. Bye." He glanced over at the women. "You guys done?"

Gia sniffed. "No."

Haven met his gaze and smiled. He smiled back. Yeah, he'd kill to protect her. Die to keep her safe.

"Ugh, you guys making goofy eyes at each other." Gia rolled her eyes.

Haven's phone rang, and she pulled it out of her tote. "It's Harry."

"Put it on speaker," Rhys said.

They moved to a quieter spot and huddled over the phone.

"Hey, Harry."

"Hi, doll face. Listen, I've got some news for you and your badass."

"He's here with me. And Gia. You're on speaker."

"Hi, Gia," Harry called out.

"Hi, Harry," Gia replied. "You still fabulous?"

"Always. So, I quietly asked some friends about Alek Volkov."

"And?" Rhys prompted.

"He's having a party at his big, faux-Mediterranean mansion in Sea Cliff tonight. Black-tie."

Haven gasped. "You think it's the auction?"

"No," Harry said. "It's a little pre-auction thing. To gauge interest."

Gia tapped a fingernail against her lips. "To see who's willing to cough up to buy a stolen painting."

"Now, I went one step further." Harry paused dramatically.

"Harry," Haven prompted.

"I got you an invite to the party!"

Rhys stiffened.

Haven grinned. "You're amazing."

"Baby doll, thing is, it's just for you. No guest. And security will be tight."

"No." Rhys' jaw clenched. He was *not* letting her go to this guy's place alone.

She spun and pressed her hands to Rhys' chest. "Rhys, I *have* to go. It's our only strong lead to finding the painting."

"Don't care."

"Rhys. Easton's out millions of dollars."

He cupped her cheek. "He has more. I care about keeping you safe."

Her face softened and Gia made a sound.

Rhys glanced over and his sister waved a hand at them. "Don't mind me. Small emotional moment."

"Oh, me too." Harry's voice from the phone. "That one's a keeper, Haven."

"I have to do this," Haven whispered.

"No," Rhys bit out.

"I'll wear a wire. You'll be right outside."

She didn't understand that things could go to hell in an instant. He'd seen it happen on far too many missions. Seen people die.

She could die before he even got to her.

"Rhys, please." Her blue eyes were pleading. "It isn't just about getting Easton's money back. It's about preserving an amazing piece of art, a piece of history. And it's also about taking charge of my life. Logically, I know I'm not to blame for the theft, but I still feel responsible. I want to sort out this mess and recover the painting, so I can be free and clear of all of this."

Fuck. "You'll wear a mic. No risks."

Her smile was beaming. "I'll go in, see what I can find, then get out."

"This Volkov might know who she is," Gia said quietly. "The art world isn't a huge one, right?"

"If he confronts me, I won't lie," Haven said. "I'll tell him that I want the painting back."

Shit. Fuck. This was too dangerous, but Rhys couldn't see any other way to find the painting. And if he said no, Haven might sneak out and go to Volkov's anyway.

She touched his jaw, stroked. "I know you don't want this."

"That is an understatement."

He dropped his forehead to hers. "What time is the party?"

"Eight o'clock," Harry said.

She smiled. "Thank you for helping me do what I need to do."

"We need to get prepped." Rhys wanted the Norcross team outside the building. Maybe he could sneak someone inside.

"Haven, you need a *fabulous* dress for this," Gia said. "Let's get searching."

HAVEN TRIED on another dress that Gia had picked. She was standing in a large, plush change room in Nordstrom.

The long, black, slinky dress was nice, but not the one.

"Here." Gia stuck her head through the curtain, holding another dress.

"Hey, I'm naked here." Haven was only in her panties.

"I've seen it all before. And I have boobs, too."

With a snort of amusement, Haven took the dress and Gia disappeared again. This one was a gorgeous, deep-green silk. She pulled it on.

Ooh.

It was a long, liquid column, with tiny spaghetti

straps that crisscrossed into a complicated design at the back. The color was beautiful. Gia had a good eye.

Her friend's head reappeared and her eyes widened. "Stunning. I knew that color would look good on you."

Haven had never done this before. Her mom had died when Haven was young, and she'd never had someone to giggle with over clothes. "Thanks, G."

Gia blew her a kiss.

A second later, Rhys slid through the curtain into the change room.

"Hey, you shouldn't be in here." She met his gaze in the mirror.

His big body moved in behind her. The sleeves of his white shirt were rolled up, and those tattooed, muscled forearms made her want to weep with need.

His hot gaze ran over her slowly, setting off tingles through every part of her.

"Rhys," she breathed.

He pushed right up behind her and dropped a kiss to her shoulder. She watched them in the mirror.

His hand touched her thigh, and slid her dress slowly upward. His lips moved to her neck, his tongue touching the mark he'd left there.

Oh, God.

Haven was on fire in an instant. His hand slid up under the dress, and a second later into her panties.

"I don't want anyone to see you in this dress." He found her clit and rolled it.

Haven writhed and bit her lip.

"They will," he continued. "But no one will see you like this. No one will touch you like me."

Her belly filled with liquid heat, her legs felt like jelly. Then he pulled his hand away and she made a small cry.

"Uh-uh. You're teasing me in all these sexy dresses, so no orgasm for you."

She ground her ass against the hardening bulge in his trousers. "Rhys."

He dropped the dress and it fell to her feet again. He gripped her hips. "Be good, naughty girl. You can be naughty later. Saxon's here to discuss things about a different case. I'll be outside."

He slid out of the change room and Haven let out a shuddering breath. *God.*

Gia reappeared. "You need the right underwear to wear under that fabulous dress, and to drive a certain Norcross brother wild." She hung a multitude of scraps of silk and lace on the hooks on the wall.

"Thanks." Haven studied the lingerie and smiled. She'd get her own revenge on Rhys.

The curtain twitched again. "Oh no, Rhys, you're not—"

Leo stepped inside.

Haven gasped. "You *can't* be here."

His nose was swollen and he had bruises under one eye. "Haven, please—"

"Just leave me alone, Leo."

He drew in a shuddering breath. "I know you don't want to see me, but I do love you."

"If Rhys sees you, he'll take you down. He's not a big fan of yours."

Leo's face twisted. "That dress for him?"

"No, it's for me. So I can sneak into a fancy party and find the painting that you had stolen from my museum."

Leo's face darkened. "Haven, look—"

The curtain wrenched open. All Haven saw was Rhys' hard face, Saxon standing behind him.

Oh, shit. "Rhys—"

Her cry was cut off as Rhys grabbed Leo and yanked him out of the cubicle.

Leo yelled, and Rhys shoved him to the ground.

"Don't hit me," Leo cried.

"Rhys," Saxon warned.

Haven raced out and saw startled, half-dressed women all looking out from the change rooms.

"Rhys." She hurried forward. "He's not worth it. Please."

Rhys shifted back, and wrapped an arm around her. Saxon stepped forward and pressed a knee to Leo's back. "Don't move."

"I'm sorry for everything," Leo spluttered. "I wanted to try to make it better. I wanted to tell you that I have a lead on the painting. They found a guy to authenticate it. I know who he is."

"God, I can't believe this!" Anger spurted inside Haven.

Rhys tugged her back. "Stand down." He looked at Leo. "Name."

"Arthur Irvine."

Haven gasped. "But Mr. Irvine's a lovely old man. He's retired."

"He does off-the-books jobs," Leo said.

"I think Becker needs a visit to our holding rooms." Saxon yanked him up.

Gia appeared. "What is—?" She stared at the scene. "The douchebag ex, I presume?" Gia patted Haven's arm. "You totally traded up, girlfriend."

"I'll take Becker into the office," Rhys said. "Sax, take Haven back to my place?"

Saxon lifted his chin. "Sure."

God, Haven's stomach turned jumpy. Was it a good idea to leave Rhys alone with Leo?

"Rhys, why doesn't Saxon—?"

Angry brown eyes cut back to her. He was beyond pissed.

"I have a few things to make clear to Becker," Rhys said, tone deadly.

"I love her," Leo declared. "And she loved me—"

"Actually, I never loved you, Leo." Everything that had happened, everything that was going down with Rhys, it had her questioning everything she'd ever known.

Something rippled over Leo's face.

"The past is done, Becker," Rhys said. "It was my cock she came on this morning, and last night. She's mine."

The raw words made Haven jolt. Wonderful, Rhys had just told the world that they were having sex. A lot of it.

Leo scowled, fury burning in his eyes.

Rhys spun, wrenching Leo's arm up behind his back. "Let's go. Feel free to cause trouble and make me punch you." Rhys looked at Haven. "I'll see you at home, angel. Stay with Saxon."

Gia slid an arm around her. "Come on. Get changed, and we'll buy that dress."

Haven pulled in a breath.

"It's a killer dress," Saxon said. "I'm partial to green." His gaze shifted to Gia's green shirt.

"Shoo." Gia flicked her fingers. "We don't need you hanging around, and Haven needs to change."

Sliding back into the change room, Haven put her clothes back on. They paid for the dress, and she said goodbye to Gia. Her friend and Saxon traded a few glares, then Haven headed with Saxon to his SUV.

It was a quiet ride back to Rhys'. She was worried about him.

"Rhys will keep it in check," Saxon said. "The man is the king of control."

He wasn't so controlled when they were in bed together. She licked her lips. "I just want this over with. I finally had my life on track, a job I love—"

"Rhys will help you get there."

"After this, Rhys and I will be over, too."

Saxon laughed. He had a deep, sexy one.

"What's so funny?" she demanded.

"Rhys isn't going to let you go."

"He'll lose interest." She looked out the window. "He'll move on." She hunched her shoulders.

"We talked a lot on missions."

She glanced over and saw that Saxon's handsome face had hardened.

"Some missions can push you to the edge, past your limits. Once, I was shot up badly."

Haven gasped. She hadn't known. She wondered if Gia knew.

"We were far from help. We got an evac point, but it was ten miles away. I could barely walk, and we had a bunch of bogeys between us and the helo."

Haven twisted her hands together.

"Rhys carried me. He carried me every step, while Vander and the others on our team provided cover. He talked to me the entire time to keep me conscious. Said he hoped everything he did in service to his country earned him something sweet. Said that when he found the right woman, he'd burn the world down to hold on to her and keep her safe and happy."

God. A burn started inside Haven's chest.

"He also said he was happy to have a shit-ton of fun until he found her." Saxon glanced over. "He's one of the best men I know, Haven."

She just stared. So many emotions writhing inside her.

Then her ringing phone cut in and she blinked. She looked at the screen. It was Rhys.

"Hi," she said.

"Angel, just wanted to tell you that I got your ex in the holding room. No blood was shed."

Her fingers squeezed on her phone. "Okay. Good."

"You all right?" he asked.

"Yeah, baby."

There was a long pause. "Baby. I like that. See you soon."

"Rhys... Thanks. For everything."

"You never have to thank me, angel."

CHAPTER FIFTEEN

H aven looked in the mirror. Her makeup was perfection, and the green dress was gorgeous. She'd left her hair loose, and it fell in waves around her shoulders. She looked like a million bucks.

She just wished she was wearing it on a night out with Rhys, instead of to some criminal's party.

She'd borrowed some jewelry from Gia, and diamonds winked in her ears.

All her own jewelry was gone. Her belly turned over, as she thought of her mom's silver bracelet. It was the only thing of hers Haven had left, and now it was gone forever. She sighed. She'd always have her memories. Those could never be stolen or destroyed.

Haven straightened. As she always did, she picked herself up and dealt with things. That was all she could do.

She walked out of Rhys' bathroom and found him in the bedroom, pacing.

He looked up and his face changed. "Angel, you look stunning."

She blushed, and absorbed the hit of pleasure. "Thank you."

He was dressed all in black—black cargoes, a tight, long-sleeved, black T-shirt. She could see the ridges of his abs outlined under the fabric. He looked dark and dangerous.

It was a reminder that tonight was dangerous.

His hands gripped her arms. "You can do this."

She smiled. She knew he really didn't want her to do this, but he was still giving her a pep talk to try and calm her nerves.

"It helps knowing you'll be right outside," she said.

He stroked his fingers along her cheekbone. "After, I'm going to bring you home and make love to you all night."

Tingles ignited through her body. "Sounds like a good deal to me."

"I've got something for you."

He grabbed a long, narrow black box off the bedside table.

Her chest hitched.

He flicked it open. Inside was a necklace. It had a delicate silver chain, with a teardrop diamond pendant.

"Rhys," she breathed.

"I've never bought jewelry before, but I know that you lost all of yours. I saw this, and I imagined it against your beautiful skin."

She turned and lifted her hair so he could put the necklace on her.

"It's so beautiful," she whispered, touching the diamond.

He turned her to face him, then kissed her. His firm lips moved over hers and she pulled in the taste of him.

"Don't ruin my makeup," she murmured against his lips.

He smiled. He was so damn sexy. He kissed her again, long and deep. She was completely in a daze, and wanted to stay right there in his arms, all night.

Then he lifted his head. "You might need to fix your lipstick, baby."

She nodded.

"I have something else for you." He held up a small, metallic box this time and flicked it open. "A microphone."

She peered in and saw the tiniest, thinnest mic she'd ever seen inside. "It's tiny."

"Vander pays for the best and latest tech. Some of it is still experimental, and not available on the open market."

The tiny microdot was cream-colored, and would blend with her skin tone.

"This adheres to your skin," he told her. "No one will find it."

She nodded. He lifted the dot on the tip of his finger, then with his other hand, he nudged the V neckline of her dress down. She wasn't wearing a bra, and as his gaze took in her breasts, fire ignited in his eyes. He ran the back of his hand against her breasts. She bit her lip, her nipples beading. "Rhys."

He pressed the small dot between her breasts. "There."

How was she supposed to concentrate on what she needed to do, when all she could think about was how much she needed Rhys?

"Time to go," he said.

His serious tone made her desire stutter, her belly tangling with knots. She quickly slipped into the bathroom and fixed her lipstick, then headed out to the kitchen. She pulled up short.

Holy cow. The mother lode of badass hotness stood in Rhys' kitchen.

Vander, Rhys, and Saxon were all dressed in near-identical, black outfits. They just needed guns strapped to them and she could picture them rappelling out of some stealth helicopter.

She took another couple of steps, and spotted two more big, broad-shouldered men. One was Rome—the dark-skinned, green-eyed hunk she'd seen at Norcross. He met her gaze and nodded.

Definitely the strong, silent type.

She looked at the final man and blinked. It took her a second to realize that it was Easton.

Sometimes she forgot that her boss was former military. He wore the mantle of successful businessman so well. Tonight, there was no designer suit. Instead, he wore black as well, and looked just as badass as the others.

Rhys came to her and took her hand.

"Haven, that dress was worth every penny," Saxon said with a sexy smile.

Rhys scowled at his friend, but Haven managed a smile.

"We'll test the microphone in the car," Rhys said. "You have your invite?"

She held up the heavy, cream invite that Harry had delivered to her. She slipped it into her small clutch, and lifted her chin. "I'm ready."

Something moved over Rhys' face, and she thought it might be pride. She basked in the light of that as they left the apartment.

They stepped into the elevator. "Rhys will act as your driver," Vander said. "The rest of us will take position outside Volkov's mansion."

Okay, it was good to know they'd all be there.

"Don't take any unnecessary risks." Vander's midnight-blue gaze bored into her.

His dark, commanding tone made her swallow and nod. There was no way she'd dare disagree with him.

"I want the painting back," Easton said. "But I want you alive and safe more."

She eyed the wall of muscle surrounding her. Each one of them was doing so much to look after her. Rhys' hand touched the small of her back.

"Thank you all again—"

"Not necessary," Vander cut her off. "One more thing. I managed to get someone inside. Rhys will update you on the way."

She nodded. Outside Rhys' building, he bundled her toward a black limo. He helped her into the back. She ran her hand nervously over the leather seat. *She could do this. She could do this.*

The limo slid smoothly into traffic.

"We'll hear everything you say, and everything in close radius around you," Rhys said from the driver's seat.

"Right," she replied.

"But you won't hear us. We can't risk an in-ear mic."

"Got it." She fiddled with her clutch.

"Vander, she coming through?" Rhys asked.

"Yes. Crystal clear." Vander's voice came from the console of the car.

"So, Vander pulled a few strings and he got a friend, actually a very good client of Norcross, into the party. He won't approach you unless you need help."

Haven swallowed. "All right."

"His name is Zane Roth, he's—"

She gasped. "A billionaire. The King of Wall Street. One of New York's Billionaire Bachelors. Voted Sexiest Man of the Year last year."

Rhys growled. "You done?"

Oops. Someone sounded put-out. "I mean, I've seen him and his friends online." The media loved the three men, and Haven couldn't blame them. Three hot men who'd met in college, gone on to be outrageously successful billionaires, and were all shockingly attractive. What wasn't to like?

Maybe her man didn't want to hear that.

"Pfft. Who wants billions, anyway? What a headache."

In the rearview mirror, she saw Rhys' lips twitch.

"I totally prefer hot badasses, with sexy tattoos and messy, thick, rock-star hair."

Rhys shook his head, but he was smiling.

The suburbs changed as they headed toward Sea Cliff. It was a wealthy neighborhood, with mansions nestled on the cliffs, offering sweeping views of the Pacific Ocean and the Golden Gate Bridge.

Soon, she was taking in the large, fancy houses that she knew were all multi-million-dollar real estate. Ahead, a line of cars was pulling up in front of a stately, Tuscan-style mansion painted a gray-green with black accents. The front garden was immaculately landscaped. More mansions flanked it, but she noted it had a large side yard, probably because the back of the house was cliffside with water views, and a driveway on the other side was blocked by security guards.

Her nerves came back, dancing a jig in her belly.

Rhys pulled up out front and she took a deep breath. The house screamed "I have money." It was a little too stuffy for her tastes.

Rhys swiveled in his seat. "Be careful, Haven. That sexy body is mine. I have lots of plans for it later."

She felt a curl in her belly. "I'll see you soon."

"Count on it."

He got out and circled the car, then opened her door and helped her out.

Security guards flanked the doors to the house. Other guests—also dressed to the nines—were heading up the stairs.

She sucked in a breath. She'd been to fancy fundraisers as part of her job. She knew how to turn it on and hobnob.

She felt the brush of Rhys' hand, then he was gone. She couldn't risk looking back. She walked up the steps, her shoulders back, making sure to show plenty of leg through the slit in her dress.

She smiled.

Showtime.

HAVEN WALKED through the crowded rooms of Volkov's mansion. There were a lot of people there, all in designer dresses, suits, and tuxedos.

Ugh. Were all these people aware the painting was stolen? Were they all interested in buying it?

No, probably not. Harry had said this shindig was to gauge interest. Probably where Volkov could drop some bait, and see who bit.

She took a glass of champagne from a white-suited server with a tray. The house was decorated in "rich, single, older-man" style, which involved a lot of dark colors, lots of wood, and heavy furniture. As she'd guessed, the back of the house was all glass windows, offering a breathtaking view of the Golden Gate Bridge. She noted a lot of San Francisco's elite were here. Some guests were out on the terrace, while others mingled inside. She wandered through the room, and her gaze caught on a painting on the wall.

She gasped. A Rembrandt. It was gorgeous. She turned and spotted a Giambologna bronze resting on a side table. It had such beautiful lines. This Volkov might be a criminal, but he was one with good taste.

She moved into an adjoining room that was less crowded. She passed a man in a suit who gave her an appraising, interested look. She kept her smile bland and moved on.

The next room was a large library.

Nice. Huge walls of shelves were covered in books. Leather chairs were grouped around, inviting people to grab a book and sit and read.

Across the room, she spotted a Cézanne landscape in a gorgeous gilt frame resting over an ornate fireplace. It should be in a museum, where lots of people could enjoy it, not just one.

She tamped down her spurt of annoyance and stopped in front of the Cézanne. It was even more exquisite up close.

"Do you like it?"

The voice behind her was deep and low, with the touch of a Russian accent.

She turned her head and saw Aleksandr Volkov standing beside her. He wore a dark, three-piece suit.

"It's stunning. I love Cézanne's work. His sense of solid substance and use of bright colors."

"Ah, a beautiful woman who knows her art."

She studied his hazel eyes. He had a wide, jovial smile on a rugged face, but his eyes were stone cold. She couldn't read him at all. Did he know who she was?

"You have an impressive art collection, Mr. Volkov."

His gaze moved over her, making the back of her neck prickle.

"I do like to collect beautiful things, Ms. McKinney."

Ugh, slime alert. She kept her smile in place. "Do you also like to collect things that belong to other people?"

At that bold statement, she could practically hear Rhys cursing her.

Volkov smiled. "I assure you, everything you see here was legally acquired."

Yeah, but what about what she couldn't see?

"I've visited the Hutton," Volkov continued. "Your museum has some excellent collections and exhibits. Especially since you took over as curator."

"I love my work." She cocked her head. "I was thrilled to acquire Monet's *Water Lilies*."

The man's face moved into solemn lines. "I heard about the theft. A terrible thing."

"Yes, terrible. I really hated the part where the thieves shot two innocent guards and beat me up."

His face remained unchanged. "I am sorry to hear that."

She pulled in a breath. "I want the *Water Lilies* back where it belongs."

Volkov eyed her. "Desperate people do desperate things, Ms. McKinney." He moved closer. "You really are very beautiful, Haven. May I call you Haven?"

Like she could say no. She gave the tiniest nod.

"I think it's best if you stay out of dangerous situations," he said.

"And not worry my pretty little head?"

He smiled. "You have an inner fire. I like that." His voice lowered, his gaze drifting to her cleavage. "A lot."

She looked back at the painting, trying not to look grossed out. A finger touched her bare shoulder and she struggled not to jerk.

"You also have very soft skin."

Crap, how did she extricate herself from this?

"Would you like to see some of my other art pieces, that aren't on display here in the main rooms?" he asked.

Go somewhere alone with him? *Nope, nope, nope.* She sipped her champagne. "Does that include the *Water Lilies*?"

Volkov just smiled.

Haven decided to go for it. "When's the auction?"

There was no surprise on his face. "Let's discuss...art some more after the party."

"I can't—"

"I insist." His smile stayed in place. "I'm a man who is very used to getting everything he wants, Haven. I'll have Ivan stay here with you to ensure you don't leave before we get a chance to talk."

Ivan was a muscled beefcake who looked like he didn't know how to smile. He was stationed at the door to the library.

Volkov ran his gaze over her again, then turned and strode back to the main party.

Oh. *Shit.* Haven's shoulders sagged, but tension sang through her body. The champagne she'd drunk turned to bugs fluttering in her belly.

"Um, Ivan, I need the little girl's room, so I'll just—"

"You stay until Mr. Volkov returns."

Great. She was trapped. She wandered across the library, turning her back to Ivan, and pretended to study the books.

"Help," she whispered.

Shit. Rhys would be really, really unhappy about now.

She eyed the window. She could try jumping out, but it was a two-story drop to the garden below, so she didn't like her chances.

She turned to eye Ivan. She was certain she couldn't take him down. He looked like an ex-wrestler.

Rhys would come. He'd get her out.

Suddenly, the door opened. "Darling, there you are. I've been looking for you everywhere."

Haven instantly recognized the handsome man in an impeccable Armani tux.

Right. She'd forgotten about her in-house rescuer. Zane Roth. Owner of Roth Enterprises. Finance billionaire.

The body under the suit looked lean and solid. Not a man who just sat at a desk. His thick, brown hair was well-cut, and his smile was as sexy as hell.

She smiled. "Zane."

"Hey—" Ivan took a step forward.

Zane ignored the bodyguard and took her hand. He winked at her. "I just needed my lovely date."

"Mr. Volkov wants to talk to her," Ivan rumbled.

"I'm afraid we have other plans." Zane tucked her close to his side and headed for the door.

Ivan sidestepped and tried to block them.

Zane's handsome face sharpened. "You know who I am?"

Ivan grunted. "Yeah."

"I'm guessing your boss doesn't want you to piss me off. So, I suggest you get out of my way."

Boldly, Zane brushed past the man and dragged her into the hall.

As they walked down the hallway, he tipped his head close to hers, voice lowered. "I'm Zane. Sorry to meet you under these circumstances, Haven."

"Hi. Thanks for the rescue."

"I don't usually get much of a chance to play knight in shining armor." He patted her arm. "Vander sent the house layout to my phone. We are to make a hasty exit out a side door and into the garden. Likely Volkov will send his goons to find you."

"I'm cursed," she muttered. "Like the crappiest luck known to man. Or woman."

"Well, you have the Norcross brothers at your back, so I'd say your luck is changing. Now, smile, and look like I'm the most handsome, charming man you've ever met."

Despite everything, Haven laughed.

CHAPTER SIXTEEN

Listening to Volkov come on to Haven, oozing his slime all over her, was one of the hardest things Rhys had been forced to listen to.

What was worse, was not being able to do anything about it.

He curled his hands, his knuckles turning white. Knowing that she was in there, alone, afraid—

Vander clamped his hand on Rhys' shoulder. "She's doing fine. Your girl is tough."

Rhys nodded. She was. He just wished she didn't have to be. She'd been through enough.

They were standing in the shadows, one house away from Volkov's mansion. Somehow, Vander had ensured the homeowners were out for the night. Rhys heard the music and murmurs of people on the terrace.

The rest of the Norcross team was spread around the area. They were all good—Ghost Ops had honed them to be the best in the world. Easton hadn't been Ghost Ops, but he'd been a damn good

Ranger. They hadn't let their skills go rusty, not even Easton.

Vander's friend, Zane Roth, was in there too. Still, the man was a billionaire businessman, not a soldier. If things went south...

Then Rhys heard Volkov's tone turn steely across the line.

"Let's discuss...art some more after the party."

Rhys' body locked. He heard Vander curse under his breath.

"I insist," Volkov said. "I'm a man who's very used to getting everything he wants, Haven."

Fuck. Anger exploded in Rhys. He took two steps.

Vander grabbed him. "You can't burst in there. There are security guards everywhere."

"That asshole wants my woman. *Threatened* her."

He could hear her fast breathing across the line. She was afraid. He listened to her trying to get out of the library using the bathroom excuse. *Smart girl.*

But Volkov's thug wasn't falling for it.

"Help," she murmured.

With a growl, Rhys shoved against Vander. Rome appeared out of the darkness. Both men shoved him against the wall of the neighboring house.

"You go in there, you put her at more risk." Vander's tone was the same one he used as commander of their Ghost Ops unit. "She needs you clearheaded."

Shit. Rhys' shoulders slumped. "Vander..."

"We'll get her out." His brother lifted his phone. "Zane, you're a go. She's being held in the library. Get out via the side exit. Schematics are on your phone."

Seconds later, Rhys heard a man's charming, yet authoritative voice on the line. Every muscle in Rhys' body went tight, vibrating with tension. Rhys listened as Zane Roth got Haven clear of the library.

The ugly noise inside him rose to deafening levels, urging him to move, run, fight, take action. That horrible burn that he'd dealt with ever since he'd left the military. The nightmares and flashbacks had faded, thanks to the counseling Vander had forced on them. But the noise never went away.

Rhys figured it, and the edginess, the need to move, was a small price to pay. He could deal with it, usually. Right now, it wanted Haven safe.

"That's it." Rhys shoved free. He strode down the narrow path beside the neighboring house. A stucco fence divided it from Volkov's place. He reached a metal side gate. It opened into Volkov's immaculately landscaped side yard.

Then across the line, he heard Haven laugh at something Roth said, and Rhys' gut stilled.

She was okay. Hell, she was laughing. How could the woman be so resilient?

A second later, Roth and Haven appeared.

They were hurrying down the path, holding hands, and damned if they didn't look like a good couple. Roth was in a tuxedo and Haven's green dress glittered in the garden lighting.

Then she lifted her head and spotted Rhys. A smile broke out on her face, and relief flooded her eyes. "Hey—"

Rhys closed the distance between them in two

strides, and lifted her off her feet. His mouth closed over hers, the kiss hard and punishing. She made a muffled sound, then kissed him back, melting into him.

Dammit, he realized now just how afraid he'd been.

Finally, he broke the kiss, and lifted his head. She looked dazed, and he pressed his forehead against hers.

Without looking at the man, Rhys said, "Thanks, Roth."

"My pleasure," the businessman replied.

Rhys glanced at the man. "I owe you."

Zane inclined his head.

"Let's go," Vander said. "Zane, you should probably go, too."

"It was a dull party, anyway."

They all moved out the gate, through the neighboring yard, and onto the street. Rome and Zane said their good-byes and headed down the sidewalk.

"I'm getting Haven home," Rhys told Vander.

His brother nodded. "We'll debrief tomorrow."

"Hey, you can have your magic mic back," Haven said.

"Vander *isn't* removing it." Rhys quickly slid his hand into the neckline of her dress, taking the dot off her skin. She gave a little shudder and he looked into her face. Her cheeks were flushed.

Vander held out a small case and Rhys pressed the mic inside.

"Night, Haven," Vander murmured. "Good work."

"Night, Vander."

Rhys towed Haven down another street to where he'd

parked his Norcross SUV. He'd found a quiet, dim spot on a street a few blocks away.

"Well, Volkov has the *Water Lilies*," Haven said glumly.

"My guess is that he's storing it and running the auction as a favor for the Zakharov family," Rhys said. "No doubt he'll get a healthy cut."

"I didn't learn much else. I'm not a very good spy."

Adrenaline still churned inside Rhys. "Your spy career is over. You're officially retired."

She gave a gusty sigh. "Shame, I liked the outfit."

His hand tightened on hers. "I'll buy you all the dresses you want and take you out somewhere fancy."

Her face softened.

His gut was still hard and wouldn't settle. He kept imagining what Volkov might've done to her. He squeezed her fingers.

"Rhys, are you okay?" she asked.

"No."

"Talk to—"

He spun her. He pushed her into the darker shadows, and pressed her against a high brick fence under a tree.

She gasped.

"No talking," he growled.

Inside him, his inner caveman had taken over. He felt a pounding need to know his woman was safe.

"Rhys," she breathed, excitement hitching her voice.

He shoved her up, until her feet were off the ground. His hands slid under her dress and he found her panties. With one twist, he ripped them off.

She gasped, then undulated against him. His mouth

took hers—hard, deep, wet. Her perfume filled his senses —sweet, just like Haven. His fingers found her pussy, stroked.

She cried out against his mouth and he swallowed the noises she made. She was wet. Wet and ready for him.

He thrust a finger into her tight warmth and his thumb found her clit.

"This is going to be fast, Haven. And rough." His voice was guttural.

She let out a low moan. "Yes."

He fumbled with his belt, then his zipper. He slid one hand under her ass. And he fitted his cock to her and thrust deep.

Haven moaned his name. Her legs clamped onto his hips and Rhys pumped into her.

"Fuck, I feel you rippling on my cock. Take me, baby."

She did, clinging as he drove into her.

"That's all for you, Haven."

"*Yes.*" Her mouth moved, touched his neck. He felt the rake of her teeth.

He kept thrusting, with no finesse, no care, just the primitive need to claim and affirm his mate.

She gave a husky cry and started coming. She bit down on his neck.

Rhys moved faster, plunging his cock deep. Haven. *His.* So fucking sweet. With one last thrust, he lodged deep and poured himself inside her.

They stayed there, with him pinning her to the wall, both panting.

Shit. He'd been wild, rough.

"Did I hurt you?" He lifted his head.

She blinked, then gave him a wide, lazy smile that he could just make out in the dim light.

"Not even a little. That was...*amazing*."

Everything in him relaxed.

"I think we should have wild, brick-wall sex at least once a week," she said.

His lips twitched. Damn, she was something.

"I might have a few scrapes on my back—"

He frowned. "You said you weren't hurt."

"I'm not. They're badges of honor."

He shook his head and pulled out of her. She moaned, and that's when he realized.

"Shit." He met her gaze in the low light. "I didn't use a condom."

She touched his cheek. "It's okay. I get a contraceptive shot, and I made sure I got tested after Leo." She licked her lips. "There hasn't been anyone since him. Um, you...?"

"Haven't been with anyone since I met you."

Her eyes widened. "What?"

"And I've always used condoms before. But I'll get checked, just to make sure." He'd keep her safe in all ways.

He stroked her swollen lips, then realized that there was only silence in his head. No noise. The driving, twisting beast inside was calm.

"Let's go home," she murmured.

Home. With Haven.

"Yeah, let's go home."

THE NEXT MORNING, Haven stood in a coffee shop with Rhys, waiting for her latte. The cute, cozy shop was just around the corner from his condo.

He handed her a takeaway cup, and she sipped her latte and moaned. When she opened her eyes, Rhys was watching her with a grin and a certain look in his eyes.

She made a show of licking the foam off the top of the lid.

His brown eyes darkened. "Tease."

He turned to get his coffee from the barista. That's when Haven spotted a pair of women sitting at a nearby table, staring at him.

She couldn't blame them. She raised a brow.

The women both smiled, and one gave her a thumbs up.

Once Rhys had his coffee, they walked outside. He kept her tucked close to his side.

Haven's heart clenched. She was starting to believe. Rhys had said he hadn't been with anyone since they'd first met. Unbelievable, but she realized that she hadn't seen him with anyone. She'd been avoiding him, but she sure had taken a lot of notice of him.

This amazing man was into her. Protecting her, caring for her.

"Come on," he said. "It's a short walk to the Hutton."

She'd wanted to get her work laptop, and some other stuff from the museum, so she could do some work at Rhys'. The museum was closed on a Sunday, but the guards would let them in.

Rhys was armed. She knew he was wearing a shoulder harness under his suede jacket. When he'd put it on this morning, it had made her want to jump him. What was it about a guy in a shoulder harness that was so sexy?

She sipped her coffee.

"You haven't asked about Becker?" Rhys said.

She glanced at him. "Because I haven't thought about him. Um, is he still at Norcross?"

"Nope. Saxon questioned him. He had nothing new for us, so Saxon let him go. If he survives Zakharov, he'll be lucky."

Haven didn't want Leo dead, but strangely, she felt... nothing. She shrugged. "I just want him to go away and stay away."

Rhys ran a hand down her back.

She was feeling far safer, but she was still just stewing over the *Water Lilies*. She wanted it back.

She was beyond pissed that Volkov and the Zakharov family thought they could just help themselves to other people's hard-earned things.

Finally, they reached the elegant façade of the Hutton. They met with the security guards, and entered the building. It was silent inside, and their footsteps echoed through the space.

Haven stopped in the main hall, staring at the empty wall. She *hated* that empty wall.

"You okay?" Rhys asked.

"I want the painting back. Easton paid so much money for it. So many people were enjoying seeing it." She sighed. "I still feel like this is all my fault. If I hadn't been with Leo, if I—"

"Hey." Rhys put a finger under her chin. "We'll get it back. This isn't your fault. I'm gonna make you repeat that until you believe it. "

"And how will you do that?"

He smiled. "I'll tie you to my bed, torment you with my hands and tongue, hold back your orgasm until you agree this isn't your fault."

Her nipples beaded and his gaze dropped. He shot her a sexy grin.

"Sadist," she said.

"Hardly. I promise you'll enjoy every second."

They headed up the stairs, and when she made it to her office, Haven dumped her empty coffee cup into the trash. At her desk, she grabbed her laptop and some files.

"I want to come into work tomorrow," she said. "I need to check in with my staff, and go over some restoration projects."

"Okay."

Just like that. He'd stay with her, keep her safe. She walked up to him and kissed him.

He raised a dark brow. "What's that for?"

She took a deep breath. "I just wanted to let you know that I really like you."

Something fired in his eyes. "I really like you too."

"I'm starting to get that."

"Finally."

She swatted his arm. "Now, we just need to find the *Water Lilies*. What do we do next?"

"Well, my plan is to question the appraiser. Irvine."

Haven gasped. "My God, with everything going on,

I'd completely forgotten about him!" This was clearly why Rhys was the investigator and not her.

"I'll ask Vander to stay with you—"

"No." She gripped his arm. "I'm coming."

Rhys scowled. "Haven."

"He's a seventy-year-old man, Rhys. I know him and he likes me." She frowned. "I'm still shocked he does illegal appraisals, but there is no risk in me coming."

"Shit, I hope you aren't always going to talk me into stuff."

She shot him a sweet smile.

In Rhys' SUV, they headed to Mr. Irvine's address, which Rhys already had.

The man lived in a small, tidy house in Glen Park. He met them at the door, dressed in slacks, shirt, and a vest. He looked like a smaller, sweeter version of Santa Claus.

"Mr. Irvine, I'm Rhys Norcross. We spoke on the phone."

"Of course, of course." The man noticed Haven. "Haven! What a nice surprise."

"Hello, Mr. Irvine."

"Come in. I just made some tea."

Inside, the house screamed "decorated by a grandmother." There were some nice prints on the wall, mostly of the English countryside. There were also lots of framed photos of Mr. Irvine, and a gray-haired, sweet-faced woman. There were also lots of children and grandchildren.

It was all so normal. Haven wanted that. Love. Family. She wanted frames all over the place filled with pictures of her life. The things she'd missed out on after her mom died.

They sat at the table in the kitchen and Mr. Irvine brought a pot of tea over.

"Not for me," Rhys said.

No, Haven was sure that badasses did *not* drink tea.

Mr. Irvine poured two cups.

"Did you appraise the *Water Lilies* here?" Haven asked.

"Oh, you know." The old man smiled. "It's just business, Haven. I am sorry the painting was stolen from the Hutton."

"My guards were shot. I was beaten."

Regret crossed the man's face. "I'm *very* sorry to hear that. I just appraise. No questions asked."

"For a very large fee," Rhys said.

"Yes. I need the money to keep the house, and help my family." The man beamed. "My oldest grandson is off to Berkeley this year. My lovely Jean died last year." Grief lined his face. "This house meant everything to her. It was her parents' home, and she grew up here. I don't commit any crimes, but I do carry out some off-book appraisals."

Haven sighed. "My ex was the one who instigated the theft of the *Water Lilies* and set this in motion. We want the painting back where it belongs, not sold to a criminal and locked away in a private collection."

Mr. Irvine sipped his tea and nodded.

"Do you have any information that might help?" she pleaded. "Do the right thing, Mr. Irvine. For Jean's memory, for that grandson going to Berkeley, for your family."

"They were all careful not to say too much around me. They took me to a warehouse in Potrero Hill. It looked like it had once been a factory."

Haven glanced at Rhys. The painting *had* been in that warehouse at some stage.

"It really is a masterpiece. Anyway, I'm an old man. A few of the guards talked like I wasn't even there."

Rhys leaned forward. "What did you hear?"

"They're planning to move the painting soon. For a private sale."

Haven frowned. "No, there's going to be an auction."

Mr. Irvine shook his head. "A private buyer made a huge offer. I think it was some prince from the Middle East." He frowned and scratched his head. "Or was it a tech billionaire from Silicon Valley?"

Haven gasped. "When? Did you hear when the sale was happening?"

"Let's see, today is Sunday, so tomorrow morning. At six am, a black, unmarked truck will leave Mr. Volkov's mansion."

She looked at Rhys. *This was it.*

"Thank you, Mr. Irvine," she said.

"Anything else?" Rhys asked. "Did you hear where the sale was happening?"

"That's all I heard. Good luck. I do hope you recover the painting. It should be in a museum. Maybe I'll drop by the Hutton soon."

It was hard to hold a grudge. Haven reached over and

touched his hand with hers. "If you do, I'll give you a private tour."

Rhys shifted her chair out and grabbed her hand. They said their goodbyes and left.

In the SUV, the tires squealed as Rhys pulled out. He drove fast, but with a quiet, confident ease she found sexy.

"I need to call Vander and plan the recovery mission," Rhys said. "We don't have much time to pull it all together.

Haven nodded. "I'll—"

"You are *not* taking part in this. And you aren't going to talk me into it this time." His voice was as hard as steel.

"I wasn't going to." Okay, maybe she was. Still. "I was going to say that I'll leave this to the experts, since I don't have badass in my DNA."

Rhys shot her a look that said he didn't believe her for a second.

CHAPTER SEVENTEEN

It was still dark when Rhys woke Haven.

He stroked her hair. She'd finally fallen asleep in the early hours after being restless for most of the night, worrying about this morning's mission.

Yesterday, he, Vander, and the rest of the Norcross team had spent the entire afternoon, planning. They'd left nothing to chance, and Vander always had more than one contingency plan.

Rhys had finally brought Haven home for dinner. She'd been nervous and twitchy, playing with her food. He'd ended up going down on her on the couch, before carrying her to bed and exhausting her in other ways.

But she'd still been restless.

Now, in the murky light of early morning, he kissed the back of her neck. She shifted, still naked, and pressed against him.

His cock went hard, and desire licked through his veins. He kissed her shoulder and she made a sexy purr.

Need swelling, Rhys pushed her onto her belly and

straddled her. He palmed her ass, kneading the soft flesh. Then he shifted, rolled on a condom, and thrust inside her.

She moaned his name.

"Take me, baby." He started a rhythm of steady thrusts, her body shaking with each one.

Her hands twisted in the covers. "Rhys."

He pulled her hips up, and leaned over her. He covered her, protected her. She was his to cherish. His to keep safe.

He bit her earlobe. "Falling hard for you, Haven."

She made a sound and whispered his name. She thrust her ass back against him.

He slid a hand under her. "Feel how you take me? How you're stretched around my cock?" He found her clit and strummed. She let out a harsh cry and her pussy rippled on his cock. "Come for me, baby."

Her back arched, and her head flew back against his shoulder. As she came, he kept powering into her, and then with a groan, he came hard inside his Haven.

Rhys dropped to his side on the bed, and pulled her close. She clung to him. Once his breathing evened out, he pressed a kiss to her temple.

"I have to go, angel." He needed to shower, get ready, then meet Vander and the others. They wanted to be prepped and ready well before six am.

"Okay, Rhys," she whispered.

He kissed her again, then climbed out of the bed. Maybe when this was over, he'd take her away. Maybe to the beach, or a cabin in the mountains. They could stay in bed all day long.

Rhys quickly showered and dressed.

When he exited the bathroom, he found Haven in the kitchen. Her hair was still a tangled mess, and she wore one of his T-shirts. It looked way too sexy on her.

"Coffee." She pushed a travel mug across the bench. "Bagel is in the toaster."

"Thanks, babe." He sipped the coffee.

She circled the island and moved in close. "You be careful." Her hands moved down his chest. "Come back to me in one piece, Rhys Norcross."

He took her mouth with his. She kissed him eagerly, and he felt the touch of desperation under it. All he could do to reassure her was to get this over with as soon as he could.

Rhys was winning against the walls Becker and life had forced her to build. She hadn't freaked when he told her that he was falling for her.

It wouldn't be long, and Haven McKinney would be all his.

"You stay here," he said. "Doors locked, alarm set. Don't leave for any reason. Ace is running comms for us from the Norcross office. You get spooked, you call him. If he doesn't answer, he's busy with the mission, so leave a message."

"Okay."

He tucked her hair back behind her ear, then toyed with the diamond that she hadn't taken off since he'd given it to her. "It's almost over."

She pressed her face to his chest and hugged him tight.

After one more kiss, Rhys grabbed his bagel and

coffee, and headed out. In the hall, he waited for her to lock the door before he made his way to the parking garage.

With a few bites, he finished the bagel, and slugged back his coffee. He left the cup near his GTS, then started his bike. He set his boot on the foothold, pulled on his helmet, then roared out of the parking garage.

He met Vander, Saxon, Rome, and Easton a few blocks from Volkov's mansion.

Vander stood by his bike, while Saxon and Easton were in one SUV. Rome was in a second SUV.

Vander handed Rhys an earpiece.

Rhys hooked it in. "Check."

"Got you." Ace's voice came through the earpiece.

Vander lifted an arm, checking his chunky Breitling Aerospace watch. "Okay, time to move."

Rhys threw a leg over his bike, checked the Glock 22 tucked securely into the holster under his arm, then pulled his helmet on. "Let's end this."

Vander revved his bike. "Hell, yeah."

They flipped their visors down. Rhys and Vander led the way, the two SUVs moving in behind them. Rhys took a corner, hugging the curve, the early morning light intensifying.

They pulled over, just down from Volkov's house.

"Six o'clock," Vander murmured.

Like clockwork, a black delivery truck pulled out of Volkov's driveway. It moved slowly down the street, turned.

"Follow," Vander ordered. "We'll stay back, then pick the right spot to approach."

Rhys really wished they knew the route, but hopefully there was a good location to pull the truck over and breach. He zipped through the light traffic, and turned to follow the truck.

They followed the truck out of Sea Cliff, and soon it was headed into the Presidio.

Where the hell were they going? Why drive through the large park? Were they headed for the Golden Gate Bridge?

The truck turned off onto a wooded side road. There were no buildings or cars in sight.

"Go," Vander ordered.

The X6s veered off, speeding ahead and overtaking the truck.

Rhys accelerated. Vander, hunched over his bike, sped ahead. He watched the brake lights on the truck flare.

Perfect.

They split, coming in fast on either side of the truck.

Suddenly, the two SUVs swerved to a stop in front of the truck, blocking the road.

The truck screeched to a halt, rocking lightly.

Rhys pulled up on his side and slid off his bike. He pulled out his Glock. Maybe this would go down easy?

The passenger door of the truck opened. A big guy slid out, lifting a rifle.

Or not.

Rhys fired. The guy spun around and laid down a volley of bullets.

Running, Rhys ducked around the back of the truck.

Vander slid in beside him from the other side.

"I've got one guy," Rhys said. "Armed with an AR-15."

"Same with the driver."

"We're closing in." Rome's deep, calm voice came through the earpiece. The guy never lost his cool.

Gunfire sounded from the front of the truck. Rome, Saxon, and Easton had engaged.

Then Rhys heard a yelp. He peered quickly around the corner of the truck.

His guy was down on one knee.

Rhys strode out of cover and broke into a sprint. He pressed his Glock to the back of the man's head. "Drop it."

The man made an angry noise, but tossed his rifle to the ground.

Saxon and Easton appeared, their weapons aimed at the man.

Rhys patted the guy down, and pulled a handgun from his waistband, and a knife off his belt.

Saxon held up some zip ties, and they quickly tied the man up.

A shout cut through the air, and Rhys turned to look through the open door of the delivery truck.

On the other side of the vehicle, he saw Vander deliver a hard front kick to the driver. The man staggered and Vander kicked the gun out of the man's hands. Next, Vander delivered a powerful side kick, followed by a punch to the face, and an elbow to the jaw. The driver went down.

Rome moved to help Vander secure the man.

"Ace," Vander said. "Call Hunt. Tell him we have some friends for him to come and collect."

"Oh, Detective Morgan will be thrilled," Ace drawled.

"Well, that was easy," Easton said.

Those words sent a tingle down Rhys' spine. A little too easy.

He strode to the back of the truck and listened. "Can't hear anyone."

As Rome and Saxon dragged the two subdued men toward the SUVs, Vander, Easton and Rhys got ready to open the back of the truck.

Vander and Easton stood to the side, weapons up.

Rhys opened the latch and swung the doors open. He whipped his Glock around and looked inside.

Then he cursed.

He heard Easton mutter some very nasty words.

The back of the truck was empty.

There were no thugs. No painting. Nothing.

"Someone set us up," Vander bit out. Fury throbbed off him.

Rhys felt a sick curl in his gut. He yanked out his phone and called Haven.

It rang and rang.

Pick up, Haven.

Dread solidified as the call cut off. The others were all watching him. He ground his teeth together and called again. Still no answer.

"Haven's not answering her phone."

"Fuck," Easton muttered.

Rhys sucked in a breath. He had no proof, but he was positive Volkov had Haven.

HAVEN PACED ACROSS RHYS' living room, swiveled, and paced back. She'd been at it for a while.

This was *torture*.

The waiting. The wondering what was going on. Were Rhys and the others okay?

She moved to the windows overlooking the balcony. The sun had risen, washing the bay and the bridge in golden light. She wrapped her arms around herself.

He'd be okay. He knew what he was doing. All the Norcross men were good.

She couldn't lose Rhys. Her throat went tight, her heart squeezing in her chest. *Oh God*. She was in *love* with Rhys.

She pressed her palm to her chest. She'd thought for a while that she would fall in love with Leo. When things between them had been good and fun.

But it had never really happened. What she felt for Rhys was bigger, bolder, and brighter than the best of anything she'd felt for Leo.

Rhys had done nothing but care for her. Sure, he could be bossy, and sometimes made her mad, but she realized now that this was real. That was life. Real love was give and take. It wasn't making yourself less so someone else felt good all the time. It was being there, through the good and bad, no matter what.

She staggered to the couch and dropped down. *She was in love with Rhys.*

Flutters started in her belly and she felt a flicker of panic. No, that was the old Haven.

He'd told her that he was falling for her. She had to trust him, trust them.

Now, he just had to come back to her.

On that thought, she started pacing again. She went over to his fancy sound system and put on some music. Then she turned it off. She needed to do something. She stomped into the kitchen and cleaned the dishes in the sink.

Then her cell phone rang and she jolted. It was barely six o'clock. It couldn't be over yet, could it?

Then she saw Harry's name on her phone.

"Hey, Harry. I thought you didn't get out of bed before seven."

"Haven."

His serious voice sent chills through her. "What's wrong?"

"I was up early. A delivery was screwed up at the gallery yesterday, so I had to schlep out to Dogpatch at the crack of dawn to the delivery company's warehouse to collect it."

"Okay."

Harry sucked in a breath. "I saw a truck. They were shifting something. I just got a glimpse. Doll face, I'm sure it was the *Water Lilies*. I recognized the frame. They loaded it into the truck."

That couldn't be right? The *Water Lilies* was in a truck leaving Volkov's mansion on the other side of the city. She froze. Was this all a ruse? A decoy?

Her mind churned. Had Mr. Irvine lied to them? *No.* More likely, the guards who'd spoken like he wasn't there were probably well aware of what they were doing.

"Harry, where are you?"

"Hiding in my car, spying out the window."

"The truck's still there?"

"Yes. For now. It looks like they're getting ready to leave soon."

"Okay, don't take your eyes off it. I'm calling Rhys and the others."

"Where's your badass?"

"Busy, but I'll get a message to him. Hold tight."

She hung up and pressed the number that Rhys had left for Ace.

It rang and rang.

"Come on."

God, had something gone wrong with the mission? There was a beep. There was no message but she knew it was recording.

"Uh, hi, it's Haven. My friend Harry called." She relayed the info that Harry had shared. "Since I can't reach you, I'll head there. I'll trail the truck until Rhys and the others can get there. Bye."

Haven raced to the bedroom, yanked off Rhys' T-shirt and pulled on some leggings, T-shirt, and running shoes. She pulled her hair up in a ponytail. She kept her diamond on, tucking it under her shirt. Then she pulled on a light sports jacket.

She grabbed Rhys' car keys and her phone, then

headed out the door. She'd have to borrow Rhys' GTS and hope he didn't get mad.

In the elevator, she texted Harry that she couldn't reach Rhys, but that she was on her way.

The elevator doors opened. The parking garage was empty and her shoes squeaked on the concrete. She bleeped the locks on Rhys' Mercedes. God, it was sexy. Low-slung and fast-looking.

She heard a noise and turned.

The garage was empty. She scanned the area, her pulse racing. Ugh, parking garages were always creepy when you were alone.

As she crossed the space, she moved the keys into her left hand, poking each one through her fingers as a makeshift weapon. She still didn't see anyone.

She picked up the pace, half running toward the car.

The dull thud of footsteps behind her. Before she could turn, beefy arms wrapped around her and lifted her off her feet. *No!* She swung her body around, and swiped out with her hand. The keys met flesh, and a masculine grunt filled her ears.

Her attacker dropped her, and she took in the big man with three fresh gouges down his cheek. "Ivan."

"Mr. Volkov wants you."

"Well, he can't have me." She scrambled back. "You can't just decide you want a person and take them. I'm not a thing."

She shook her head. Why did she attract crazy guys? Rhys excluded, of course.

Oh God. When Rhys learned she'd left the apartment and this had happened...

She'd have to soften him up and distract him.

"You're coming with me," Ivan rumbled. "I don't want to hurt you."

"Just leave. My boyfriend is going to be pissed."

"Zane Roth?"

"Um, no. He's actually not my boyfriend."

Ivan looked confused, then his face hardened. He advanced on her.

Haven held up her hands. "Please—"

She darted left and ran between two cars.

She heard him chasing after her, and she circled a Chevy SUV and sprinted. She needed to get to the stairs.

Breaking out from behind a car, she pushed for speed, her chest heaving. Damn, she needed to go to the gym more.

Unfortunately, Ivan was faster than he looked. He tackled her, and they both smacked into the concrete. *Ow.* The wind was knocked out of Haven and her bones rattled.

Before she could catch her breath, Ivan rose and yanked her up.

Haven fought. She tried to scratch and kick, and she wriggled like crazy.

Nothing worked. The man was unmovable.

He maneuvered her toward a plain, silver sedan. He yanked open the back door and shoved her into the back seat. Despite her struggles, he managed to duct tape her wrists together, then her ankles.

Shit. Damn. Fuck.

Tears pricked her eyes but she fought them back. She couldn't afford to lose it.

Ivan shoved her again, and she fell flat on the seat. She glared at him as he shut the door, then climbed into the driver's seat. "My boyfriend is going to be pissed as hell. And I'm telling him that you're an asshole."

"He won't find you. Mr. Volkov has plans for you."

Those ominous words sent a wave of nausea through her. That didn't sound good.

Rhys would find her...right? "We'll see." Haven dredged up all the bravado she could. "Rhys is going to—"

"Quiet. I don't want to hear your jabbering."

She flopped back against the seat. "I don't like you, Ivan."

That got her a grunt.

Then he turned, and leaned through the gap between the front seats. "We have a drive ahead of us, and Mr. Volkov wants you out for the ride."

Ivan held a syringe in his hand.

"No!" she cried.

She tried to fight, but he was too strong. There was a brief, sharp prick in her neck.

As she blinked her eyes, Ivan pulled back into the driver's seat. A second later, the car pulled out of the parking garage. Haven bit her lip as her vision blurred. *Oh, shit.*

Then, there was nothing but darkness.

CHAPTER EIGHTEEN

H aven groaned.
Her head was throbbing, her mouth dry. She opened her eyes. She was lying on a leather couch. She blinked a few more times, and the room came into view.

It was a spacious, light-filled office, with pale, glossy, wooden floors and a large, wooden desk set in front of French doors. Sunlight streamed in. There was lots of wood around the room and everything was decorated in shades of brown and tan. The French doors offered a gorgeous view of... She propped herself up on her elbow. Grapevines. Rows and rows of grapevines.

Haven sat up, looked around and jolted.

The *Water Lilies* was leaning against the far wall.

Her pulse spiked. It looked fine. There appeared to be no obvious damage to it. *Thank God.*

She rubbed her hands. The duct tape was gone, but there was still sticky residue on her wrists. She caught movement out of the corner of her eye, and she jerked her head around. Aleksandr Volkov came out of an adjoining doorway.

"Ah, you're awake," he said.

She glared at him, but inside she was quaking.

"Do you need some water?" he asked. "The drugs can leave your mouth dry, I hear."

"I don't want anything from you. You can't just kidnap me!"

He moved to the desk and leaned his hip against it. "I can do anything I want, Haven. I always have, I always will."

"You're going to regret this."

"I'm not afraid of Zane Roth."

"Zane is a friend of my boyfriend's. He's not mine."

Volkov cocked his head, a furrow forming on his brow. "It doesn't matter, you're mine now."

Annoyed, Haven leaned back against the couch. "Seriously, what is it about me that attracts obsessive, creepy men?"

Volkov's eyes flashed. "Careful. I don't allow disobedience or insolence."

The tone of his voice sent a tremor of fear through her belly.

"I can give you so many things, Haven." He spread his hands. "Dresses, shoes, jewelry, the finest of everything."

"You really think I care about that?"

He tilted his head. "I should've known you'd have more class. I have art that you'll love to see. As soon as the buyer arrives—" he nodded at the Monet "—and I complete the sale of the painting, my good friend Sergei Zakharov will transfer me my share."

Scumbag. Her nails bit into her palms.

"Then we'll head to my oceanside estate in Mexico. You'll love it. My art collection is incredible."

She tasted bile in her mouth. "I'm not going anywhere with you. Rhys will come for me."

Volkov looked unimpressed. "The boyfriend?"

"Yes, Rhys Norcross."

The older man straightened like he'd been stung by something. "Norcross?"

She lifted her chin. "Yes."

He muttered a curse. "Related to Easton and Vander?"

"Their brother."

The look on Volkov's face turned unhappy and disturbed. Then he shook his head. "No one will find you here, not even the Norcross brothers. After the buyer arrives from Silicon Valley, we're leaving. We'll be long gone before any Norcross can track you down."

Haven glared at him.

"I want you to go into the adjoining bathroom. I have an outfit in there that I want you to change into." He gave her activewear a slight sneer.

She crossed her arms over her chest. "No."

Volkov smiled coldly. "If you don't reconsider, I will undress you myself."

Ick. She didn't want this man's hands anywhere near her.

Glaring at him, Haven stomped through the doorway he indicated. Inside was a small, but nicely appointed bathroom with brown-granite countertops shot through with gold.

Hanging on a hook on the wall was a fire-engine-red dress, and a pair of strappy, silver shoes with four-inch heels. Ordinarily, she'd drool over the shoes, but since Volkov had bought them, she didn't. The dress wasn't nice, though. It was far too short, far too clingy, and far too low-cut to be something she'd usually wear.

Annoyed, she pulled her gear off and slid the dress on. Great, she looked like a high-class escort. She slipped the shoes on and decided to leave her ponytail. She wasn't pandering to him any more than she had to. She strode out, glaring at him.

His eyes lit up. "Good. Soon, we'll be on our way." He strode out.

Haven pressed her hands to her face. Shit, she hoped that wasn't true. Rhys would come.

She dragged in a shaky breath.

Damn, she really wished she'd told him that she loved him.

Okay, well she wasn't going to sit around hoping to be rescued like some lousy damsel in distress. She definitely wasn't going to let herself be whisked off to a skeevy bad guy's estate, no matter how much art he had.

First, she checked the French doors. Locked, and no key in sight. She figured smashing the glass would make too much noise.

She walked back to the bathroom and searched it. She found a small air freshener spray in the cupboard under the sink. It wasn't mace, but it would do.

Back in the office, she glanced at the desk. Maybe

there was a phone? A jolt of adrenaline rushed through her and she hurried to the desk. She checked everything. One drawer was locked, one had nothing but a notepad and pen, and the others were empty. Nothing else, not even a stapler.

She huffed out a breath. *Dammit.*

She moved over to the main door, expecting it to be locked. The handle turned, and she swallowed a gasp.

Haven peeked into the hall.

There were no beefy guards waiting. She guessed they were around somewhere, or Volkov wouldn't have left the door unlocked.

Quietly, she slipped into the hall. The house was gorgeous, and much nicer than Volkov's San Francisco mansion. The wooden floors were beautiful, and the place had a relaxed, rustic edge to it.

She walked on her toes so she didn't make any noise with the heels, and reached the end of the hall. She saw a large, open plan living area. Nice, comfy suede couches dominated the space. There was a monstrous flatscreen TV on the wall next to a large, stone-lined fireplace.

There were lots more French doors, all opening onto a large, flagstone terrace. Beyond that, she saw a pool and gazebo, and beyond that vines as far as she could see.

Okay. Get to the vines, hide, and run. Maybe she could find a road and flag down a car or something.

Haven darted across the living room. The first French door was locked, but on the second one, she got lucky.

She pulled it open, grinning as she slipped outside. She pulled in a deep breath of fresh air.

She loved Napa. Maybe after all this was over, she'd convinced Rhys to come away with her for a long weekend.

Sex, wine, and Rhys. *Mmm.*

She darted along the terrace, her heels clicking. First, she needed to get out of here.

Then she heard voices. *Crap.* She ducked down behind some outdoor couches. Her heart drummed so loudly that she was sure the people would hear it.

"All clear," a deep voice said. There was a pause. "Vehicle on approach. Acknowledged." Another pause. "Yeah, the Citation is fueled and waiting at the airstrip."

Oh, shit.

Silence. Haven waited a few more seconds, and prayed the guard had moved away.

Time to go.

She jumped up and ran. She rounded the gazebo structure by the pool and ran smack into a hard chest.

"Oof." She stumbled back.

A tall, blond guard in a dark suit scowled at her. "Hey, you aren't—"

She lifted the air freshener and sprayed it in his eyes.

He threw his hands up and cursed. She tossed the can at him and it hit his head.

Haven ran. *Get to the vines. Get to the vines.*

Damn these stupid high heels. The heels kept sinking into the grass. She should have kicked them off earlier, but she hadn't been thinking straight. She hadn't gone far when a hand grabbed her ponytail and yanked.

She yelped. *Oh, that hurt.* It felt like her scalp was on fire.

She was swung around to face a scowling Ivan.

"You again," she cried.

He wrenched her arm behind her back and marched her back toward the house. The blond guard met them, his eyes red and streaming with tears.

"Bitch," he snapped.

"I've been abducted and held against my will, what did you expect?" She heard a noise from Ivan and glanced at him. "Did you just laugh?"

"No."

She frowned at him. "Sounded like a laugh."

"Lipinski, flush your eyes out," Ivan ordered. He shoved Haven inside the house.

He marched to the office and Volkov met them at the doorway.

"Lucky I like a spirited woman, Haven."

She rolled her eyes. She was too pissed off to feel scared anymore.

"But not too spirited. Ivan, tie her to the chair."

Ivan shoved her into a chair in front of the desk. He pulled out his handy roll of duct tape.

"Is a roll of duct tape part of the henchman's essential toolkit?" she asked sarcastically.

He ignored her, and taped her arms and legs to the chair.

Just great. Rhys, please be the hotshot investigator you are and find me.

Fear rose again, making her throat tight. She tested her bindings but she was tied up tight.

Another guard appeared in the door and nodded at Volkov.

The older man smiled. "Good, the buyer is here. Once the transaction is complete, we can be on our way, Haven."

Her stomach lurched sickeningly.

Rhys, please hurry.

FUCK.

Rhys had never felt this frantic. He picked up Haven's cracked phone off the concrete and the keys to his GTS.

He scanned the parking garage, his jaw creaking under the pressure of grinding his teeth together. He had no idea where she was.

Vander watched him like a raptor, clearly ready to subdue him if Rhys lost it.

Vander's phone rang and he pulled it out. "Ace, what have you got?"

"Take a look." Ace's voice came out on speaker.

Rhys peered at Vander's phone and they watched the security footage flicker across the screen. A big bruiser chased Haven through the parking garage, before catching her and manhandling her into a silver sedan.

"She called him Ivan," Ace said.

Rhys cursed. "Volkov's goon. The one who tried to detain her in the library."

"I'll contact Hunt," Ace said. "Get the SFPD looking for the car." Ace drew in a breath. "I'm sorry, Rhys. I missed her call when you guys were taking down the truck. Her friend Harry spotted the painting being loaded into a truck."

Rhys bit back his frustration. He knew it wasn't Ace's fault, but he wished that Ace had taken the damn call. "It's okay. Let's just focus on finding her."

She should never have left the apartment. When he got her back, he was going to tan her sweet ass.

If he found her in time.

He dragged in a breath. "I gave her a necklace. It has a tracker in it. Ace, can you activate it?"

Saxon raised a brow. "You put a tracker on your girl-friend? Man, you have balls."

"I was ensuring my woman's safety."

"Did you tell her?" Saxon asked.

"Hell, no."

Vander shook his head.

"I got it," Ace said. "It's showing that she's in...Napa."

"Napa," Rhys breathed.

"Volkov has an estate there," Vander said.

"Yeah," Ace added. "Confirmed. She's at Volkov's estate."

Rhys' hands curled into fists. The fucker was going down. "I'm going to kill him."

It would take well over an hour for them to drive to Napa. Too damn long.

"Ace, get the helo ready," Vander ordered. His cool gaze swept over them. "We'll get back to the office, get prepped, then go in hot."

"Nice," Rome murmured. His teeth flashed white as he grinned.

Rhys jumped back on his bike. Soon, they were all

back at the Norcross office, in the team locker room off the gym.

It didn't take them long to get ready since they had already prepped for the truck breach. Rhys pulled on a Kevlar vest and strapped it on. Next, he pulled an M4 assault rifle out of the weapons locker. It was what they'd used in the military.

He turned, finding Vander, Saxon, Rome, and Easton all ready, the same as him.

They headed up to the roof, where a helo—a sleek, black Sikorsky—was waiting for them.

Vander waved to Magdalena "Maggie" Lopez through the cockpit window. Vander had lured the young pilot away from the Navy. The woman was always smiling, swore like a sailor, and was brilliant at the controls of a helicopter.

They all boarded, and a moment later, they lifted off and swept over the city, then the bay, heading northeast.

It was like the old days, heading off on a mission. For a second, Rhys saw desert below. Then he blinked, and Alcatraz Island appeared.

This wasn't a Ghost Ops mission. This one was much more important—saving Haven and bringing her home.

Rhys tried not to fidget on the flight. But as San Francisco Bay gave way to San Pablo Bay, the pressure built inside him—the noise, the fear—it all curdled together. He tapped his boot on the floor.

Be okay, Haven. Be fucking okay.

Vander touched his knee. Rhys looked up at his brother, then Easton, then the others. They all gave him steady looks. They had his back. They had Haven's back.

He wasn't alone, and his woman was smart, resilient, and resourceful.

He nodded.

"Hold on, baby," he murmured.

Soon, the grapevines came into view. They spread out over the hills in long, marching rows.

Maggie brought them in lower. He saw Vander's mouth moving, and knew he was talking with the pilot.

They circled around Volkov's estate, and Vander pointed. Rhys took in the sprawling house.

His focus solidified, zooming in on the mission objective. *Rescue Haven.*

Maggie flew them away from the house. They didn't want to alert Volkov and his goons. A helicopter flying in Napa was common enough. The helo touched down on a flat area of grass near some sheds. They exited, and moved into formation, weapons up.

"Shoot to incapacitate," Vander said.

They moved silently and fast, covering the distance to Volkov's quickly. They approached the house, circling a large pool.

A guard appeared, raising his weapon, and Vander took him down with a shot to the leg. It took Saxon seconds to disarm and secure the man.

The team split up. Vander and Rhys went left around the house, while the others went right.

Rhys ran into two more guards, and he felt savage satisfaction in taking them both down with several hard hits and punches.

He and Vander left the men trussed up.

They approached a long bank of French doors. Rhys peered into a large living area, but no one was in view.

He pointed farther on, and Vander nodded. They kept moving along the building.

Ahead was another set of glass doors. As they neared, Rhys heard the murmur of voices and held up a hand. He and Vander stopped.

Carefully, Rhys peered inside.

He saw Volkov talking to two guards. They were in an office, and the guards were stationed by the far door.

His gaze swept over the room and then he saw Haven. His chest hitched.

"She's alive," he murmured. She was tied to a chair, looking gloriously pissed.

The *Water Lilies* rested against the wall. As he watched, Volkov grabbed the painting, and left the room.

"Volkov walked out with the painting."

Vander nodded. "I'll enter through the living room and take him down. Can you handle the guards?"

Rhys glanced at his brother.

"Right," Vander said. "Try not to kill anyone."

Inside, Rhys heard Haven talking. She sounded angry. She jerked on the bindings holding her to the chair.

The guards frowned at her.

Rhys decided to enter fast. He took a few steps back, then ran. He lifted his arm and closed his eyes as he crashed into the French doors, glass shattering.

Haven screamed.

Rhys aimed and fired. The first guard jerked and

collapsed. The second was moving, but Rhys swiveled and took him down, too.

He marched over and kicked the guards' weapons away. Both were groaning. "Try anything, and I'll kill you."

Both went still and stayed silent.

Then Rhys strode over to Haven.

"Rhys!"

"It's okay, baby." He pulled his knife and cut through the tape, freeing her. "I'm getting you out of here."

Suddenly, the door to the office flew open. Volkov strode in, two guards with him.

Fuck. Vander hadn't found him yet. The guards lifted their handguns.

"Shoot him!" Volkov yelled.

Rhys leaped away from Haven. If they shot at him, he didn't want to risk her getting hit. He dove behind the desk and bullets ripped into the wood. *Fuck.*

"Stop!" Haven screamed.

Rhys popped up, and shot one guard, then dropped down again.

There was another hail of bullets.

He popped up again, and saw Volkov rushing toward Haven, who was pressed against the far wall. The man had a gun in his hand.

Fear swamped Rhys. Without thinking, he moved toward her.

Bam.

The bullet hit Rhys' chest. As his body jerked, he got a shot off. The guard yelled and fell.

"Rhys!" Haven screamed.

He dropped behind the desk on one knee and grunted. Fuck that hurt. He touched his vest and tried to pull in a breath. It was agony.

"Rhys, no," Haven cried from the other side of the room.

He gripped the edge of the desk and pushed himself up. The pain was outrageous and made his head swim. *Hold it together, Norcross.*

Volkov held Haven in front of him, his gun pressed to her head.

Rhys' gaze met hers. Her face was pale, her eyes wide and shimmering with tears.

"Drop your weapon," Volkov barked.

CHAPTER NINETEEN

error had claws, and they were ripping at Haven's belly.

Rhys had been shot. No. *No*.

Volkov grabbed her, pressing the gun to her head. But she didn't care. She stared at the desk where Rhys had gone down. *Rhys*. His name was a cry inside her. She couldn't breathe.

Then, he rose, looking shaky. She blinked. He didn't have any blood on him, and she suddenly realized he was wearing a vest.

Rhys and Volkov glared at each other. Rhys had his gun aimed at Volkov's head.

"Put the gun down." Volkov shoved the barrel against her cheek and she winced. "Do it, or I'll hurt her. Put it down and kick it over to me."

Rhys moved, circling around the desk and lowering his gun.

"Rhys, no." He'd be defenseless.

He set the deadly-looking rifle down, and kicked it across the wood floor. "I'll do anything to keep you safe."

Her lungs compressed.

"Handgun as well," Volkov added.

Rhys pulled a pistol out of the holster strapped to his thigh and tossed it down.

I'd do anything to keep you safe.

Any lingering doubts she'd had about how Rhys felt about her, or how she felt about him evaporated. For a beat, it was just the two of them in the room, looking at each other. He'd die for her, do anything in his power to keep her safe.

She loved him. *Oh, God.* And it was her job to do the same for him.

She was *not* letting him die here.

Turning slowly, she stomped her high heel down on Volkov's foot.

He yelped. She shoved him and arms flailing, he slammed into the wall. She leaned down and yanked one of her shoes off. The shoes he'd forced on her.

She flew at him, and whacked his chest with the heel. She felt it gouge in. She did it again.

"You asshole! You shot my man. You put me in this cheap dress."

Volkov staggered. She whacked him in the arm and his gun went flying. She stabbed the shoe again, hard enough for the heel to break skin.

With a cry, he fell backward and Haven leaped on him, slapping his face.

Rhys kicked Volkov's gun well out of the way. "Okay, Wonder Woman." He lifted her off the man.

Volkov curled into a ball on the floor.

"I'm not done," she bit out.

There was a noise at the door and Vander strode in.

"You're late," Rhys said.

"Sorry, ran into a little trouble." He eyed Volkov, his eyebrows rising. "What happened?"

"Haven beat the shit out of him."

She tossed her head back. "And I'm not finished."

Vander's lips twitched and he crouched down, binding Volkov's hands. "Stabbed with a high heel?"

"Beaten up by a beautiful woman," Rhys added.

Vander shook his head, dragged Volkov up, and shoved the man into the chair Haven had been tied to. With a few zip ties, Vander had Volkov immobilized. "Move and I'll shoot you."

Volkov swallowed and stayed silent.

"I'm glad you two find this so amusing," Haven said. "He shot Rhys in the chest!"

Vander's face turned serious and he rose. "You okay?"

"Vest caught the brunt of it."

"Still hurts like a—" Vander looked at Haven "—a lot?"

"I'll deal with it later, but first..." Rhys gripped Haven's arms. "What the hell were you thinking, attacking him like that?"

Her eyes widened. "You're mad at me?"

"He had a *gun* to your head," Rhys barked. "He could've killed you."

"And he could have killed you! He'd already shot you, and I wasn't letting him shoot the man I love again."

She froze. *Oh God, she'd just said that aloud.*

Rhys stared at her and something moved through his eyes. Then he yanked her into his arms and kissed her.

Haven stayed frozen for a second, then kissed him back. His tongue plunged into her mouth, and she sank her hands into his hair. *More.* She needed more.

When he finally broke the kiss, she was panting. He pressed his face to her hair, his arms tight and secure around her.

"At least you won't complain about my shoes or shoe shopping again," she said quietly.

He shook his head and smiled.

"Where's the *Water Lilies*?" Vander asked.

Haven stiffened. "Volkov took it out of here. Didn't you find it?"

Vander shook his head and touched his ear. "Saxon, any of you guys got eyes on the painting?" He must have gotten a response because a second later, Vander shook his head.

Oh, God. "Volkov said the buyer arrived. Please don't tell me the asshole took it already."

"No vehicles have left since we arrived." Vander toed Volkov. "Where's the painting?"

"Fuck you," the man said back.

Vander crouched and murmured something too quiet for Haven to hear.

Volkov's eyes widened and his lips trembled. "Cellar level. The buyer drove in to collect it, and we completed the deal."

"Let's move," Vander said.

Haven kicked off her other shoe and followed the men out. Rhys was keeping her close.

They jogged down the hall.

"Ace, I need fast access to the cellar level," Vander said.

In the living room, Saxon, Rome, and Easton joined them.

"Haven." Easton hugged her.

"I'm okay."

"This way." Vander led them through a massive kitchen. The appliances and countertops all gleamed. He opened a door and wide stairs led downward, lights flicking on automatically along gorgeous stone walls.

In the cellar level below, one long wall was lined with impressive shelving filled with bottles of wine. There were also several stacks of large barrels, and as they continued on, they passed a tasting room with a long table and chairs.

At the end of the corridor, Vander pushed through a door. Just beyond it was a delivery area, with doors open, revealing a driveway leading up. A van was parked inside, its back doors open wide.

Two men turned around and saw the Norcross team. They instantly lifted their hands in the air.

"The buyer is some tech billionaire," Haven said.

"Where's your boss?" Rhys asked.

The men shrugged.

"The painting?" Rhys asked.

"Mr. Allcroft hasn't come back with it yet."

Vander cursed and reached in and yanked the keys out of the truck. "Spread out," he told his team. "Find him."

Rhys turned to Haven. "I want you to find a place upstairs and stay—"

"Nope." She turned, heading back toward the stairs. "I'm going to find that damn painting, Rhys."

He glared up at the ceiling, and it looked like he was fighting the urge to handcuff her to something.

"Come on," she said. "No time to waste."

She heard Rhys mutter under his breath. She was pretty sure it was something about her always getting her own way.

RHYS MOVED up the stairs in front of Haven. He paused at the top. There was no sound in the kitchen. They'd taken out a lot of Volkov's guards, but the man struck Rhys as the kind of guy who'd have his own private army.

He waved to Haven to follow him across the huge kitchen.

Suddenly, a large body barreled out of a doorway. The guard slammed into Rhys.

Haven screamed. "Rhys!"

His Glock went flying and hit the tile floor. The guard jerked an elbow up, and Rhys blocked it. They crashed into each other and slammed to the floor.

Rhys heaved, and they rolled across the kitchen floor, grunting as each of them tried to get the upper hand.

They rolled again, hitting a cupboard. Plates rained down, smashing on the floor.

Rhys landed a punch to the man's gut and the guard made a pained sound. Gripping the man's legs with his, Rhys twisted, sliding an arm around the guard's neck in a choke hold.

The man made an enraged noise. He bucked hard, almost dislodging Rhys.

With a cry, Haven appeared. She was holding a broom. She whacked the handle downward, hitting the guard's side. He grunted and jerked.

Rhys struggled to subdue the man and when Haven hit again, this time the broom whacked Rhys' back.

"Shit, Haven."

"God, sorry. I'm trying to help."

He tightened his hold on the guard until the man slumped into unconsciousness. Once he was out, Rhys jerked his head. "Get some zip ties out of my pocket."

She crouched, grabbed them, and set about tying the guard's hands. Tight.

"Babe." Rhys rose. "You'll cut off his blood flow."

"My tolerance for assholes is low, Rhys. Very low."

He cupped her cheek. "Let's find the *Water Lilies*."

He snatched his Glock up, and they headed into the living room. There was no sign of anyone, nor a multi-million-dollar painting.

"Rhys, look," Haven hissed.

He followed her gaze. One of the French doors leading outside was open.

Quietly, they moved that way. Once they got closer, he saw a slim man in a suit holding the *Water Lilies*, making his way past the pool.

"Oh no, he doesn't," Haven muttered.

They rushed outside.

"Stop!" she yelled.

The man jerked, and for a second, Rhys thought he was going to fall in the pool.

The man faced them, and swallowed, his Adam's apple bobbing.

Rhys recognized the man. Mark Allcroft. Rhys had seen him in the news. He owned some social media company teenagers loved. He was young, with a slight build, and a face covered in freckles.

"Don't move," Rhys warned.

Allcroft swallowed again, nervously eyeing Rhys' gun. "Please—"

"Shut up," Haven snapped. "That painting is stolen."

"It is?" The man lied unconvincingly.

"Oh, please. You knew." She strode up to him.

Rhys stayed still, his gun aimed on the man.

Haven snatched the painting out of Allcroft's hands. "Thank God. I'm returning this to where it belongs."

"But...but...I paid for it."

"Oh, you paid money for a stolen painting? Boo-hoo."

Rhys moved closer. "You can explain it to the police."

"The police?" Allcroft's voice went high and squeaky, his face stark white.

Haven sniffed, then before Rhys realized what she had planned, she shoved the businessman.

With a cry and windmilling arms, Allcroft fell into the pool with a big splash.

Rhys shook his head. Haven tossed her ponytail back. "That felt good."

He tucked his gun into his holster, then took the painting and set it on a deck chair.

Her eyebrows rose. "What are—?"

He picked her up and kissed her. With a husky noise, she wrapped her legs around his waist and kissed him back.

It felt so right. Holding her, kissing her. He kept kissing her, drinking her in as she writhed against him. She was safe, and that was all that mattered.

Then Rhys heard a clearing throat. He lifted his head and saw Vander and the others standing on the terrace.

"You'll be happy to hear that we cleared the house." Vander eyed the man flailing in the pool. "That our buyer?"

"Yes." Rhys set Haven down, but kept her close.

"Cops are on the way," Vander said.

"How did he end up in the pool?" Rome asked.

"Haven pushed him in," Rhys replied.

She lifted her chin. "I'm not sorry."

"Get him out," Vander said.

Saxon and Rome started around the pool.

Haven leaned into Rhys. "Thanks for coming for me."

He tipped her face up. "You didn't think I would?" Fuck, he'd thought he was finally getting through to her.

"I knew you would, I just wasn't sure you'd find me before Volkov flew me off to Mexico." She grimaced.

Rhys' gut hardened. He wanted to hurt Volkov all over again. "I'm the best investigator in San Francisco, remember?"

Saxon, walking past him with the sodden tech billionaire, snorted. "You're not going to tell her about the tracker?"

"Tracker?" Her eyes widened and she gripped the diamond resting against her chest. "You put a tracker on me?"

"Haven—"

She grinned. "Considering what happened, I'm totally okay with that." She smacked a kiss to his lips.

He slid a hand into her hair, and so many things moved through him. Damn, she turned him inside out.

"Police are two minutes out," Ace said in their earpieces.

"It's over," Haven murmured. She looked at the painting, then scanned Volkov's house. "The danger, it's done."

"Yeah, baby."

She started shaking. "Oh, God. I held it together this long, why am I freaking out now?"

"Adrenaline crash. It's normal."

"You aren't shaking."

"I'm trained to deal with it." He pulled her close, his hand resting at the nape of her neck, massaging gently. "Just breathe, Haven."

"I'm tired of freaking out. I'm definitely tired of being kidnapped."

Rhys' mouth moved into a flat line. "I'm tired of that, too." He scooped her off her feet and into his arms. "But you don't have to worry about that anymore." He headed inside. He'd raid Volkov's cellar and find her something to drink.

She'd need to give a statement to the cops, but she could do it while he held her.

"Wait," she said, "the painting."

Fuck the painting. "We'll get it later."

She looked like she was going to argue, but then she relaxed into him, and snuggled against his chest. "Okay."

CHAPTER TWENTY

Haven moaned, straddling Rhys, riding him hard. His fingers dug into her hips. Flesh slapped against flesh.

She looked down to find his hot gaze on her face. His hand stroked her jaw, and he slid his finger in her mouth. She sucked on it hard.

She was lost in him. The pleasure was so intense that she felt it everywhere. She sucked his finger deep, and he cursed, his hips bucking up beneath her.

"So fucking beautiful, Haven. *Mine.*"

His hands left her hip, sliding around to find her clit.

She leaned over him, her hips moving faster. Her release was building, shimmering. She was right on the edge and she wanted to jump.

She slammed down, his thick cock stretching her, his thumb on her clit. Then the edge was gone and she was freefalling.

"*Rhys.*" Her hoarse scream echoed off the walls.

"Yes, Haven. I'm here. Watching how gorgeous you

are taking my cock, coming on my cock."

Everything inside her spasmed. With a growl, he surged up.

In a blink, she was on her back with Rhys over her, moving inside her with fast, hard thrusts.

God, he was beautiful. *Magnificent.*

With a groan, he came, his muscles straining, his face twisting.

They lay collapsed on the bed, skin cooling. She traced one of the tattoos on his arm. "I need to get moving. I'm due at the museum."

He grunted, kissed her, and rolled off.

As she headed to the shower, she glanced back. A little thrill went through her.

All those gorgeous, hard muscles stretched out on the bed. It had been four glorious days since they'd recovered the *Water Lilies* at Volkov's estate in Napa.

The first two days, they'd spent in bed. They'd had an insane amount of creative sex, eaten, slept, watched movies. They'd discovered that they both loved the sci-fi genre. She'd been sure he'd prefer action movies, but the inaccuracies drove him crazy. He'd been sure she'd love chick flicks, but the over-the-top, embarrassing situations in rom-coms made her wince.

Now, they were both back at work. She was safe, and the Monet was hanging back on the wall in the Hutton where it belonged. Life was back to normal.

She glanced at the sexy man on the bed. His body was relaxed, but for the last couple of days, he'd seemed... preoccupied. Even now, she saw the small furrow on his brow.

A lump formed in her throat and she ducked into the bathroom. She flicked the shower on.

Haven looked in the mirror. Her hair was a mess. It looked like she'd just had wild sex. Her cheeks were flushed, her eyes sparkling. She had a hickey on her neck. Anytime it faded, Rhys bit her again.

She shivered, feeling it between her legs. She'd told him that she loved him, but he hadn't returned the words.

Her smile faded.

Maybe he wanted her gone? She was essentially living with him, and the dangerous circumstances that had forced the situation were gone. Maybe he was tired of her?

She touched the mark on her neck. *No.* The distrusting, uncertain Haven was gone. She'd been through hell and survived. She was stronger.

Rhys liked her. He felt something for her. And her feelings were her own. She'd offered her love to him, and she wouldn't demand anything from him in return.

She was safe. She had a hot man in her bed. She was back at the job she loved.

Life was good.

It was time she searched for a new apartment though. Her insurance payment would come through soon. She'd borrowed Rhys' laptop earlier and pulled up a few websites, and looked at apartments in her price range.

The thought of leaving Rhys' place made her belly clench. She glanced at her toiletries lined up on the sink. She liked cooking with him, waking up beside him every day.

But she had to finish regaining back control of her life, and she didn't want to overstay her welcome.

She slipped into the shower and then got ready for work. Finally, makeup done, hair up in a twist, and wearing a black skirt and crisp, white shirt, she walked into the kitchen.

She found a shirtless Rhys drinking coffee against the island. *Yum*.

"Breakfast?" His gaze lingered on her skirt.

"I need to run. We're almost ready to go live with the interactive exhibit, and I have things I need to double-check."

"Mmm."

He was clearly distracted by her skirt. The man had a thing for her skirts.

"We also have the fundraiser party to finish planning. It's this weekend. With all of the excitement and interest after the theft—" She pulled a face. It hadn't been so exciting for her. "—Gia said we should capitalize on it. Get donors to open their pockets for our charity." The charity was one she'd selected that provided art resources to schools.

"That sounds like Gia." Rhys dropped a kiss to Haven's lips. "Have a good day, angel."

"Don't get shot at."

He smiled.

"Or get in a car chase."

He shook his head, amused.

"Or rescue some beautiful damsel in distress who'll fall for you, forcing me to scratch her eyes out."

His smile faded. "Only you, baby."

That was nice. She gave him another quick kiss, then waved as she headed out the door.

She walked to the museum. She had to admit, she was still getting used to being safe on her own and knowing that she could walk anywhere she wanted. No thug was going to try and snatch her.

When she reached work, she dumped her bag in her office. Then she got sucked into a whirlwind of tasks.

She checked on the interactive exhibit. The touch-screens were all ready to go. It would be wonderful, and allow guests, especially kids, to interact and understand the art more. Instead of art being untouchable, something expensive up on the wall, it would be something they could savor and enjoy.

"Haven."

She spun and saw Gia walking toward her. Her friend wore a dark-blue dress with a snug skirt, her hair in a French roll. But despite looking her usual, put-together self, there were lines of strain around her mouth, and dark circles under her eyes.

"Hey." Haven hugged her. "You look tired."

Gia glanced away. "Busy. So busy."

"With work?"

"Yes. Work's always busy."

It wasn't like Gia to be evasive. "G?"

Her friend sighed. "You know Willow."

Haven kept her face impassive. Willow was Gia's friend from high school. Apparently, they'd been best friends growing up, both dreaming of college, and opening a classy PR firm together.

Only, Willow had been caught having sex with her

professor, flunked out of college, and later gotten into drugs. She sporadically cleaned up and reconnected with Gia.

The random contact always made Gia unhappy.

"She has a thing," Gia said.

Haven squeezed her friend's arm. "Sorry. Especially when you've just finished dealing with my thing."

"Which wasn't your fault." Gia straightened and dragged in a breath. "I'll do what I can to help Willow, but try to steer clear at the same time."

Haven nodded. A part of her admired her friend's loyalty. "Hey, you want to come with me to check out apartments later?"

Gia frowned. "Apartments?"

"Yes. Mine blew up, remember?"

"But you're living with Rhys."

"Because I was in danger. Now I'm not."

Gia's frown deepened. "Have you told Rhys?"

"Not yet."

"Mmm. Okay, I have to run. I have some ads for the fundraiser for you to approve."

"Email them to me."

They kissed each other on the cheek.

"You need a killer dress," Gia said. "It's only a few days away."

"Which reminds me that I need to talk with the caterer." Haven's mind whirled as she did a mental To-Do list. "And talk to my team about decorations. Go, get out of my hair."

With a wave, Gia left.

Haven checked with her team working on a new

sculpture exhibit. Then she checked on the location for the party—a large exhibit hall with a wall of windows and a long balcony outside. They'd be decorating with fairy lights and lanterns. It would look amazing.

Her heels clicked as she moved back into the main hall and stopped in front of the *Water Lilies.*

A sense of rightness moved through her. Things were up in the air with Rhys, but she was happy. She drank in the painting, and for a second, everything was right in her world.

"Haven."

She stiffened and turned. Leo stood several feet away. He wore dark slacks and a dark shirt, his hands in his pockets.

This couldn't be happening.

"Don't call security," he said. "I'm not staying long."

She just looked at him. For a brief moment, she could see why he'd once attracted her. He was a handsome man.

"I just wanted to say..." He blew out a breath. "I'm sorry. For everything."

She nodded, but she realized she didn't care. Leo was her past.

He eyed her face. "Fuck, you really are over me."

"Yes, Leo."

"Does he make you happy?"

"Yes. I know I can trust him, that he will be loyal and always keep me safe."

Leo nodded. "I want you to be happy." He turned, and started to walk away.

"Leo?"

He glanced back

"Are you safe?" she asked.

He nodded. "The tech buyer already paid the money before your man got the painting back. The money got Zakharov off my back."

Ugh. It felt wrong that criminals had still gotten a payday out of all of this.

"That said, some mysterious hacker took most of the funds. All the Zakharov family got was a small fraction. Still, it was more than what I owed them, so I'm off the hook."

A mysterious hacker? She frowned. Rhys had mentioned that Ace was a good hacker.

Leo was looking at her.

"Find your happy, Leo. Preferably without the help of the Russian mafia."

He smiled. "Goodbye, Haven."

He left. And finally, she hoped she would never see him again.

"Haven." An assistant rushed in. "We need your help with some restoration decisions."

"Coming."

RHYS ENDED his phone call and looked at his desk. He had two new cases waiting for him. He'd already put out some feelers to contacts for one.

"Hey." Vander appeared in the doorway.

Rhys flicked a finger at his brother.

"Spoken to Gia lately?" Vander asked.

"No."

"I talked to her this morning. Willow is dragging her into some shit again."

Rhys grimaced. No one in the Norcross family, bar Gia, could stand the woman. Even as a teen, she'd been wild. She'd come onto Rhys and his brother so many times they'd lost count. Once, she'd been sleeping over with Gia, and he'd caught Willow trying to sneak into his bed naked.

She was needy and selfish, and Gia refused to give up on her.

"We need to monitor that," Rhys said. "Gia likes to pretend she's tough, but she's got a marshmallow heart under it all."

"Yeah, I'll do it since you're busy with domestic bliss."

Rhys grinned. "Yep."

Haven was clear of Becker's mess, and safe. The *Water Lilies* was back in Easton's museum. Volkov was in jail. And Haven was in his bed every night. Best of all, she loved him.

His chest tightened. She loved him, now he just needed to keep convincing her that they were good together. He wanted her to stay, and when the time was right, he wanted to marry her.

"You think Ma would want to help me pick out a ring?" Rhys asked.

Vander raised a brow. "You're going to put your ring on Haven?"

"Yes." Soon. Because then not long after that, he

wanted kids. He wanted to see Haven swollen with his baby.

Vander shook his head. "You take Ma with you, you'll get no say in what ring you pick."

True, Clara Norcross was opinionated with a capital O.

"I think I'll head over to the Hutton and take Haven out for lunch."

"You mean take her for a lunchtime quickie."

Rhys smiled. "You should get a woman, Vander."

His brother shook his head and left quickly. *Coward.*

Rhys opened his laptop. He'd deal with a couple of emails, then head out to find his woman.

Saxon appeared, a major scowl on his face.

"What's bugging you?" Rhys said.

"Vander said Willow is messing with Gia again. I hate that woman."

Sax seemed pretty worked up. "Well, we'll keep her from dragging Gia in too far."

"She needs to cut that bitch off."

"Gia hasn't in all these years, so I'm not sure she can."

A muscle ticked in Saxon's jaw, then he stomped off.

Rhys opened his browser and found a tab open. He frowned. It was a real estate website, with searches for rental listings.

What the fuck?

He flicked through it. Haven had been looking at apartments? She'd favorited several of them. She was planning to move out? *Hell, no.*

He grabbed his keys and phone, and headed out. He

stewed all the way to the Hutton, and he parked out front. He waved to the security guards as he strode inside.

He found Haven in a side gallery, talking with two assistants. They were hanging some paintings. Haven was smiling as she directed them. He watched her give a few suggestions, smile, then stop to fix a small statue resting on a pedestal.

Fuck, he could watch her work all day. She just lit up.

Finally, she noticed him.

"Rhys." She smiled and he realized that she looked at him the same way.

He closed the space between them, and saw her eyes widen.

"You are *not* moving out."

She blinked. "What?"

"I found your apartment searches. You are not moving out."

Her face eased into smooth, unreadable lines. "I'm safe, now. There's no danger anymore. I can't stay with you forever."

He noted her assistants watching them with rapt attention, but he didn't care. "Why not?" he demanded.

Her mouth tightened. "Because."

"Because why?"

"Because you haven't asked me to live with you!" The words burst out of her. "Because you haven't told me that you love me."

Rhys blinked slowly. "I thought I've been showing you how much I needed you, how much I want you to stay?"

Her chest was rising and falling fast. "I need the words, Rhys. Since my mom died, no one's said them to me." Her nose wrinkled. "Except Leo, and he doesn't count."

"Don't say that fuckwit's name." Rhys wrapped an arm around her, pulling her up on her toes. She let out a little squeak.

"Haven Amelia McKinney, I'm totally, completely, one-hundred-percent in love with you."

Her face softened, a glimmer of tears in her eyes. "You are?"

"Yes." He brushed her lips with his. "You're not moving out, because I won't let you."

"You're a bit bossy."

"And you like it." He kissed her properly—deep, and filled with all the love he felt.

Behind them, her assistants started clapping. Haven laughed, hugging him close. "I love you, Rhys. Thanks for being there for me when I needed you."

"That's my job now. I'll always be there for you, angel."

GLASSES CLINKED, the conversation was lively, and the party was amazing. Haven hoped it inspired everyone to donate. A lot.

She was so excited for the art charity to get enough money to help all the schools in the San Francisco area.

She wound her way through the gala, calling out greetings to guests, checking the servers were all okay, scanning the art on the walls and pedestals dotted around the room. Everything looked fabulous.

She glanced up. The ceiling was filled with floating red lanterns, and the walls dripped with fairy lights. It looked magical.

Although, she was well aware the party was bursting at the seams because of the notoriety of the theft of the *Water Lilies*. She was certain everyone was hoping something shocking would happen.

She'd worn black tonight. The dress was cut stylishly low in front, then hugged her body to her knees before it flared out in a mermaid-style bottom. The entire dress shimmered with strands of silver.

She nodded at some guests, and spotted Easton hobnobbing and looking dashing in his tuxedo.

Close by, Vander stood with their parents. Mr. and Mrs. Norcross looked like they were enjoying themselves. Mrs. Norcross looked like an older version of Gia and looked fabulous in her gray dress. While all the siblings looked more like their mother, Mr. Norcross had passed his tall, fit body onto his sons. He'd also given Vander and Easton their blue eyes.

Mrs. Norcross had not hidden any of her elation when she'd found out that Haven and Rhys were together. In fact, she'd dropped by the museum the day before and left Haven a stack of wedding magazines.

Haven looked around and wondered where her hot Norcross brother was.

As Haven glanced around, she spotted Gia talking with a group of men, waving one arm, her other hand clutching a champagne flute.

Tonight, Gia wore a midnight blue, one-shouldered dress. It floated to the floor and she looked like a tiny Greek goddess. A large split flashed a lot of slim leg.

G was no doubt charming the rich, old men into giving lots and lots of money to the cause.

Smiling, Haven walked along the wall, checking the artwork. The *Water Lilies* hung in a place of pride on the wall. She smiled at it. After bribing Rhys with several sexual favors, he'd admitted that Ace had hacked the account of the Zakharov family, and taken back as much of the money as he could. It'd all been given to the police, and the rumor was that it was going to be donated.

An arm snaked around her and tugged her into a shadowed alcove.

She didn't worry or panic about another potential kidnapping, instead, she snuggled into her captor's hard body.

"You look edible," Rhys murmured in her ear.

Despite them having quick, delicious sex on the vanity in the bathroom before they'd come to the party, she'd spent a lot of time ogling him tonight. He looked hot in his tuxedo with his messy shock of dark hair. He was gorgeous, and all hers.

She tilted her head back and kissed him.

"How long until we can leave?" His hands skimmed down her body.

"A few hours, unfortunately."

He let out a frustrated growl. "I want to get you home and strip this sexy dress off you." He nipped her earlobe.

Haven moaned. Home. *Their* home. Rhys' place was now officially their place.

"I love you," she murmured.

"Love you too, angel. I'm very, very happy I managed to scale those walls of yours."

She smiled. He hadn't scaled them, he'd obliterated them.

She'd called her dad and told him about Rhys. He'd been happy for her in his distant way. Her mom would have *loved* Rhys.

"We could probably sneak off to my office." She looked up at him. "No one would miss us for a little while."

His grin was sharp and predatory.

Suddenly, there was a commotion in the party. Frowning, Haven turned.

The crowd was looking out onto the balcony. A few of the guests were out there, enjoying the evening air. Haven tried to peer over the heads of the crowd.

"What's going on?" she asked.

Rhys frowned and tugged her forward. "Not sure."

People gasped and the crowd parted.

Haven's eyes popped open. *What the hell?*

A man in a tuxedo was striding along the balcony. Through the glass, she saw him draw a handgun. The air locked in Haven's chest and she felt Rhys stiffen.

A few cries of alarm went up.

The man was normal-looking. He had an ordinary face—not handsome, not unattractive, just bland. He had an ordinary build—not tall, not short.

Haven swung her head.

He was aiming the weapon at *Gia*.

Haven's chest locked. Her best friend strode along

the balcony from the other direction, her blue dress flaring out behind her. She reached into the slit of her dress, and pulled out her own gun.

Oh, my God. Rhys' hand convulsed on Haven's.

The man fired and Gia didn't even flinch as the shot went wild. Then, cool as a cucumber, Gia fired. The man dodged.

Then Gia spun, and ran, her dress trailing behind her like a flag.

The man leaped up, fired, then gave chase. He and Gia disappeared out of view.

Haven saw Saxon move. He sprinted through the crowd, burst through the doors onto the balcony, then raced after them.

Vander brushed past them, Easton one step behind him.

"Rhys, stay here. Control the crowd, and look after Haven, and Mom and Dad."

"Got it," Rhys replied.

"Be safe," Haven said.

She watched Vander and Easton head out the door and rush after their sister. Rhys slid an arm around her.

"Gia will be fine," he said.

Haven nodded. God, they'd just gotten everything on an even keel and now this. She sucked in a deep breath, fighting back a skitter of fear. She lifted a hand, signaling to the uniformed security guards to close the balcony doors.

"Ms. McKinney." Her head guard reached her. The woman wore a neat pantsuit in dark gray, her salt-and-pepper hair in a neat bob. "We want everyone to stay inside until we know what we're dealing with."

"Of course, Rachel."

The woman nodded. "We'll get everything under control, so don't worry." Rachel glanced at Rhys. "And your brothers can handle themselves."

Rhys lifted his chin and the woman strode off, barking orders at her guards.

Right now, Haven was more concerned about Gia. "Well, one thing is for sure, our life is *not* boring."

He dropped a kiss to the top of her head.

Hiding her worry, Haven cleared her voice to address the guests. "Well, never a dull moment at the Hutton."

Titters of laughter broke out.

"Please, eat, drink, and continue to enjoy yourselves. Our excellent security team has everything in hand." *Please have it in hand, and please stay safe, Gia.*

Haven grabbed a drink for herself and gulped it.

Rhys took the glass away. "Don't worry."

"I'm going to worry, Rhys. A man *shot* at Gia and she shot back."

He lowered his head and nipped Haven's lips. "Guess I'll have to find a way to distract you."

She melted into him. She knew now that she could lean on him and he'd help hold her up. She didn't have to shoulder everything alone. "I love you."

"Love you back."

Haven knew that she could depend on her hot investigator and his love, every day, for the rest of their lives.

I hope you enjoyed Haven and Rhys' story!

There are more Norcross stories on the way. Stay tuned for **THE TROUBLESHOOTER**, starring feisty Gia Norcross, coming in October 2020.

If you'd like some more sexy, fast-paced contemporary romance, then check out my Team 52 series about a covert black ops team (Vander Norcross even makes a cameo in one book!)

Read on for a preview of the first Team 52 book, *Mission: Her Protection*.

Don't miss out! For updates about new releases, free books, and other fun stuff, sign up for my VIP mailing list and get your *free box set* containing three action-packed romances.

Visit here to get started: www.annahackett.com

Would you like a FREE BOX SET of my books?

PREVIEW - MISSION: HER
PROTECTION

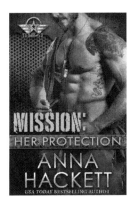

I t was a beautiful day—ten below zero, and ice as far as the eye could see.

Dr. Rowan Schafer tugged at the fur-lined hood of her arctic parka, and stared across the unforgiving landscape of Ellesmere Island, the northernmost island in Canada. The Arctic Circle lay about fifteen hundred miles to the south, and large portions of the island were covered with glaciers and ice.

Rowan breathed in the fresh, frigid air. There was nowhere else she wanted to be.

Hefting her small pickaxe, she stepped closer to the wall of glacial ice in front of her. The retreating Gilman Glacier was proving a fascinating location. Her multidisciplinary team of hydrologists, glaciologists, geophysicists, botanists, and climate scientists were more than happy to brave the cold for the chance to carry out their varied research projects. She began to chip away at the ice once more, searching for any interesting samples.

"Rowan."

She spun and saw one of the members of her team headed her way. Dr. Isabel Silva's parka was red like the rest of the team's, but she wore a woolen hat in a shocking shade of pink over her black hair. Originally from Brazil, Rowan knew the paleobotanist disliked the cold.

"What's the latest, Isabel?" Rowan asked.

"The sled on the snowmobile is almost full of samples." The woman waved her hand in the air, like she always did when she was talking. "You should have seen the moss and lichen samples I pulled. There were loads of them in area 3-41. I can't *wait* to get started on the tests." She shivered. "And be out of this blasted cold."

Rowan suppressed a smile. *Scientists*. She had her own degrees in hydrology and biology, with a minor in paleontology that had shocked her very academic parents. But on this expedition, she was here as leader to keep her team of fourteen fed, clothed, and alive.

"Okay, well, you and Dr. Fournier can run the samples back to base, and then come back to collect me and Dr. Jensen."

Isabel broke into a smile. "You know Lars has a crush on you."

Dr. Lars Jensen was a brilliant, young geophysicist. And yes, Rowan hadn't missed his not-so-subtle attempts to ask her out.

"I'm not here looking for dates."

"But he's kind of cute." Isabel grinned and winked. "In a nerdy kind of way."

Rowan's mouth firmed. Lars was also several years younger than her and, while sweet, didn't interest her in that way. Besides, she'd had enough of people trying to set her up. Her mother was always trying to push various *appropriate* men on Rowan—men with the right credentials, the right degrees, and the right tenured positions. Neither of her parents cared about love or passion; they just cared about how many dissertations and doctorates people collected. Their daughter included.

She dragged in a breath. That was why she'd applied for this expedition—for a chance to get away, a chance for some adventure. "Finish with the samples, Isabel, then—"

Shouts from farther down the glacier had both women spinning. The two other scientists, their red coats bright against the white ice, were waving their arms.

"Wonder what they've found?" Rowan started down the ice.

Isabel followed. "Probably the remains of a mammoth or a mastodon. The weirdest things turn these guys on."

Careful not to move too fast on the slippery surface, Rowan and Isabel reached the men.

"Dr. Schafer, you have to see this." Lars' blue eyes were bright, his nose red from the cold.

She crouched beside Dr. Marc Fournier. "What have you got?"

The older hydrologist scratched carefully at the ice with his pickaxe. "I have no idea." His voice lilted with his French accent.

Rowan studied the discovery. Suspended in the ice, the circular object was about the size of her palm. It was dull-gray in color, and just the edge of it was protruding through the ice, thanks to the warming temperatures that were causing the glacier to retreat.

She touched the end of it with her gloved hand. It was firm, but smooth. "It's not wood, or plant life."

"Maybe stone?" Marc tapped it gently with the axe and it made a metallic echo.

Rowan blinked. "It can't be metal."

"The ice here is about five thousand years old," Lars breathed.

Rowan stood. "Let's get it out."

With her arms crossed, she watched the scientists carefully work the ice away from the object. She knew that several thousand years ago, the fjords of the Hazen Plateau were populated by the mysterious and not-well understood Pre-Dorset and Dorset cultures. They'd made their homes in the Arctic, hunted and used simple tools. The Dorset disappeared when the Thule—ancestors to the Inuit—arrived, much later. Even the Viking Norse had once had communities on Ellesmere and neighboring Greenland.

Most of those former settlements had been near the coast. Scanning the ice around them, she thought it unlikely that there would have been settlements up here.

And certainly not settlements that worked metal. The early people who'd made their home on Ellesmere hunted sea mammals like seals or land mammals like caribou.

Still, she was a scientist, and she knew better than to make assumptions without first gathering all the facts. Her drill team, who were farther up on the ice, were extracting ice core samples. Their studies were showing that roughly five thousand years ago, temperatures here were warmer than they were today. That meant the ice and glaciers on the island would have retreated then as well, and perhaps people had made their homes farther north than previously thought.

Marc pulled the object free with careful movements. It was still coated in a thin layer of ice.

"Are those markings?" Isabel breathed.

They sure looked like it. Rowan studied the scratches carved into the surface of the object. They looked like they could be some sort of writing or glyphs, but if that was the case, they were like nothing she'd ever seen before.

Lars frowned. "I don't know. They could just be natural scoring, or erosion grooves."

Rowan pushed a few errant strands of her dark-red hair off her face. "Since none of us are archeologists, we're going to need an expert to take a look at it."

"It's probably five thousand years old," Isabel added. "If it is man-made, with writing on it, it'll blow all accepted historical theories out of the water."

"Let's not get ahead of ourselves," Rowan said calmly. "It needs to be examined first. It could be natural."

"Or alien," Lars added.

As one, they swiveled to look at the younger man.

He shrugged, his cheeks turning red. "Just saying. Odds are that we aren't alone in this universe. If—"

"Enough." Rowan straightened, knowing once Lars got started on a subject, it was hard to get him to stop. "Pack it up, get it back to base, and store it with the rest of the samples. I'll make some calls." It killed her to put it aside, but this mystery object wasn't their top priority. They had frozen plant and seed samples, and ice samples, that they needed to get back to their research labs.

Every curious instinct inside Rowan was singing, wanting to solve the mystery. God, if she had discovered something that threw accepted ancient history theories out, her parents would be horrified. She'd always been interested in archeology, but her parents had almost had heart attacks when she'd told them. They'd quietly organized other opportunities for her, and before she knew it, she'd been studying hydrology and biology. She'd managed to sneak in her paleontology studies where she could.

Dr. Arthur Caswell and Dr. Kathleen Schafer expected nothing but perfection from their sole progeny. Even after their bloodless divorce, they'd still expected Rowan to do exactly as they wanted.

Rowan had long-ago realized that nothing she ever did would please her parents for long. She blew out a breath. It had taken a painful childhood spent trying to win their love and affection—and failing miserably—to realize that. They were just too absorbed in their own work and lives.

Pull up your big-girl panties, Rowan. She'd never been abused and had been given a great education. She had work she enjoyed, interesting colleagues, and a lot to be thankful for.

Rowan watched her team pack the last of their samples onto the sled. She glanced to the southern horizon, peering at the bank of clouds in the distance. Ellesmere didn't get a lot of precipitation, which meant not a lot of snow, but plenty of ice. Still, it looked like bad weather was brewing and she wanted everyone safely back at camp.

"Okay, everyone, enough for today. Let's head back to base for hot chocolate and coffee."

Isabel rolled her eyes. "You and your chocolate."

Rowan made no apologies for her addiction, or the fact that half her bag for the trip here had been filled with her stash of high-quality chocolate—milk, dark, powdered, and her prized couverture chocolate.

"I want a nip of something warmer," Lars said.

No one complained about leaving. Working out on the ice was bitterly cold, even in September, with the last blush of summer behind them.

Rowan climbed on a snowmobile and quickly grabbed her hand-held radio. "Hazen Team Two, this is Hazen Team One. We are headed back to Hazen Base, confirm."

A few seconds later, the radio crackled. "Acknowledged, Hazen One. We see the clouds, Rowan. We're leaving the drill site now."

Dr. Samuel Malu was as steady and dependable as the sunrise.

"See you there," she answered.

Marc climbed onto the second snowmobile, Lars riding behind him. Rowan waited for Isabel to climb on before firing up the engine. They both pulled their goggles on.

It wasn't a long trip back to base, and soon the camp appeared ahead. Seven large, temporary, polar domes made of high-tech, insulated materials were linked together by short, covered tunnels to make the multi-structure dome camp. The domes housed their living quarters, kitchen and rec room, labs, and one that held Rowan's office, the communications room, and storage. The high-tech insulation made the domes easy to heat, and they were relatively easy to construct and move. The structures had been erected to last through the seven-month expedition.

The two snowmobiles roared close to the largest dome and pulled to a stop.

"Okay, all the samples and specimens to the labs," Rowan directed, holding open the door that led inside. She watched as Lars carefully picked up a tray and headed inside. Isabel and Marc followed with more trays.

Rowan stepped inside and savored the heat that hit her. The small kitchen was on the far side of the rec room, and the center of the dome was crowded with tables, chairs, and sofas.

She unzipped and shrugged off her coat and hung it beside the other red jackets lined up by the door. Next, she stepped out of her big boots and slipped into the canvas shoes she wore inside.

A sudden commotion from the adjoining tunnel had Rowan frowning. *What now?*

A young woman burst from the tunnel. She was dressed in normal clothes, her blonde hair pulled up in a tight ponytail. Emily Wood, their intern, was a student from the University of British Columbia in Vancouver. She got to do all the not-so-glamorous jobs, like logging and labelling the samples, which meant the scientists could focus on their research.

"Rowan, you have to come now!"

"Emily? What's wrong?" Concerned, Rowan gripped the woman's shoulder. She was practically vibrating. "Are you hurt?"

Emily shook her head. "You have to come to Lab Dome 1." She grabbed Rowan's hand and dragged her into the tunnel. "It's *unbelievable*."

Rowan followed. "Tell me what—"

"No. You need to see it with your own eyes."

Seconds later, they stepped into the lab dome. The temperature was pleasant and Rowan was already feeling hot. She needed to strip off her sweater before she started sweating. She spotted Isabel, and another botanist, Dr. Amara Taylor, staring at the main workbench.

"Okay, what's the big issue?" Rowan stepped forward.

Emily tugged her closer. "Look!" She waved a hand with a flourish.

A number of various petri dishes and sample holders sat on the workbench. Emily had been cataloguing all the seeds and frozen plant life they'd pulled out of the glacier.

"These are some of the samples we collected on our first day here." She pointed at the end of the workbench. "Some I completely thawed and had stored for Dr. Taylor to start analyzing."

Amara lifted her dark eyes to Rowan. The botanist was a little older than Rowan, with dark-brown skin, and long, dark hair swept up in a bun. "These plants are five thousand years old."

Rowan frowned and leaned forward. Then she gasped. "Oh my God."

The plants were sprouting new, green shoots.

"They've come back to life." Emily's voice was breathless.

THE CLINK of silverware and excited conversations filled the rec dome. Rowan stabbed at a clump of meat in her stew, eyeing it with a grimace. She loved food, but hated the stuff that accompanied them on expeditions. She grabbed her mug—sweet, rich hot chocolate. She'd made it from her stash with the perfect amount of cocoa. The best hot chocolate needed no less than sixty percent cocoa but no more than eighty.

Across from her, Lars and Isabel weren't even looking at their food or drink.

"Five thousand years old!" Isabel shook her head, her dark hair falling past her shoulders. "Those plants are millennia old, and they've come back to life."

"Amazing," Lars said. "A few years back, a team working south of here on the Teardrop Glacier at Sverdrup Pass brought moss back to life...but it was only four hundred years old."

Isabel and Lars high-fived each other.

Rowan ate some more of her stew. "Russian scientists regenerated seeds found in a squirrel burrow in the Siberian permafrost."

"Pfft," Lars said. "Ours is still cooler."

"They got the plant to flower and it was fertile," Rowan continued, mildly. "The seeds were thirty-two thousand years old."

Isabel pulled a face and Lars looked disappointed.

"And I think they are working on reviving forty-thousand-year-old nematode worms now."

Her team members both pouted.

Rowan smiled and shook her head. "But five-thousand-year-old plant life is nothing to sneeze at, and the Russian flowers required a lot of human intervention to coax them back to life."

Lars perked up. "All we did was thaw and water ours."

Rowan kept eating, listening to the flow of conversation. The others were wondering what other ancient plant life they might find in the glacial ice.

"What if we find a frozen mammoth?" Lars suggested.

"No, a frozen glacier man," Isabel said.

"Like the Ötzi man," Rowan said. "He was over five thousand years old, and found in the Alps. On the border between Italy and Austria."

Amara arrived, setting her tray down. "Glaciers are retreating all over the planet. I had a colleague who uncovered several Roman artifacts from a glacier in the Swiss Alps."

Isabel sat back in her chair. "Maybe we'll find the fountain of youth? Maybe something in these plants we're uncovering could defy aging, or cure cancer."

Rowan raised an eyebrow and smothered a smile. She was as excited as the others about the regeneration of the plants. But her mind turned to the now-forgotten mystery object they'd plucked from the ice. She'd taken some photos of it and its markings. She was itching to take a look at them again.

"I'm going to take another look at the metal object we found," Lars said, stuffing some stew in his mouth.

"Going to check for any messages from aliens?" Isabel teased.

Lars screwed up his nose, then he glanced at Rowan. "Want to join me?"

She was so tempted, but she had a bunch of work piled on her desk. Most important being the supply lists for their next supply drop. She'd send her photos off to an archeologist friend at Harvard, and then spend the rest of her evening banging through her To-Do list.

"I can't tonight. Duty calls." She pushed her chair back and lifted her tray. "I'm going to eat dessert in my office and do some work."

"You mean eat that delicious chocolate of yours that you guard like a hawk," Isabel said.

Rowan smiled. "I promise to make something yummy tomorrow."

"Your brownies," Lars said.

"Chocolate-covered pralines," Isabel said, almost on top of Lars.

Rowan shook her head. Her chocolate creations were gaining a reputation. "I'll surprise you. If anyone needs me, you know where to find me."

"Bye, Rowan."

"Catch you later."

She set the tray on the side table and scraped off her plates. They had a roster for cooking and cleaning duty, and thankfully it wasn't her night. She ignored the dried-out looking chocolate chip cookies, anticipating the block of milk chocolate in her desk drawer. Yep, she had a weakness for chocolate in any form. Chocolate was the most important food group.

As she headed through the tunnels to the smaller dome that housed her office, she listened to the wind howling outside. It sounded like the storm had arrived. She sent up a silent thanks that her entire team was safe and sound in the camp. Since she was the expedition leader, she got her own office, rather than having to share space with the other scientists in the labs.

In her cramped office, she flicked on her lamp and sat down behind her desk. She opened the drawer, pulled out her chocolate, smelled it, and snapped off a piece. She put it in her mouth and savored the flavor.

The best chocolate was a sensory experience. From how it looked—no cloudy old chocolate, please—to how it smelled and tasted. Right now, she enjoyed the intense flavors on her tongue and the smooth, velvety feel. Her mother had never let her have chocolate or other "unhealthy" foods growing up. Rowan had been forced to sneak her chocolate. She remembered her childhood friend, the intense boy from next door who'd always snuck her candy bars when she'd been outside hiding from her parents.

Shaking her head, Rowan reached over and plugged in her portable speaker. Soon she had some blood-pumping rock music filling her space. She smiled, nodding her head to the beat. Her love of rock-and-roll was another thing she'd kept well-hidden from her parents as a teenager. Her mother loved Bach, and her father preferred silence. Rowan had hidden all her albums growing up, and snuck out to concerts while pretending to be on study dates.

Opening her laptop, she scanned her email. Her stomach clenched. Nothing from her parents. She shook her head. Her mother had emailed once...to ask again when Rowan would be finished with her ill-advised jaunt to the Arctic. Her father hadn't even bothered to check she'd arrived safely.

Old news, Rowan. Shaking off old heartache, she uploaded the photos she'd taken to her computer. She took a second to study the photos of her mystery object again.

"What are you?" she murmured.

The carvings on the object could be natural scratches. She zoomed in. It really looked like some sort of writing to her, but if the object was over five thousand years old, then it wasn't likely. She knew the Pre-Dorset and Dorset peoples had been known to carve soapstone and driftwood, but this artifact would have been at the early point of Pre-Dorset history. Hell, it predated cuneiform—the earliest form of writing—which was barely getting going in Sumer when this thing had ended up in the ice.

She searched on her computer and pulled up some images of Sumerian cuneiform. She set the images side by side and studied them, tapped a finger idly against her lip. Some similarities...maybe. She flicked to the next image, chin in hand. She wanted to run a few tests on the object, see exactly what it was made of.

Not your project, Rowan. Instead, she attached the pictures to an email to send to her archeologist friend.

God, she hoped her parents never discovered she was here, pondering ancient markings on an unidentified object. They'd be horrified. Rowan pinched the bridge of her nose. She was a grown woman of thirty-two. Why did she still feel this driving need for her parents' approval?

With a sigh, she rubbed a fist over her chest, then clicked send on the email. Wishing her family was normal was a lost cause. She'd learned that long ago, hiding out in her treehouse with the boy from next door—who'd had a bad homelife as well.

She sank back in her chair and eyed the pile of paperwork on her desk. *Right, work to do.* This was the reason she was in the middle of the Arctic.

Rowan lost herself in her tasks. She took notes, updated inventory sheets, and approved requests.

A vague, unsettling noise echoed through the tunnel. Her music was still pumping, and she lifted her head and frowned, straining to hear.

She turned off her music and stiffened. Were those screams?

She bolted upright. The screams got louder, interspersed with the crash of furniture and breaking glass.

Team 52

Mission: Her Protection
Mission: Her Rescue
Mission: Her Security
Mission: Her Defense
Mission: Her Safety
Mission: Her Freedom
Mission: Her Shield
Also Available as Audiobooks!

One former Navy SEAL. One dedicated archeologist. One secret map to a fabulous lost oasis.

Finding undiscovered treasures is always daring,

dangerous, and deadly. Perfect for the men of Treasure Hunter Security. Former Navy SEAL Declan Ward is haunted by the demons of his past and throws everything he has into his security business—Treasure Hunter Security. Dangerous archeological digs – no problem. Daring expeditions – sure thing. Museum security for invaluable exhibits – easy. But on a simple dig in the Egyptian desert, he collides with a stubborn, smart archeologist, Dr. Layne Rush, and together they get swept into a deadly treasure hunt for a mythical lost oasis. When an evil from his past reappears, Declan vows to do anything to protect Layne.

Dr. Layne Rush is dedicated to building a successful career—a promise to the parents she lost far too young. But when her dig is plagued by strange accidents, targeted by a lethal black market antiquities ring, and artifacts are stolen, she is forced to turn to Treasure Hunter Security, and to the tough, sexy, and too-used-to-giving-orders Declan. Soon her organized dig morphs into a wild treasure hunt across the desert dunes.

Danger is hunting them every step of the way, and Layne and Declan must find a way to work together...to not only find the treasure but to survive.

Treasure Hunter Security
Undiscovered
Uncharted
Unexplored
Unfathomed
Untraveled

Unmapped
Unidentified
Undetected
Also Available as Audiobooks!

Edge of Eon

Touch of Eon

Heart of Eon

Kiss of Eon

Mark of Eon

Claim of Eon

Also Available as Audiobooks!

Galactic Gladiators: House of Rone

Sentinel

Defender

Centurion

Paladin

Guard

Weapons Master

Also Available as Audiobooks!

Galactic Gladiators

Gladiator

Warrior

Hero

Protector

Champion

Barbarian

Beast

Rogue

Guardian

Cyborg

Imperator

Hunter

Also Available as Audiobooks!

Hell Squad

Marcus

Cruz

Gabe

Reed

Roth

Noah

Shaw

Holmes

Niko

Finn

Theron

Hemi

Ash

Levi

Manu

Griff

Dom

Survivors

Tane

Also Available as Audiobooks!

The Anomaly Series

Time Thief

Mind Raider

Soul Stealer

Salvation

Anomaly Series Box Set

The Phoenix Adventures

Among Galactic Ruins

At Star's End

In the Devil's Nebula

On a Rogue Planet

Beneath a Trojan Moon

Beyond Galaxy's Edge

On a Cyborg Planet

Return to Dark Earth

On a Barbarian World

Lost in Barbarian Space

Through Uncharted Space

Crashed on an Ice World

Perma Series

Winter Fusion

A Galactic Holiday

Warriors of the Wind

Tempest

Storm & Seduction

Fury & Darkness

Standalone Titles

Savage Dragon

Hunter's Surrender

One Night with the Wolf

For more information visit www.annahackett.com

ABOUT THE AUTHOR

I'm a USA Today bestselling romance author who's passionate about *fast-paced, emotion-filled* contemporary and science fiction romance. I love writing about people overcoming unbeatable odds and achieving seemingly impossible goals. I like to believe it's possible for all of us to do the same.

I live in Australia with my own personal hero and two very busy, always-on-the-move sons.

For release dates, behind-the-scenes info, free books, and other fun stuff, sign up for the latest news here:

Website: www.annahackett.com

Printed in Great Britain
by Amazon

86439684R00171